To my aunt,
The angel who guided me as I wrote my first novel.
You've been the biggest inspiration to me.
Thank you, you've changed my life.

For the little girl,
Who knew one day she'd do something big with the cards she'd
been dealt. I hope this story brings hope for those who are
fighting battles we don't see.

The Moment Promised

By Amber Evergreen

Second edition.

Cover art by Silver Grace at bittersagedesigns.com

Editor: Amy Briggs, Briggs Consulting, LLC www.editsbyamy.com

ISBN 979-8-9889690-2-0

ISBN 979-8-9889690-1-3

THE MOMENT PROMISED

AMBER EVERGREEN

IMPORTANT NOTE

This book contains scenes of domestic violence and addiction. Please take these triggers into consideration. Your mental health matters.

I

I like to play this game inside my head where I go back in time to whatever stupid thing I've done and undo it. In this case, I wouldn't have pressed the lock button in my ancient car while the keys were still inside before starting my eight-hour shift.

If I hadn't, then I wouldn't be in my current predicament.

A dark parking lot. Alone.

With a can of pepper spray…that's locked in my car along with the keys.

I might as well hold up a neon sign that reads *Kidnap me, please!*

I close my eyes and curse my past self for not realizing her keys weren't occupying the pocket of her black pants like they do every shift. At least then I could've asked a coworker for a ride home.

I could go back into Pete's, but I have a feeling my boss —Pete—wouldn't be too happy to find me snoring in one of the booths when he opens tomorrow. If he knew one of his employees was left stranded in the parking lot, he'd be so guilt ridden. Especially since he's the one who always closes. Me closing today is a one-time thing since he needed to leave early for a doctor's appointment, and I insisted he take the rest of the day off.

I have two options. I can walk two miles to my house in the pitch black, or I could stand my five-foot four self on the side of the road with my thumb up, and pray I've done enough good deeds to get picked up by a nice family on their way home from church.

Considering it's Friday, and nearing midnight, the latter option's not looking very plausible.

A salty breeze whips my auburn hair up and around my head. It rattles the *Welcome to The Florida Keys* sign, which would've startled me if the streetlamp losing power hadn't beaten it to it.

Grab your keys and then *lock your car, Adeline!*

The summer's heat still scalds me in the dead of night. Headlights flood the dark, followed by a car door slamming shut.

There are footsteps against the gravel.

They belong to the presence behind me, nearing frighteningly fast. My fight or flight response must be broken because my body freezes, and my scream lodges in my throat the way it does in a nightmare, as firm hands grip my small shoulders. I'm about to squeeze my eyes shut, but before I do, a familiar voice eases my terror.

"Adeline Miller, what the hell are you doing out *here* at *this* hour?" He spins me around in one swift movement, making my stomach swoosh.

It's hard to make him out in the dark, but the moonlight casts a dark blue shadow across his dimpled smile.

2

"Finn!" I shriek, squeezing his torso and sighing in relief.

After only a few short moments of hugging my best friend, he pushes me an arm's length away from him with an expectant look on his face. "What are you doing out here, in the dark, alone?"

I sigh. "I locked my keys in my car," I say, ashamed.

He shakes his head a few times and pulls me back into our hug.

"How did you know I'd be at Pete's?" My question cuts into the silence.

"Your car wasn't at home, so, I figured you'd be at work." He suddenly shudders at whatever image haunts his imagination. "You're lucky I got here when I did."

I'd rather not imagine myself lifeless with yellow caution tape drawing attention to the scene, so I change the subject to catching up over how long it's been since we last saw each other—five weeks. "Two months sooner than I expected to see you. Why aren't you at FSU?" I cross my arms and tap my foot, switching the judging gaze onto him.

"I was failing economics." He shrugs. "So, I dropped the class before it could mess up my GPA." He turns and walks toward his car, still talking.

I take fast strides to keep up with his long legs.

"I was only taking the one class, and a stupid elective to get the credit. I figured it was a waste of time to stay up there for just the elective at this point." He pulls a car key out of his pocket and unlocks the car with the press of a button. "So, you have me all to yourself for the next two and a half months."

I can't ignore the smile that overtakes my face.

His hand skims the small of my back as I near the

passenger side of his black car. His forearm grazes my shoulder as he reaches past me to open my door.

I slide onto the red leather seat. I bite my cheeks as he holds firm eye contact until he's at the driver's side door, scooting in next to me.

His car smells strongly of him. Leather and a hint of deodorant that smells like expensive cologne. It's a scent he started wearing in high school, and when I'd asked him what cologne it was, he shrugged and told me his mom got him a new deodorant, which was always amusing to me. But it made up the unique scent I've grown to love.

Despite what a passing stranger might assume by his fragrance, Finn isn't one of those guys into their own appearance. I don't think he even looks in the mirror before leaving the house. Yet he always manages to appear put together and smells like his wallet is bursting at the seams. And he's oblivious to all of it.

"How generous of you." I squint my eyes to meet his, as if I were under harsh lighting.

"We'll get your car in the morning. You *do* have a spare key, right?" he says in a teasing voice, putting the car in reverse, and backing us out of the parking spot.

I roll my eyes. "You have an F in economics, right?"

"You're funnier than that, love." He calls me the nickname he's been calling me for years, but for some reason my stomach warms at the sound.

He pulls onto the one main road, a highway that connects all the islands that make up The Florida Keys. We live on the closest island to the mainland—Key Largo.

I glance at the time displayed on the dash. It's a little past midnight, June fifteenth.

I wag my eyebrows in the birthday boy's direction and start to sing "Happy Birthday."

"You know how much I love hearing you sing, but for the sake of our passengers...keep it down."

I roll my eyes. We're the only two people in this car. I belt it out, but he places his entire hand over my mouth, and once my muffled singing goes quiet, he removes his hand only to put it on my knee.

I clear my throat to put my suddenly shallow breath at bay. *It's only Finn.*

"So, wise *twenty-year-old man*, have any wisdom to pass down to the younger generation?" Finn is only two months older than I am. But I never let him forget it.

My lips upturn, giddy to be back in my best friend's presence, but it quickly turns to a frown. "You passed my street."

"You can sleep at my parents' tonight." His voice is suddenly hoarse.

"But I have to check on my mom! What if—"

"Where is your house key?" His amber colored eyes are dark as he focuses straight ahead, already knowing the answer while my mind tries to catch up.

I picture my keys, trapped in my locked car. I shift uneasily in my seat, bringing the tip of my thumb to my mouth as I bite the nail.

"She'll be okay," Finn whispers, grabbing my wrist, pulling it toward the center console as he holds the steering wheel with his left hand. "It's just one night, love," he coos, and my anxiety eases for a second.

It's the middle of the night. My mom is surely passed out by now, unable to open the door and let me in anyway.

I let my eyes follow the world whizzing by through the window. The streetlights dance around my vision as Finn speeds past them. Before I know it, we're pulling into a driveway.

Finn Walker's childhood home hasn't changed one bit. The driveway is still made of tiny white rocks, like most here in the Keys. The rainbow windmill we made together when we were kids still catches the breeze in the yard, and Finn's dad still has his collection of seashells in a flowerpot by the front door.

Being here feels so…

"Nostalgic," I say, as Finn unlocks the door.

He holds it open and gestures for me to enter. "Ladies first, madam." He gives me a sarcastic smile and bow of his head.

I don't say thank you, instead I stick out my tongue like the nineteen-year-old I am.

"Nostalgic." Finn throws my observation back at me.

The moon coming through the window is the only light source. My eyes adjust, taking in my surroundings. *Home.* A smile tugs at the corner of my lips, and Finn's eyes twinkle in amusement as he watches me.

"You look nice, Ad," he says without a hint of sarcasm.

I glance at him warily, and then down at my clothes. I'm wearing black jeans and a striped red and white polo shirt that reads Pete's with a few grease stains. My name tag reads Adele, since that was the girl who quit before me, and Pete figured it was close enough when he handed it to me with a shrug.

My eyes meet his. I get lost in them and can't look away, like catching the last glimpse of a rainbow hanging in the sky after a storm. His expression is serious, not even a hint of a shadow where his dimple hides.

I clear my throat, forcing my eyes anywhere but his.

"I think I'll go shower." I toss my thumb over my shoulder, toward the staircase that leads to a series of bedrooms and bathrooms.

He nods, and his lips straighten into a thin line.

I quickly spin around, face planting into the shoe rack. Mother fu—

Someone laughs behind me, and I slowly turn my head toward Finn, who is biting his bottom lip to keep from laughing more.

"I will be going now." I turn around, slowly this time, and walk up the stairs. I feel Finn's penetrating gaze on my back, but I refuse to peek back at him.

I pass his parents' room, the first on the left. Then Finn's.

When I open the door to the guest room, I look around in confusion. "What the hell?" I whisper to no one.

"My parents turned it into a gym."

My hand flies to my chest as I gasp, turning around to see Finn. How the hell did he get here so fast?

"Guess I'm sleeping on a treadmill tonight," I say, as if my night of inconvenient events couldn't get any worse.

"You'll sleep in my bed," he says casually.

The light from the guest r—*gym*—floods into the dim hallway, and I can finally really see Finn since running into him in the dark parking lot.

It's only been five weeks, but he looks so much older. My eyes sweep over his hair. The brown strands are shorter on the sides and longer on the top of his head, like he's found a new barber other than the one he'd been going to since he was a kid. He probably doesn't even notice the difference between the two styles, but this one makes him look different. Like he's a man instead of a boy. His gleaming eyes are finally visible in the light, and just as alluring as they were downstairs. His T-shirt is loose along his torso but tight around his shoulders, like he's been working out.

My breath catches in my throat like it did earlier when he touched my knee. My childhood best friend is nowhere in sight. The man standing before me is…attractive.

I shake the thought loose from my head. *It's just Finn.* I'm tired from working all day and in need of a *hot* shower.

I blink a few times, and realize Finn is waving his hand in my face.

"Hello. Earth to Adeline…"

"Sorry." I blink again. "What did you say?"

"You'll sleep in my bed," he repeats himself with a bored expression, like he's used to my daydreaming.

"Um, you know what, I've always wondered what it would be like to sleep on a treadmill…" I laugh awkwardly.

Finn stares at me like I have grown another head. "This is what you get for befriending the weird ones. Just go get a shower and meet me in my room." He starts to walk away, but I burst.

"Wait! Won't it be weird sleeping together?" I whisper-scream, like the act of us sleeping in the same bed is too dirty to discuss at full volume.

He turns around and stares at me head on, suddenly I can't look into his eyes. "Why would that be weird? We've been sleeping in the same bed since we were kids?"

"Um, well I guess it's not—"

"Look, if you're uncomfortable I can sleep on the floor or somethi—"

"No!" I shout, cringing at the volume since his parents are sleeping down the hall. Finn's my best friend, I've never seen him as anything but that. I'm being ridiculous.

"Um, okay." And with that, he slowly turns around and disappears inside his room.

I lock myself in the guest bathroom and sink to the floor.

2

TEN YEARS AGO

I quietly shut the door to my bedroom behind me, and lock myself in. My stomach sinks, and tears blur my vision. Is it normal to cry this much? I can't relate to the girls at school. All they worry about is who has the most impressive pencil collection.

It just seems so insignificant compared to everything else. When my mom picked me up from school today, she wouldn't look at me. She wore big chunky sunglasses. When I tried to talk to her, she just turned the radio volume up. I even noticed a tear roll down her cheek.

There weren't any chairs at the table for me to do my homework when we got home.

They were just *gone*.

Sometimes things in our home go missing.

We never talk about it, but we all know it's because my dad, Jason, broke them in a fit of rage. When I think or talk about my dad when he isn't around, I call him Jason. I don't like to think of him as my dad. It makes my stomach hurt.

I didn't even have the chance to ask my mom to sign my field trip form for the zoo trip tomorrow because she disappeared to her bedroom.

I just sit on my bed, clutching my backpack to my chest. At first, it was quiet down the hall behind their bedroom door, but now it's so *loud*.

I wonder if the girls at school fear someone's voice.

The walls vibrate, and even my chest feels the bass in my father's shouting. I can't move. Something thuds against the wall. I close my eyes and hum to myself.

My tears taste salty when they silently drip down my face into my mouth. My shaky hands struggle to empty my backpack. Folders and a few dull pencils roll across my floor. In their place, I stuff a sweater and fresh outfit. I pack away my favorite stuffed giraffe. There are only a few sips left in my water bottle, but I put it in my bag for safe measure.

I can't stay here anymore. I'll live somewhere else.

I have the perfect new home for me. It's got swings and slides, and the only screaming at the playground is of excitement.

I peer out of my bedroom window. The ground is so far away. There's a tree branch a few feet down. If I can jump onto it, I'll be able to climb the rest of the way down.

I lift my rusty window, it squeaks and whines, and I close my eyes and hope his shouting drowns out the sound. I throw my backpack out the window first.

I clutch onto the edge of my window with wet hands as waves of something make me spasm from head to toe. I'm going to throw up or pass out. Or both.

I can't do this—

"*Fuck you!*"

His voice goes right through my chest, moving me into action. I lift myself over the window, quickly bringing the tips of my toes to the tree branch.

Another loud bang comes from my parents' room, and my hands slip.

I fall.

My feet land on something wobbly. I slowly open one eye, realizing I made it onto the branch.

I maneuver my body and climb down the tree, jumping the last few feet.

A rush of excitement ping pongs throughout my belly. That was *fun*.

I pick up my backpack and run down the street as fast as I can, heading for the playground my dad never lets me use. I need to get out of sight in case my dad sees me out his window. I don't stop running until I feel the spongy mulch of the playground beneath my feet.

The swing is hot and burns the back of my legs, but I kick, and I swing and—I can't escape the sadness that wraps its arms around me. So tight. So strong. It squeezes my chest, and I can't breathe.

I can't.

I can't.

I burst.

My face falls into my hands. I'm crying so hard I think I might drown in my own tears. I might flood the entire earth with my pain.

No one likes school. My classmates buzz with excitement as the end of the day nears. They squeal and run to their parent's car when it comes into view at carline.

Me? I stare at the clock and wish it would stop moving. When I'm sitting at my desk holding my wooden pencil,

I'm the happiest I've ever been. Because even when the girls secretly judge my yellow pencil with the pink eraser, I am safe. I pretend having wooden pencils instead of mechanical ones is my biggest struggle in this world.

"Hey," a boy with brown hair says as he sits on the swing next to me.

I gasp, quickly wiping my tears away. Is he talking to me? I glance around, I'm the only one on the playground besides a pretty lady sitting on the bench. She must be his mom.

She smiles at me.

"Hi." I sniffle, embarrassed that the boy saw me crying, but he doesn't draw attention to it. Instead he asks, "Want to see something cool?" He brings his cupped hands close to my face before I can even answer. "I caught him over there in the grass." He reveals a tiny lizard in his hands. The reptile tries to jump out, but the boy cups his hands together, trapping it.

And the craziest thing happens.

I smile.

"Here, you can hold him." The boy smiles at me again, this time I notice a dimple on his cheek.

"I've never held a lizard before."

"It's a baby gecko," he says. "I catch them all the time here."

"He's kind of cute."

"Hold out your hands." He places the tiny creature into my palms. I stare in awe. How could something so small, so fragile, survive in this big cruel world?

I shriek as the gecko jumps out of my hands and runs back into the grass.

"Sorry!" I say with wide eyes.

He laughs, easing my guilt. "Don't worry, that happens

to me all the time." He brings the back of his hand to his forehead to wipe the sweat gathered there. "My name is Finn, what's yours?"

Finn. It's a kind name for a kind boy.

"I'm Adeline."

3

NOW

My skin is rubbed raw, but I think after a good scrub, I'm back to normal. You know, not all bobble headed looking at my best friend's shoulders. Besides, I'm not the type of girl to turn to mush over biceps and pretty eyes.

When your heart's been shredded to pieces in the past, all you can do is grow a protective shell around it and hope no force can break through.

Images of an angry man flash before my eyes, chilling my skin and speeding my heart. I close my eyes and shred the memory of my father, like I've trained myself to do.

I'm single because I choose to be, not because the option of an alternative hasn't arisen. My lack of mingling with the opposite sex doesn't bother me. I sleep just fine knowing I'm nineteen and haven't even had my first kiss.

Don't get me wrong, I believe in love... I'd be an arrogant fool not to.

But love is a temporary feeling, just like any emotion. I

mean, come on, a brain can only make so much oxytocin; eventually it will run dry.

I wrap my towel around my body and reach for my clothes... *No!*

I forgot to bring clothes into the bathroom. All I have are my filthy work clothes I'd hate to put back on my body after taking a shower.

I can just go ask Finn to borrow some clothes, he won't think it's weird I'm in a towel. I probably wouldn't have thought twice about it before today. It's not like he'd look at me like *that*.

I pull my shoulders back, grip the towel wrapped around my body with white knuckles, and open the door.

Steam rolls into the gym which was once a guest room. I walk with false confidence to Finn's door and push past it.

He's laying above the comforter, legs crossed at the ankles, in only a pair of sweats, staring intently at the novel opened in his hands. His eyes slowly travel away from the pages as I hover in the doorway, suddenly unsure of how to ask for a shirt to sleep in. It's as if my brain forgot the entire English language the moment I saw his bare chest. My brain was not wrong about Finn's new workout habits. Whoa.

His gaze travels over me, invisibly touching every inch of skin beneath my towel, up my lips and nose, then straight into my eyes.

"Shit, sorry. Let me get you something to wear." His gaze is down as he gets out of bed, as if trying to avoid looking at me again.

"It's fine." It's not. I want to melt into the floor. My cheeks burn, and I'm sure if Finn wasn't actively trying *not* to look at my nearly naked body, he'd see the blush all over me.

A piece of cloth hits my face, then falls to the floor.

"Fuck," Finn curses. "Sorry." He bends to pick up the black T-shirt he threw at my face and extends it out to me along with a pair of boxers.

I inhale a slow breath, then quickly exhale it. "Could you turn around?"

His eyes go wide, but he does as he is told.

I let the towel drop and step into the boxers, then pull his ginormous T-shirt over my head. "You can look now," I say, crawling into the bed and getting beneath the covers.

Finn just stands by the other side of the bed, his back toward me.

I think I'd rather be in the parking lot right now.

"What are you doing?" I ask.

"Just—" He holds up a hand. "Give me a minute," he says, just standing there.

"You're not even doing anything," I point out.

"Adeline," he says sternly, like that should be the end of the conversation.

"I mean you're quite literally just *standing* there, facing the wall." I laugh. "I mean are you that disgusted by the idea of me being naked that you have to—" I gasp as he turns around, revealing the very obvious bulge in his pants.

"Do I look *disgusted* to you?" He stares at me, and all I can do is stare at…it.

Finn's *it*.

Ohmygod.

"Oh, wow. Um." I force my gaze to the ceiling. "Proceed." I cringe at myself.

Finn chuckles at that.

"What?" I ask, feeling defensive and a touch embarrassed at my naivety. "I only meant you should continue doing whatever it was you were trying to do to manage that…situation."

"I think you having clothes on now will definitely help my *situation*." He fights back an amused smile, scooting into bed beside me.

I stare at him in shock. "I just saw the outline of your…" I let that part hang loose in the air, "and you're fine with it?" The idea of me naked in his room caused that?

No. There's no way. We're best friends and he certainly doesn't see me that way. It would be completely inappropriate given our strictly platonic relationship. I try to forget it even happened and the way it causes a warm sensation lingering deep within my belly.

He doesn't respond to that, he only says, "Goodnight, Miller." He turns the lamp off, leaving me alone in the dark with my thoughts.

～

I wake up to the sound of comforting voices singing "Happy Birthday."

No, I'm not losing my mind, really, there are voices.

Everything is black when I open my eyes, there's fabric suffocating my face. I shove it off me, my hair is a mess around my face.

"Happy birthd—*Ah!*" Finn's mom, Jill, shrieks at my sudden presence, arms flailing.

I blink a few times, then slowly turn my head to Finn's dad, Burt, who squints at the floor, defeated.

My eyes travel down to where Burt's frustration lies, at the remains of a cake splattered all over Finn's bedroom floor.

"Mom. Dad… What the hell?"

"I'm sorry! I didn't know Ad was here, and when she

popped up from the covers, well..." Jill gestures to the mess.

My cheeks warm, I sink a little further into the bed.

"I guess it was a good thing I forgot to buy the birthday candles," Burt jokes with his wife, who doesn't seem to find the humor in it.

Finn's parents walking in on us having a sleepover wouldn't normally feel awkward, but since we are now older, it feels like we were caught doing something more than sleeping...

And the more I think of how wrong they could interpret this, the more my face burns.

I can only imagine my appearance right now, in Finn's T-shirt with wild hair like we—

That would never, in a million years, *ever* happen. I've never even thought about it...but now that I have, I wonder what it would be like—*no*. That would ruin everything between us.

"I would've told you guys she was spending the night if I had known. I found her stranded at Pete's with no key to her house."

"She could handle her own, right Addy?" Burt holds a fist out to me, I awkwardly pull my hand out from beneath the covers to meet his, appearing even more guilty.

Jill glances between Finn and I, slowly backing into the doorway. "Um, well honey, we better go get started on that paperwork we have..." She tosses a thumb over her shoulder.

"We don't have any paperw—" Burt starts.

Jill widens her eyes at him, and then focuses her gaze on us. He clears his throat. "Oh, right...*that* paperwork." He not so subtly winks at his wife, walking toward the doorway. "Happy twentieth birthday, son."

They disappear down the hall, but he shoots out one last comment. "I had *lots* of fun in my twenties."

A slapping sound, of what I can only imagine was Jill's rear end, makes her shriek, "Burt!"

"My mom wants *us* to happen so bad she's making scenarios up in her head." Finn laughs as if the idea of *us* is an absurd suggestion.

And I don't know why, but something caves in my chest. Do I want there to be an *us*?

I clear my throat and change the subject, unwilling to dive too deeply into these new feelings about Finn. "I know you probably envisioned intoxicating yourself to the point of slumber with your head in the toilet for your birthday, but since you're home, you'll have to spend the evening eating dinner with me." I flatten the mess of hair around my face.

He doesn't say anything, just pulls the covers off his half naked body. Pulling on a black T-shirt over his head, he walks toward his bathroom.

"Sounds good, love."

It feels like I swallowed a bunch of moths. They throw themselves at the wall of my stomach hearing Finn's nickname for me.

Finn talks through the bathroom door, "You should come with me."

"Where?"

"To FSU. Just think about it, Ad. You can take some prerequisite classes toward your associate degree, or something."

"I can't leave, Finn."

"Adeline." The bathroom door swings open, Finn's hair is still tousled, but in a more organized way. He has some dried toothpaste in the corner of his mouth, my eyes zero in on the curve of his lips as they move.

I blink a few times, realizing they produced words. "What?"

"I said you have to start living life for yourself, Adeline, not your mom."

It's hard to concentrate when he looks at me so intensely. The gray comforter is a much easier place to look, so I focus on the fabric and the way it was weaved together.

"Ad." He sighs, stepping right in front of me and kneeling so we are eye level. Damn it, my plan failed. "You got into FSU," he says, like it was some big accomplishment. "You said you were going to take a gap year, but you haven't even signed up for classes. When are you going to start your life?" He speaks with no judgement, just sympathy.

It's sweet but infuriating all in one. "I have started my life." My voice comes out harsher than I intend it to. "I have a job."

"At Pete's," he says, like it justifies his point. "Did he even make you interview?" He sounds genuinely curious and doesn't say it demeaning, but it still stings.

I didn't interview. I've known Pete as long as I've known Finn. His restaurant has been a second home to us.

I don't respond because my answer makes this conversation even more pathetic.

"Look, college isn't all its jacked up to be without you there." He runs a gentle finger through a strand of my hair, then neatly tucks it behind my ear.

I try to pull as much oxygen into my lungs as I can, but a much greater force sucks the air out of the room.

I try to focus on his eyes, but mine keep shifting to the

pale pink of his lips. What would they look like after being pressed against mine? Would they swell into a deeper pink?

"I have to go." I hate the way my voice comes out. So small, so fragile. Like a hint of rejection from Finn will sweep me up like a feather caught in the wind, only to drop me in a pile of trash.

Finn sighs, like I'm upset by the conversation.

Maybe I would be if I wasn't thinking of ways to commit an exorcism. Because clearly, I've been possessed by a horny ghost last night.

"I'll walk you home," he offers.

I refuse, needing relief from his presence immediately. Besides, it's a short walk to my house. I just hope my mother is awake to let me in.

Reality sits heavy upon my chest.

Time to step back into the real world. One without pools of amber and bugs that tickle my insides.

I might drive this pencil right through my eye.

I don't hold a pencil, but there's a sharpened one laying innocently upon the pile of dishes with spoiled food on my kitchen counter.

I don't know whether to be relieved or concerned that my front door was unlocked this whole time. I'll get back to that one some other time.

There's a smell coming from the living room, probably the couch cushions soaking up my mother's urine. I pull urine filled air into my nostrils, expelling it as fast as possible. "Mom, I'm home." I'd rather be anywhere but.

I continue my daily search for her. She's not in the

living room. I grab the bunched-up tissues covering the floor, right by the couch.

There's a wet stain on the light blue fabric. Lovely, I get to scrub a couch today.

I glance out the window at our pool…just in case, then release a breath of relief because it's empty, other than a brown palm frond floating on the surface. The patio surrounding the pool I once considered my safe space sinks into the ground. It cracks around the edges, as if one more rainfall will send it deeper into the earth like a sink hole.

My mom hasn't worked in years. She was a small business owner of a local boutique, but she gave that up a few years ago. She doesn't need to work. The inheritance she got from her parents was enough to keep her comfortable. They both died before I was born.

My mother kept the story of their love alive when I was a little girl. She didn't read me books before bed. Instead, she told me about her mom and dad, and how strong their love was.

In the end, my grandma passed away from cancer. It was a long, brutal journey, but my grandpa stood by her side in sickness like he vowed. He died of a heart attack a week after her passing.

Sometimes I wonder if their love was a tale my mother made up to shelter me from reality. From what was happening to her. I wonder if she needed to tell the stories more than I needed to hear them.

Sometimes I wonder if I'll ever experience anything like it. A love strong enough to give a healthy man a heart attack.

But she loved her boutique; she loved fashion and picking out special pieces to display in her store. I miss that version of her.

The stairs are cold beneath my bare feet, and I slowly creep up them, knowing there's only one last place she could be. The door to her bedroom is cracked. I brace myself for whatever disaster lays on the other side.

I lightly tap on the white chipped paint. "Mom, I'm home." Bile rises to my throat at the smell of vomit.

I step over the obstacle of clothes mixed with garbage to get to her side of the bed. "Hi, Mom," I whisper to the shell of her left behind, limp on the sheetless mattress.

I wonder if it will ever hurt less to see her like this.

A sound similar to a groan vibrates through her body.

I gasp as she shoots up from lying face down, quickly grabbing the salad bowl next to her vomit-stained pillow.

I touch my chest while I catch my breath.

"Fucking A," my mom curses into the bowl between dry heaves.

I stand still, watching the aftermath of her binge drinking play out like I do every morning. Only some days consist of puking, when she surpasses her limit.

When she finally runs out of stomach acid, she sits up in her bed, leaning against the headboard. "Hi honey, I checked on you before I went to bed last night, but you were asleep."

I don't bother calling her out, explaining how I was at Finn's last night. I'm just glad she made it to her room without falling down the stairs or something. "Thanks, Mom." I smile. "Do you need a Gatorade or something?" I turn on my heel, ready to grab her one from the stash beneath her bed.

"You look different," she says, not answering because I'm already ducking beneath the bed to pull out a purple one.

I screw off the lid, handing it to her. "I haven't gotten any taller since yesterday."

She holds it to her cracked lips, cringing at the taste. I watch her pull open the drawer to her night table, grab a bottle of clear liquid, and take a large gulp of it.

I cower a little, but there's no use in explaining the detriments excessive alcohol consumption has on the body.

She knows. She's the one living it.

"Would you grab me my pills, puffin?" She gulps her vodka between Gatorade sips.

"Does your foot even hurt?" I attempt to talk her out of "needing" her pain killers, but she just rolls her eyes and holds out her hand.

Her doctor prescribed her pain killers when she broke her foot, but that was nearly five years ago. I don't even want to know where she gets the pills now, but she claims the doctor forever messed up her foot, that the pain is *so bad* she needs medicine to put it to rest.

I twist open the white cap while reading the prescription for a lady named Betty, which is obviously not my mom's name. I hesitantly hand her two pills. She shakes her head in disappointment, grabs the bottle from my hand, and shakes a few more pills into her palm.

Each rattle of pills against pills sends my organs into failure, or at least it feels that way.

"Don't you have to be at work?" she asks after swallowing who knows how many pills.

"It's Saturday."

"So?" She stares up at me through fierce yellow-green eyes.

"I don't work Saturdays," I remind her for the hundredth time.

"Oh yeah." She slowly lays back down, resting her head

on the stained pillow.

I watch her for a few moments, the way her breath slows, and a snore takes over the quiet. I try my best not to make noise as I snatch the vodka from the nightstand, walk over to her bathroom, and replace it with tap water.

Once I've set the bottle back where she left it, I carry on with my day.

Saturdays are my only days off, so I always try to make the most of them, starting with *the shower.* I exfoliate the skin on my legs and shave extra good, making sure not to miss any spots. I give myself a voluminous blowout, since the auburn strands look like a lion's mane any other day.

By the time I finish my second romcom movie of the day, it's six in the evening, which means Finn will be here any minute.

Only moments later, headlights shine through my blinds. I run down my stairs and out the front door. The white pebbles seem to find their way into my flip flops with every step toward Finn's car.

He's silent as I get settled in, but not in an awkward way. Finn and I can spend hours talking but can just as easily sit in the silence and not be bothered by it.

He puts the car in drive and heads south, following the one main road on the island. He doesn't bother asking me where we're going, knowing I'll just tell him when to turn.

The next island, Islamorada, has the cutest restaurant on the water where we can eat the freshest seafood while watching the sun go down. I've always wanted to go, and it seemed too date-ish to do with my best friend, but since it's a special occasion—Finn's birthday—it feels okay to eat there.

He glances at me, "I miss your freckles." He says, "I can hardly see them."

I tuck a strand of hair behind my ear, "I haven't been in the sun much lately." The hard-to-see freckles that line my nose and cheeks become more visible in the summer, except for *this* summer. This summer, I've spent every day indoors, without giving the sun a chance to kiss my fair skin.

"We need to change that. You love being outside." His eyes are on me again. "I like what you did with your eyes, by the way."

My cheeks heat. "I put on mascara." I hardly ever put on makeup.

I see the name of my favorite song on the tiny screen of his dash. I turn the radio up. It blares in my ears, exactly how I like it. I press a button, rolling down the windows. My hair slaps me in the face, strands sticking to my lip-gloss. The whole world whizzes by, as if only Finn and I exist.

I stick my arm out, and the air kisses all my pores. I move my hand in a wave motion to the momentum of the wind. It's hypnotizing.

I feel alive for the first time in months.

"Your hair is hitting me in the face, Adeline!" Finn's shouts to get louder than the music.

I awaken from my hypnotic state, pulling my arm inside the car.

Finn rolls up my window.

"Hey!" I complain, pulling the sun visor down to glance in the mirror. My hair sticks up in every which way. I attempt to smooth the mess, but it's a lost cause. Maybe closing the window was for the best if I want to appear at all presentable for dinner.

I lower the music to a more appropriate volume, focusing on nothing for a few heart beats. "What do you think the meaning of life is?"

Finn doesn't question my question, he just asks, "In what way?"

This is how our friendship is. I pick his brain and he entertains me with the beautiful abyss of his mind.

I point to a silhouette of a man running on the sidewalk. Pinks and golds morph into purples as the sun starts to set. I hope we make it to dinner before it fully descends behind the horizon. "That guy could be doing literally a million other things right now, but he chose to spend *this* moment running on *that* sidewalk."

"So?"

"The only thing really promised is now." I sigh. "That's it."

I point between me and him. "You and I spend our only promise from the world driving on this massive rock, floating in space."

His eyes fixate on the road in front of him, but they twinkle in amusement.

"No one knows why we're here, or what we're supposed to do. All we can do is choose how to spend our precious seconds," I say.

"I can't think of a single thing I'd rather be doing right now," he says, no hint of sarcasm in his words. Even so, I still can't help but hear the echo of my insecurities, telling me he's lying.

I raise my chin, signaling to my subconscious to *shut the fuck up*.

"Waitressing has really shown me how lost some people are," I tell him. "Some couples sit there and just…eat." I shake my head. "Like that's it. They don't talk about their day or compliment one another. They sit down, order their food, stare at the wall or their phones, and eat."

We stop at a traffic light. His face glows red, and the

Saturday night traffic reflects onto his perfectly sharp features. His eyes are a liquified amber. I get lost in the way the world before us is pocketed into them.

"I know what you mean. So many people just go through the motions of the day." He turns on his right turn signal, pointing directly to Pete's.

He pulls into an empty parking spot next to my car.

"Let's get my car after dinner. There's no point in both of us driving there," I tell him, thankful I remembered to bring my spare key.

"We're having dinner here, love." He puts the car in park and shuts off the engine.

"You want to eat *here* for your birthday?" I am appalled, staring at Pete's in front of me.

"Yes, Adeline. It's the best pizza place in town. Why wouldn't we eat here?"

"Finn, I know you're a man of habit, but we could go somewhere *nice*. I was going to take you to this place in Islamorada."

"But this is *our* place." He unbuckles his seatbelt. I don't budge. "Besides, I haven't seen Pete in ages." He unbuckles my seat belt for me.

I surrender with an obnoxiously loud sigh. "Don't move." I push my door open and step onto the same parking lot I was stranded in yesterday.

Of course, Finn doesn't follow orders. He shuts the door behind him innocently walking with his hands in his pockets to the front of the car, where I stand.

"Dude, what part of *don't move* do you not understand?"

"I understood. I just didn't care." He shrugs.

"Get back in the car." I cross my arms over my chest in attempt to be taken seriously.

"Why?" He lifts a brow.

"Because."

"Because *why?*"

"Please?" I batt my eyelashes.

"No."

"I wanted to open the door for you and be all gentle-woman-like for your birthday, but you ruined it." I throw my hands up. "You know what? You can make it up to me by holding the door on the way in, and then scooting my chair out for me," I say, matter-of-factly.

"Yes, ma'am." He puts his hands up in defense, eyeing me like I've lost my mind.

It's a breezy night and my hair is blowing in every direction, so I pull it into a ponytail as we walk to the front door. Finn does as he is told and opens the door for me causing the bells at the top to jingle. I give him a nod of approval. The mouthwatering smell of pizza makes me feel like I just walked into an eight-hour shift.

"Well, if it isn't my favorite employee and customer!" Pete says from across the restaurant. He makes his way to us. "You want the usual?"

"Of course," Finn answers.

We rode our bikes here almost every day as kids. Pete stopped making us pay for our food years ago, saying he sees us as family.

He never had any kids, and his wife, Linda, passed away ten years ago, around the time we met. He should be retired, but I think he enjoys the social aspect of being here.

When I asked him for a job last year, he hired me on the spot. I couldn't go to college hours away from my mom. She'd probably aspirate on her own vomit and go months without being found.

I could've done some online classes, but the thought

really bummed me out. I wanted to go off to college like everyone else, I just didn't have the luxury of a self-reliant parent.

"One large pizza, half meat-lovers half cheese, coming right up!" Pete starts toward the kitchen, but I interrupt.

"Pete!" I call after him. "How are the ducks behaving?" I ask, already knowing the answer. He talks about his pet ducks every time I come in for a shift. Finn and I got them for him last Christmas.

My coworker, Ava, puts two glasses of water in front of us.

"Finn." Pete widens his eyes as he's about to tell a story. "Who would've known a couple a ducks could get into so much trouble? Daffy started bullying my dog—you met him I think—Gus Gus. Anyway, Daffy chases Gus Gus around the pool. Does this scary thing with her wings to make herself seem all big and tough. Poor dog's too scared to go out back now. I gotta go home and walk him every few hours so he doesn't pee in the house." He laughs easily. He doesn't take life too seriously; I wish I could be as carefree as Pete sometimes.

Finn laughs at the image. "Man, poor Gus Gus."

"Yeah well, what about you two? Datin' yet or what?"

The tips of my ears burn, I focus anywhere but Pete or Finn. What a horrible time to ask that question. You know, with the horny ghost possession and all.

"No, sir," Finn answers politely.

"Come on, Finn!" Pete slams his palm against the red table. "Make a move already. I haven't got all the time in the world like you two do. You've tortured me enough for ten somethin' years, watching y'all do that flirty banter thing you've got going on."

"Pete, we need you in the kitchen!" one of my coworkers yells from the back.

"Saved by the bell. You two, enjoy your meal." He winks at Finn and walks to the kitchen.

We are left alone, Pete's words still lingering in the air, making it extremely hard to look Finn in the eye.

"Do you think you're truly living, Adeline?" Finn picks up our earlier conversation, right where we left off.

"Yes," I lie.

"That doesn't sound very convincing."

"I just worry about everyone else who isn't," I tell him truthfully.

"Of course you sit around and worry for strangers' well-being." He drums his straw against the table to get the paper off. "Adeline, you spend every day taking care of your mom and serving people pizza. How are you any different than the strangers you worry about?" His words sit heavy on my chest.

I don't have a choice. My mom needs me, and I need a job. Since I don't have a degree or a clue of what career path I want to take, waitressing is the only option right now.

"Maybe I'm not, but at least I don't mask my pain like everyone around me. They scroll for hours on their phones pretending they live a different life… Or drink into oblivion." I grab the paper from Finn's straw, ripping it to pieces, and then rolling each piece into a ball.

I try to convince myself the words I'm speaking are the truth, but a memory of my bruised mom and terrifying dad parade around my mind until I do what I always do, burying it deep inside.

It's the only way I survive.

"That's their choice, Adeline." He doesn't miss a beat. "You don't have to give up your life for *their* choices." He doesn't say her name, but we both know he's talking about my mom. "I don't know the meaning of life, but it's definitely not spending it trying to save someone who doesn't want to be saved."

My stomach sinks. "Ouch."

"Ad, I didn't mean—"

"No," I interrupt, not letting him get away with this so easily. "Addiction isn't a *choice*." I correct his ignorance. "And I would rather spend my time helping my mom than the rest of my life regretting *not* helping her." I blow out a breath. "I'm all she has." My voice cracks.

Finn's hand stills my shaking ones. "You can't fix her."

"She just needs—" I start.

"Just like she couldn't fix your dad," he interrupts.

The heaviness of his words in the air weighs between us.

"What do you recommend I do?" I ask, knowing there's no right answer to the problems in my life.

"She could go to rehab," he suggests.

"She doesn't want to admit she has a problem," I counter.

"You could come to FSU with me and hope she finally acknowledges her problem," he says hopefully. "Think about it. Without you there to make every area of her life easier, she'll figure out real fast how much her addiction really disables her."

If I left, I would worry the whole time I was gone if she'd be alive when I came back. "I can't leave," I say. "But you make a good point; maybe I'll try to be less helpful."

Finn smiles, like he's proud of me.

"I guess sometimes you have to give someone a shove to rock bottom." I give a weak smile. I know I'm not going to like this.

"I do know the meaning of life." Finn lightens the

mood with this goofy grin.

"Oh yeah?" I ask, flicking a paper ball at him.

"Yeah." He flicks it back at me, missing and hitting the lady sitting behind me. "Shit," he murmurs.

I laugh, by some miracle, after the conversation we just had.

"The meaning of life can be anything you make it to be," he says. "Adeline, the guy on the sidewalk's meaning of life is different from yours. From mine." He catches his breath. "In *this* moment, the moment promised, I'm going to have fun. That's it." He leans back. "It will probably change in the future, but I don't worry about that. You said it yourself, tomorrow isn't promised, only this second is."

"The moment promised," I repeat, a smile tugging at my lips. "I like that. It perfectly encapsules what life is. Individual moments woven together to create an exhilarating story."

"We've cracked the code, Miller." He lightly taps his knee against mine.

I have his full attention when he asks, "How's the moment promised going for you?"

He already knows the answer. Horrible, pathetic, *boring*... I spend each day repeating the previous one on an exhausting loop.

I look up at him, "I want to have fun." The weight of the world lifts off my shoulders with one sentence.

He smiles, and for a moment his eyes drop to my lips. His voice comes out hoarse, "Then let's have some fun."

Ava places a pizza in front of us.

"Thanks, girl."

The melted cheese smells so good.

Finn grabs a slice from the meat-lovers side. "We can't have fun if you spend every day working," he points out.

I grab a slice from my side, burning my finger on the cheese. "Ow! How are you eating right now? It's so hot!"

Finn shrugs with a mouthful of pizza.

"Are you suggesting I quit my job?" I cut into my pizza with a fork and knife since it's too hot to pickup with my hands.

He nods, trying to finish chewing the ginormous bite he took.

"I can't quit," I whisper, since I'm literally having this conversation at the place I work.

"You hardly spend any money, I'll bet dinner you have a pretty hefty savings." He watches me expectedly.

"That is not the point." I take a sip of my water. "Pete needs me. I have an obligation to this place and—"

"Pete!" Finn interrupts, calling across the restaurant to Pete, who wipes down a table.

I kick Finn over and over beneath the table when Pete starts walking over.

"Adeline needs the summer off, is that cool?" Finn asks nonchalantly, as I frantically shake my head.

"Sure, thing kiddo, how long?"

"Couple months or so." Finn answers before I can.

"I don't need the summer off," I squeak.

Pete looks between us. A grin grows across his face. "You know what, I'm going to make it mandatory. You work too hard, and if Finn thinks you need a couple months off, then time off is what you'll get." He doesn't give me time to protest before he walks away.

"How could you do that?" I lean across the table, pointing an angry finger in Finn's face. I have enough money saved that I could go a few months without working, but that's not the point.

"You're making a scene, love," he says, relaxed, grabbing

another slice of pizza.

"I need to use to ladies' room." I throw the napkin occupying my lap on the table. On my way to the bathroom, I spot Pete. "Psttt. Pete, come over here quick."

"What's up, lava girl?" He's called me this since I was a kid because of my red hair. I don't mind though, it's just Pete. If anyone else called me lava girl, I'd probably rip them a new one.

Since Finn basically got me fired for the next two months, I'm going to make something happen I know he'll hate. "Can you do one of those embarrassing restaurant birthday songs that makes everyone look at Finn?"

"I'll see what I can do, you want a molten lava cake?"

"You know it's our favorite." I smile.

Pete tosses a rag over his shoulder, making his way back to the kitchen.

I wash my hands in the bathroom to waste time, then walk back to my seat. I bite my cheeks, not to smile.

"What's with the knowing smile, Adeline?" Finn asks.

Crap.

"Pete told a really funny joke on my way to the bathroom." I look down. Maybe Finn will think my flushed face is a reflection from the red table.

"Okay," he says, wary, as he cocks his head.

I turn around at the squeak of the kitchen door flying open. Pete walks out with a plate of lava cake, and a sparkler stuck in the middle. My now ex-coworkers clap in sync.

A smile overtakes my face from ear to ear.

Pete sings his own version of "Happy Birthday." My laughter gets lost as the guests clap and sing along. I glance at Finn, his nostrils flare, and he is giving his famous death glare to everyone in the restaurant.

Tears spill out of my eyes from laughing so much. It

gets to the part of the song that says, "Happy birthday dear..." and everyone pauses because they don't know his name.

I stand up and yell, "Finn Walker!" Pete gives me a cheeky smile and a thumbs up. The singing ends with the slice of lava cake set in front of Finn. By the time the attention is off our table, Finn gives me a murderous glare.

He yanks my hand, inspecting the ring he once bought me years ago for my birthday. "Oh Adeline. Adeline, Adeline, *Adeline*. You can't possibly think I'm going to let you get away with this." He pulls the ring off my index finger and gets down on one knee. Is he about to...*no*. I grimace.

I immediately start shaking my head aggressively.

Please no.

I silently plead with Finn not to do the thing I think he is about to do.

He speaks painfully slow, "Adeline Marie Miller—"

"Sh! Stop it," I whisper, smacking his shoulder.

He looks up with devilish eyes. "Will you marry me?" he asks, so loudly conversations all around come to a halt. I think I hear Pete giggling somewhere.

I stare at him wide eyed. Red patches light up my face and neck. I want to crawl into a hole and never leave. I hate all the eyes on me, I feel like each one is burning a new hole into my skin. To get this over with I just nod my head and Finn jumps up with hands in the air of victory.

"She said yes!"

The restaurant goes wild with whistling and cheering. I'm sure the whistling is coming from Pete. I turn my head to see but Finn pulls me into a hug.

Before I can hide in his embrace, warm lips slam into mine.

4

NINE YEARS AGO

Are you thirsty? We have juice, water, soda, if your parents allow you to drink it, of course." Jill gives me a maternal smile.

"No, thank you," I say sweetly.

"I'll have some orange juice!" Finn says.

"You have two working legs and two working arms. Get up and get it for yourself," she tells her son. Half-jokingly.

"How come Adeline gets special treatment?" He rolls his eyes.

"She *is* special."

"Yeah, we like her better than you sometimes," Burt says, walking into the kitchen, a rolled-up newspaper in hand. "Got anything for me today, Adeline?" He sits on a barstool, pulling a pencil from behind his ear to complete his daily crossword puzzle.

I smile. "Yes, I do." I empty my backpack onto the center island. Seashells scatter onto the granite.

"You've really outdone yourself!" He nods with approval.

"Do you really need any more seashells, Burt? I think we have more in this house than the entire Gulf of Mexico," Jill jokes.

Burt walks over to his wife, a lifetime of love still evident in his eyes. He tucks a strand of hair behind her ear, giving her a sweet kiss on her cheek.

"A man can never own too many shells, dear," he says, picking one up to observe. "Do you know what this one's called, Adeline?"

"Hmm. Looks like angel wings." I smile at the way the two shells are connected together.

"It does, doesn't it? It is called a Sunray Venus, did you know—"

"All right, Burt, stop holding up the poor girl," Jill interrupts the beginning of her husband's tangent, handing me a juice box since I never got the chance to answer which drink I wanted.

I beam. It's my favorite flavor, and we never have anything but water at our house. "Thank you."

"We're going to the beach." Finn walks toward the door that leads to his garage, directing me to follow.

"By yourselves?" his mother asks.

"We are ten years old, it's not a big deal." He gazes down, like she's embarrassing him.

"All right, all right. Go. Have fun guys, bring your phone, Finn!" she shouts, as Finn drags me toward the garage.

The way Jill worries about her son is nice. My parents don't even know it's spring break. They think I'm going to school every day, but really, I come to the Walker's house.

Surfboards line the walls of the garage, along with a few skateboards. Burt surfs every Sunday morning, and sometimes Finn and I go with him.

The Walkers treat me as their own, and sometimes I wish his parents were mine. I know it's selfish, and I hate myself for even thinking it.

"You can ride the one with the basket." Finn points to the smaller of the two bikes. "Think fast!" He tosses me a helmet with a second's notice.

I don't catch it in time, and it clatters against the ground.

"Too slow," Finn teases.

I roll my eyes at him like I always do.

We ride our bikes side by side on the neighborhood street, not bothering to use the sidewalk.

The beach is only a half mile from Finn's house. You need a special key to get past the gate, which only the residents of his neighborhood have.

The air smells like rotten eggs. It blows against my face as I petal faster to keep up with Finn.

"It's an eggy day out," Finn says.

"A what?"

"An eggy day. It's what my dad calls it when it smells gross outside. Like rotten eggs." He makes a disgusted face as I glance over at him.

I laugh a little at the expression.

Sometimes I wonder what I would be doing if I never met Finn last year. I dread the thought. I hope our friendship lasts forever. I don't know what I would do without him.

I used to wake up every day feeling like I had a hundred pounds sitting on my chest. I loathed being home, and I hated being at school because all I could think of was how horrible it was going to be when I got picked up.

I still don't like being at home, but I don't spend the

39

time I'm away from it dreading going back, because now I have someone I'm *excited* to see every day.

A blue Volkswagen Beetle drives by as Finn says, "Punch buggy blue no punch backs!" and punches my arm, making me lose balance and fall.

Pain suddenly engulfs my knee. The skin burns as I scrape it against the asphalt. Tears well in my eyes and my blood stains the road beneath me.

"I'm sorry! Are you okay?" Finn's voice shakes.

I wipe my eyes like my dad always tells me to. *"Don't cry. You're not a fuckin' baby."* His voice is always around, even when he's not.

My chin quivers, and I try to stop the tears.

Gentle arms wrap around me. "It's okay," Finn tells me.

"I'm sorry. I don't mean to cry."

"You can cry, here let me call my mom. She can pick—"

"No!" I scream.

"Why not?"

"Because I don't want her to call my parents. It's fine, I'll wash my knee in the ocean."

"But your knee is bleeding a lot, you need a bandage."

"Please, Finn. Really, I'm okay," I plead. "I'll get in trouble. My parents think I'm at school and my dad gets mad if I get hurt."

He pauses for too many heart beats, like he's battling something within himself, and then says, "Okay."

I wipe my eyes and get back on the bike.

Finn doesn't say a single word to me. Not while we ride our bikes, not when he's putting them on the bike rack, and not as we walk through the sand.

The water is biting. I take a deep breath and walk further in until my knee is fully submerged. I wince at the pain.

Finn finally breaks silence. "What did you mean when you said your dad gets mad when you're hurt?"

Images of an angry Jason flash through my mind.

"I don't know." I shrug. "He says I shouldn't be falling around, and I need to watch where I'm going."

He steps into the water beside me, "Sometimes you can't help it. Accidents happen."

I wish Jason would see it that way.

I squeeze my fists. The truth sticks to my tongue. I'm not supposed to tell anyone what happens in our house. My mom told me it would be very bad if anyone found out. Carrying this secret with me everywhere I go has gotten so heavy, I fear it will crush me whole. Before I can help it, the words are falling from my mouth. "The last time I got hurt he blamed it on my mom. He was so mad he slammed her face against the wall."

Finn chokes on his own breath. His eyes widen as he realizes I was serious. "He hits her?"

I should say no. I should laugh and pretend I was making a sick twisted joke. "Yeah." I look down, my blood colors the water surrounding it.

"Why is she still with him?"

I've wondered this too lately. They are opposites in every possible way. He's like a storm crowding her sunshine.

No.

A hurricane.

"I don't know. I sometimes wish my mom would break up with him," I admit, feeling guilty for wishing such a terrible thing.

"Like...divorce?" he asks.

I nod. They aren't happy like Finn's parents. Jason doesn't look at my mom and smile like Burt does when he sees Jill. Instead, he tells her everything she is doing

41

wrong, even if it's right. I mean, I'm pretty sure he *hates* her.

He faces me fully, there's a tremble in his voice when he asks, "Adeline, does he—" He winces, and swallows like he's stalling. Like he's afraid to even ask. "D-does he hit you?"

I answer too fast, like I'm supposed to be standing up for my dad instead of telling his secrets. "No." It's the truth. He'd never laid a hand on me… Not even for a hug. But his words throw punches at my chest until my heart bleeds, and I can't breathe.

"Do you like your mom better than your dad?"

"Yes." I don't have to think twice about my answer.

Finn's eyes flash with sorrow. I feel regret in the pit of my stomach, but it's the truth.

"What about you? Do you like your mom or dad better?" I ask.

"I can't decide. I love them both." He kicks a piece of washed-up coral.

Something sharp stabs my stomach. Jealousy. I want that life. The one where deciding which parent gained more of your love seems impossible.

"Please don't tell anyone," I whisper.

Finn looks like he's grinding his teeth, like he wishes I never asked this of him. "But, Adeline—"

"Finn, I'll have to move away," I plead. My skin burns and my hands tremble and a bead of sweat drips down my back. I shouldn't have told him. I've heard stories of what happens to families when someone tells. The kids get taken away and only once in a blue moon do they go somewhere kind. Somewhere safe. Somewhere loving. *No.*

No.

"You can't say anything. Please, Finn. Not to your mom and dad. Not to anyone. They will take me away. They could put me with a family that *does* hit me. *Please*, Finn." I don't even realize I'm crying until a soft fingertip brushes over the wetness coating my cheek.

And I watch it happen. Right through his eyes I see a crack forming in his soul under the weight of the truth. Truth too heavy for anyone to carry. And yet I so easily placed a million tons onto his back and ask him to never set it down.

I hate myself.

"Okay," he says, then he does the craziest thing.

My skin raises in goosebumps as he splashes me.

I laugh, and forget about Jason, divorce, and the rest of my life. When I'm with Finn, none of it exists.

I run after him, chasing him along the shore. His footprints are bigger than mine, and it's hard to reach him since he is faster than me.

I finally catch up when he trips and I crash into him. We roll around in the sand, laughing together.

"Am I your best friend?" He sits up, wiping the sand off his shorts.

"Yeah… Am I yours?" I'm a little afraid of his answer.

"Duh," he says like it's obvious.

I smile. I've never had a best friend before. The wind picks up, I wrap my arms around my legs.

"Do you think we will be best friends forever?" I ask, hopeful.

"No," he says quickly.

I frown.

"Because I'm going to marry you," he says matter-of-factly.

I laugh. "Gross. I would never marry you."

He smiles, but it doesn't touch his eyes like mine does.

5

NOW

The noisy restaurant goes quiet in my head. My body catches up before my brain does because I am parting my lips and letting my best friend's tongue sweep over mine. His hands are everywhere, moving swiftly down my arms, up my back, into my hair.

I'm bursting and I'm souring.

I'm dying and I'm living.

Up is down and right is left and…

Everything changes… Everything.

A gentle sound escapes my throat and Finn catches it with his mouth.

I have no thoughts except for words flashing against the blackness of my mind like a neon sign. Passion. Bliss. Desire. Three words burn into my brain and suddenly my stomach because I'm burning from within.

He places one last kiss on my lips, resting his forehead against mine. With his amber eyes so close I can see worlds in them. My eyebrows pull together with so much emotion.

I've never felt anything more intense than this moment. It's as if I've been brough to life.

"I told you I'd get you to marry me," he whispers.

The world spins a billion miles per hour until suddenly it stops and everything around me can be heard again. What just happened?

"Atta boy!" Pete's voice echoes in my head, reminding me of where we are.

Finn's eyes leave mine to glance at my lips before breaking away, taking along the piece of my heart he captured with his kiss.

I focus on the checkered floor to avoid all the stares heating up my skin.

From the corner of my eye, I see Finn taking his seat again. I still don't look at him when I sit back down and pull the scrunchie from my hair, the wild pieces shielding me from the watchful eyes of ex coworkers and customers.

When I glance up, Finn is laughing. He fake proposed as a joke to get back at me for embarrassing him, but it didn't *feel* like a joke.

Kissing my best friend shouldn't feel so...*good*. My best friend's lips shouldn't have the power to light my insides on fire, to make me feel something I've never felt before.

I try to act like nothing happened. Like I haven't dropped ten degrees without Finn's touch. "I swear, Finn, this will be the last birthday you ever have." Or maybe I'm the one who won't see their next birthday because I'm pretty sure I'm having a heart attack.

"We'll see, love," he says easily, completely unaffected by what just happened.

Maybe I'm the weird one for feeling as if my world has turned sideways from something as trivial as a kiss. But it didn't feel like just any kiss between friends.

"Congratulations, you two." Pete winks at Finn.

Never have I ever thought I'd be stealing from the Walkers' liquor cabinet, but life is a funny thing sometimes.

This could look bad without context...with my mom being addicted to this stuff and all.

Being a good friend apparently entails stealing your best friend's parents' liquor, while they distract said parents.

"Oh shit," Finn curses from the living room after something shatters.

If all is going to plan, he "accidentally" knocked over the ceramic vase on the TV stand.

"Finn!" Jill's voice is clipped.

I flinch, hating the idea of causing Finn's parents' stress. But as it turns out, this is how the birthday boy wanted to end the night, and I'm in no position to turn down his wishes after my "I want to have fun" proclamation.

"I'll go grab the broom," Burt says.

I hear shuffling, like someone just got off the couch. "I'll get it!" Finn says, suspiciously rushed.

I try to focus on the task at hand. The vodka is just out of reach, almost as if the Walkers didn't want their kid to get into it.

Ironic.

Footsteps near awfully fast and my entire body freezes as I stand in front of the forbidden cabinet.

"How's it going?" Finn whispers.

I jolt, startled by his presence in the kitchen.

"Can't. Reach." I struggle on my tippy toes.

He easily reaches past me, grabbing the alcohol as he peeks over his shoulder. He puts the bottle in my sweatpants. The glass is cold against the skin between my stomach and pelvis.

I pull my hoodie down to cover the bulge and stick my hands in the pockets, trying desperately to hold the bottle in place so it doesn't fall down my pant leg.

His proximity mixes with the adrenaline from what we're doing, causing my eyes to drop to a dangerous place. His lips.

Where mine were only thirty minutes ago.

To him, kissing me was just a way to make the fake proposal more believable so I'd feel even more embarrassed. I wonder if he realizes it was my first kiss.

I take a step back from him, but my spine meets the bottles of wine displayed on a lower shelf, causing the entire structure to wobble. I squeeze eyes tight, expecting the Walkers' collection of alcohol to shatter against my skull.

Before any of that can happen, Finn stills the cabinet with his hands, caging me in between his arms.

We're closer than before. His chest is against mine, rising and falling together, in perfect synchronicity. Like a perfectly balanced poem, falling on the same note, rhyming on the same vowels.

It's as if we're stuck in a trance. Both of us are unmoving, as if we want to linger in this moment a little while longer. "Are you coming with the broom?" Jill calls. I hear her get off the couch, her footsteps getting closer.

I push past Finn, walking toward the back door in a hurry. "I'll meet you out there," I whisper.

My sense of reasoning has turned to mush, and I haven't even had a sip. I shouldn't be lusting after Finn, and I plan to put a stop to it immediately.

Finn's presence is so loud.

When I'm in the same room as him everything surrounding us just disappears.

This feeling, it's so strong and unnerving... It's intoxicating. I don't like it one bit.

I pace back and forth along his back patio. The pool glows blue under the moonlight. Large palm trees sway with the breeze. The atmosphere smells like salt from the ocean that's only a block away. A carved wooden sign screwed into the base of the closet tree reads *DANGER FALLING COCONUTS.*

My eyes pull away from the words at the sound of sliding glass doors slamming shut.

Stepping into view with a smile plastered to his face, Finn says, "I'm going to remind you how to have fun, love." He walks past me, onto the sidewalk that leads to the neighborhood's private beach.

I follow close behind, looking up to the stars, but they're invisible because of light pollution.

I unscrew the cap, taking a large swig of vodka.

Finn turns around. "Hey! We haven't even toasted yet and you're taking a shot?" he asks, personally offended.

"A toast? It's just us," I say, stating the obvious.

He grabs the bottle from my hands. "Exactly. To us having the funnest summer yet." He holds the bottle to his lips.

"For the record, funnest isn't even a word." I take the bottle as he hands it to me.

I giggle to myself after what feels like an hour of walking silently. It's probably been ten minutes at most. The world around me starts to spin. Well, I guess it's always been spinning, just too slow for me to notice. I wobble a little.

"Woah," I say when Finn's hands grip my shoulders to balance me.

His eyes roam my body from head to toe, his expression barely changes, but I notice.

"Your hands are so big."

He raises a brow.

"It's just that one day you were this kind boy and now you're this…man. With big hands." I widen my eyes for emphasis.

He tightens his hold on me, and amusement flickers across his smile. He has such pretty eyes. *How did we get so close?*

I can feel the warmth of his breath against my face. "I think that was enough 'hand' discussion for one day. At this rate we won't make it to the beach before tomorrow." He links our arms, so I walk besides him. The innocent touch feels like electricity is shooting through my entire body.

We are quiet the rest of the way, and I'm only thinking about the kiss we shared earlier. It seems to have shifted things. It feels like a line has been crossed. I can only hope things don't change between us in a bad way. I can't lose him.

I take off my shoes, leaving them in the sand since no one is here to take them. "Don't you love how soft sand is?" I grin.

Finn looks at me amused, walking lazily toward me. "Yup. So soft." He sets the alcohol down by my shoes.

"I *love* the moment promised." I give my attention to the ocean.

The waves crash into the shore, creating a beautiful sound.

I feel Finn right behind me. He takes up so much room, he's not just behind me. He's everywhere.

In the ocean we've swam in together a thousand times.

The sand we've built into castles as kids.

My heart.

My soul.

My—okay. I'm definitely drunk.

I spin around, crashing into his chest. He holds me still with two firm hands, then slowly slides them down my arms to grab my hands.

We stay like this for only a moment before Finn starts swinging our arms back and forth. "Dance with me."

"There's no music."

He sings the *Friends* theme song.

I lift my face to the stars, a laugh easily escaping. It gets lost in the breeze.

He twirls me, and my feet splash in a wave that rolls higher into the sand.

These lyrics feel a little too personal. Except my love life is nonexistent by choice. I've never met a guy who knows basic human decency and respect. Well, except for Finn. He's my only exception. To everything.

"You're special," I say.

He leans back but doesn't pull his hands from mine. He still swings them side-to-side, humming the rest of the song, waiting for me to explain.

"Every guy I know sucks. Just plain sucks," I start. "They are either misogynistic, incredibly rude, or selfish." I draw a half circle into the sand with my big toe.

"I'm touched, truly." He pulls a hand away to touch his chest, sarcastically.

I shake my head. "But you're good. You aren't like those other guys." I shrug. "You're special."

His eyes glimmer from the moon's light. "Adeline." He shakes his head. "You were raised by a couple who demonstrated a toxic…*abusive* relationship to you. But that's not all that exists." He sighs, "Don't close yourself off to love, okay?"

I shrug.

He doesn't seem pleased with my silent reply, but he doesn't prod.

"I'm going swimming," I say casually.

Finn raises a brow at me.

I giggle, pushing him aside and running toward the pitch-black waves. I pull my shirt over my head, throwing it back at Finn. I dive into the salty water, getting some in my mouth. I spit it out when I breach the surface.

"I hope you know it's the sharks' dinner time," Finn's voice calls out.

"Sharks don't exist." I wave him off, splashing around like a drunken idiot.

"Yup, that'll scare them." My eyes adjust to the dark enough for me to see him pulling his shirt over his head. "Splash around some more, love. The sharks won't think you are a dying seal or anything." He kicks off his shoes, running to join me in the water.

I scream as his arms wrap around my waist. "Please, spare me—" I'm thrown into the water, salt burns my nose since I didn't have time to plug it. I surface and take a deep breath before going after him. "Oh, you are so gonna get it." I go to push his bare chest, but he grabs my wrists before I can.

His expression goes from playful to serious as his eyes meet mine.

Kiss me again. For real this time.

I take off sprinting to shore, running from these thoughts, hoping they will fall out of my head like items in an open trunk of a car speeding down the highway. As the wind on my wet skin makes my teeth chatter, I realize I'm terrified. Terrified of ruining a friendship that has been my safety boat since I was nine. Terrified of a world without Finn. These feelings complicate something that used to be so *un*complicated.

I want them gone.

6

EIGHT YEARS AGO

om and Dad are getting a divorce. I smile to myself in my bedroom mirror.

They haven't told me yet, but they're fighting downstairs. It started like every other fight they have: Something small made my dad mad, and each sentence that leaves his mouth gets louder and angrier by the syllable.

"I'm getting a fucking divorce, Marsha!" His voice chills me down to the bone, but the words attached lift me up.

"Okay, Jason, just calm down—"

"Fuck you! Adeline?" Angry footsteps stomp up the stairs.

I rush to my bed. My eyes widen as my door swings open. Jason stands in the doorway, visibly shaking. "Get your fucking shit. We're leaving."

"No!" My mom steps into view, tears stream down her face. Her body trembles, but her voice is strong with conviction I've never heard from her before. "You're not taking my daughter. Adeline, *don't* move."

Jason's face turns bright red. "You really think you're gonna sit there and tell me what I can and can't do with my own fucking kid? Get out of my house!" he shouts, foam spitting out of his mouth.

I can't move.

I can't speak.

He's getting closer.

His hand grasps my arm so tightly, tears sting my eyes and my entire body tenses. "Let's go." His voice is so strong it could kill me right now with the way it wraps around my throat and cuts off my airway.

I can't breathe.

I'm going to *die*.

My heart beats so rapidly I fear it will explode.

I don't have a say in what my body does because it stands up and follows Jason to the open doorway, and past my mother.

"Where are you going?" She sounds how I feel, like she can't breathe.

I turn my head to see her, her knees bend like she can't hold herself up. Her expression would make my heart sink if I could feel my body. But I can't. I look down at myself from above, wishing so badly to be anywhere but here.

In this body, in this moment, in this *fear*.

"Your mother's fucking crazy. Don't listen to that bitch," he seethes.

I want to disagree with him, but I'm too scared to be on the other end of his anger. I simply nod my head and don't look back.

The car ride is a blur of honking horns and sharp corners. I have no idea how long we drive or where. I choke back the taste of bile and the urge to scream, knowing I'll likely get backhanded if I do either.

I don't remember pulling into this strange neighborhood, or unbuckling my seatbelt, or watching my dad ring the doorbell to a house I didn't realize we were standing in front of. I'm a shell, a zombie, moving without my control.

The door swings open and a woman I've never seen before smiles at me. "Hi, sweetie!" Her voice sounds forced, like she's doing an impression of an annoying cartoon character.

"Um, hi." I shy away from her, slowly stepping back.

Jason walks through the door, giving her a kiss on the way in.

Oh—

Jason is cheating on my mom.

I'm burning from the inside out. Red is all I can see, and it's in this very moment I decide to hate Jason.

"I've heard so much about you, Abagail!" The woman holds out a welcoming hand, but I hate her too.

"It's Adeline," I correct, stepping around her and following Jason into her house.

The walls are a dark brown, her furniture is burnt wood, and the lights are a depressing yellow. I feel my lungs expanding with darkness and hate each inhale I take.

I want to run far away, but I'm caged in.

"I've been waiting so long to meet you, but your dad wouldn't bring you over."

Her smile slithers up my spine and sinks its teeth into my neck like a venomous snake.

"Grab me a beer, Erin," Jason orders, flipping through the channels on the TV.

Erin does what she's told with a smile plastered to her face. When she hands it to him, she looks me up and down, then rolls her eyes.

The rest of the afternoon is spent in Erin's depressing

house. I remain quiet, only saying a few words when I'm spoken to.

Erin puts on a façade in front of Jason, acting sweet, but the second his back is turned, she gives me dirty looks.

It's dinner time, and she made meatloaf. I hate meatloaf. I move it around with my fork; the smell brings bile to my throat.

Jason pushes out his chair and gets up, walking toward Erin's bathroom.

The one I locked myself in seven times today.

"So." She scrutinizes me like I'm nothing. "Is that really the color of your hair?"

"Yup." My fork clatters against the plate when I drop it.

"It's…unique." She sizes me up and down for the millionth time today, and my cheeks burn with anger.

"Oh, are you embarrassed, honey?" She laughs to herself. "You can always dye it when you're older," she whispers, glancing at the bathroom door.

"I like my hair."

"Boys don't like girls with red hair." She pulls her shoulders back like she's won some unspoken competition.

I lean into the table on my elbows, narrowing my gaze. "My dad always tells my mom how pretty her red hair is, so I think I'll be fine." Actually, my dad hates my mom. I think he hates all women who don't serve him the way he wants, but I don't say any of that.

She clicks her tongue, putting her face closer to mine. "You little—"

The bathroom door opens, and Erin pulls back. I think of a bad word, one that starts with B and ends in H.

I pick up my fork and smile at her. "I'm full. Dad, we better get going, I have school in the morning."

"You can sleep in the guest room!" Erin pipes up, grabbing my plate. "We can save your leftovers for breakfast since you hardly ate any."

"Sure." Jason sits back down at the table, and I'm left standing by my chair completely dumbfounded.

"But," I shake my head, "my clothes are at home."

"You can wear that." Jason looks at me pointedly.

I peer down at my clothes that reek of Erin's cooking and the smell of her house.

Erin walks with a pep in her step, her annoying voice infiltrating my ears, "Let's go, sweetie. I'll show you your room." She holds out a hand for me to grab, but I walk past her.

She closes the door to the guest room, trapping me. "Your dad loves me."

I ignore her, walking over to the bed and pulling down the brown, itchy comforter.

"He hates your mom's hair," she spits out, leaving me alone in the dark room.

I sink into the bed, finally able to let myself feel everything that happened today. I grab a throw pillow, stifling my sobs with it.

"I wish you were here, Finn," I whisper into the dark, pulling my knees to my chest in the fetal position. I close my eyes, picturing the Walker's bright, colorful home. I long for their smiling faces and welcoming hugs.

Anger builds and builds like a rolling snowball. "I want to go home!" I shout. Rage brings down the wall of fear I've built. "Take me home! I want to see my mom!" My screaming stings my throat.

The door flies open and my dad looks angry. Erin is right on his heels with a pleased expression on her face.

"Shut the fuck up and go to sleep!" he shouts, coming up to the side of the bed.

I kneel, almost eye level with him. "I want to go home!" I repeat, begging.

Jason pushes me onto my back. Every ounce of fear slams into me like a highspeed train. He becomes blurry from my tears.

Erin steps beside him. "You're not going home, so stop crying like an ungrateful brat," she yells, but not with the same fire as Jason.

I squeeze my eyes shut, turning into a crying sobbing mess.

"Shut your fucking mouth!" Jason screams even louder.

I open my eyes, expecting him to be directing his orders at Erin, but he stares right at me.

"Me?"

"Who the fuck else?" He turns, grabs Erin's hand, then slams the door behind him with enough force to rattle the walls.

Everything in my body shatters.

I pretend I'm somewhere else with Finn.

We're swimming at the beach.

Everything is okay.

But when I open my eyes, everything is not okay.

7

NOW

If there's a point beyond rock bottom, my mother managed to surpass it.

I've spent the last week doing absolutely nothing for her, but I've never felt so drained. She's screamed out in frustration many times. She's fallen over from drinking too much. She hasn't had me there to help her back up.

She's a miserable, help deprived, mess.

Watching her struggle is beyond anything I can imagine, and it tears me apart, but sometimes tough love is the only thing you can do to save someone. I won't enable her anymore; it pulls her deeper into the hole of addiction, further away from getting the help she needs to get sober.

One day she'll see this was my way of saying I love you.

If she makes it to that day.

I try to push those thoughts aside. Hope is the only thing getting me from point A to B.

There are five stages of grief, or so I've been told. My mother hasn't died, but in a way, she has. I've been stumbling back and forth between the five stages since her addiction began.

Right now, I bargain.

If Jason were still here, would she have started in the first place? No, something else would have been killing her instead—Jason's abuse.

But if he had never been in the equation to start with, if she had met a better guy, then maybe she wouldn't feel the need to escape reality.

Maybe if I had said something, did something...

It's too late. No matter if any of those thoughts are true, it's still too late.

I try not to think about how I haven't seen Finn in a week, as I stare up at my ceiling fan. The whirling puts me in a trance as I recall everything that happened the last time we were together.

The fake proposal...the kiss...the way I wanted it to happen again on the beach.

Maybe a week is what I needed to get over these ridiculous feelings.

But I can't help but feel like I've wasted the gift of time we've been granted. Before I know it, he'll be driving back up to college.

Without me.

I grab my phone off my nightstand. The light from the screen illuminates my bedroom. It's already three in the morning and I haven't gotten any sleep.

I accept this is going to be another night of insomnia, so I click on Instagram and scroll for a few minutes.

A video of a dolphin retrieving someone's phone who dropped it off the side of a boat makes me laugh, so I send it to Finn. His username is green, meaning he is online too. A jolt of excitement electrifies my stomach.

I blame it on my sleep deprivation.

@Adeline.miller: You're up late.

@Finn_Walker03: I always stay up late. You on the other hand should've been tucked in 5 hours ago.

@Adeline332: Too much on my mind.

@Finn_Walker03: Cold Cow is open 24/7. I'll pick you up in 5 minutes.

He's right on time. Horizontal lights luminate through my blinds. I grab my purse, slip on some sandals, and climb out the window.

I wave at the blacked-out windows of Finn's car, and when I grab the door handle—*Honk!*

A loud screech leaves my mouth before I'm leaning down to glare through the window. I can't see anything through the tints.

Honk!

"I have sleeping neighbors!" I whisper-scream so he can hear me from inside his car. I pull the door handle, but it's locked.

He must let his foot off the brakes because the car rolls forward a foot.

I sigh. Let's try this again. Before I can yank the handle, he moves forward. Again.

Third time's a charm. When I pull the handle, the door finally opens. I fall into the leather seat and Finn's raspy laughter fills the air.

"You're not funny," I say without humor.

"Oh, I'm hilarious. You get all red and cute when you're flustered." He continues to laugh.

Surely his use of the word cute means something completely different than the way my heart took it. I'll be looking up the technical definition later, just to be sure.

He shifts gears and backs out of my driveway. I turn up

the volume. The playlist I made for him is playing, and the music puts me at ease.

He turns it up even louder, so even my own thoughts can't be heard. It's a nice change for once.

I close my eyes and rest my head against the window while my knee bounces to the beat of the music.

After a few minutes of this, his fingertips graze my leg, startling me. He glances over at me amid his hilarious attempts at dancing, since we are in a car. I laugh at the way he moves. Only with me. The world doesn't get to see this Finn Walker, only I do. It brings a selfish smile to my face.

The song ends, and my favorite one replaces it.

Now I'm the one singing and dancing in my seat like a moron. I swing my arms around, bopping my head. I don't care how silly I look, I'm safe and warm. Finn would never judge me, so I let loose in front of him.

Only him.

It's one of those sleep deprivation highs, where you're completely giddy and everything is hilarious. Tears well in my eyes from laughing so much, my body flops around like a fish out of water. The thought makes me laugh even harder until it's soundless and I can't breathe.

This right here is how it feels to be alive. Simply laughing with Finn makes me feel alive. But nothing in my life has ever been simple. I need to cherish this moment. I store the memory safely in my brain to remember on a rainy day.

I haven't smiled in a week. Coincidentally, it was the last time I was with Finn.

Once we get to Cold Cow, the best ice cream place on the island, Finn puts the car in park and turns down the radio.

"Those were some sick ass moves back there, Ad."

"Much better than *yours*." I touch my hair, twirling it between my thumb and index finger.

His eyes graze over my features, focusing on the piece of hair I twist with a tick of his jaw. "Why are you up so late?"

"I wasn't tired." I shrug, grabbing the door handle.

I gasp as his hand quickly covers mine, trapping me in the car with him.

"You don't have to do this alone." His gaze is hot, and I feel like I could melt right into the seat. He's so close, I forget how to breathe.

I can't meet his gaze any longer, instead I stare at his hand as it engulfs mine. "I know," I whisper.

"So then let me help you." He tightens his grip. "Let me listen to all the things keeping you up at night."

"You already get my mind off those things."

He looks like he wishes he could be given a bigger task.

He just doesn't realize he's the only one who has ever made me forget about the ugly in my life. He's been bringing out the beauty all these years. He unintentionally held me above the water while my entire world flooded.

Without realizing it, he's doing it now too.

"You're going to try my ice cream." His smile returns.

I internally thank him for switching the subject. "I'm not eating chocolate ice cream with sour gummies. It's just wrong." I cringe.

"We'll see."

Finn convinces me to try *a bite* of his ice cream. I gag and wrinkle my nose as the sour gummies sting my taste buds. "Absolutely atrocious." I mock gasp. "It tastes like battery acid only robots can eat—wait a minute." I peer around, pretending what I'm about to say is top secret, lowering my voice. "That explains everything… You're a robot!"

Finn remains stoic as he sticks his germ filled fingers into my cup of water.

"Hey!" I complain.

"If I was a robot I would short circuit or something from the water."

I dunk my phone into the already contaminated cup. "You're waterproof." I demonstrate with my phone, that is also waterproof.

He grabs my phone out of the cup and dries it on his shirt. Before he can give it back to me, a notification chimes, feeding his curiosity.

"Who's Eddie? And why does he think it's okay to text a girl at three in the morning?"

I grab my phone from his grasp, unlocking it to see the message.

Eddie: Sup, Ad. Few friends from high school are having a bonfire, you should come. I can pick you up.

I hide a smirk because I've only spoken to this person maybe once, but I wouldn't mind dragging this out to toy with Finn.

"See." I shove my phone in front of Finn's face. "Innocent."

"That is not innocent."

I laugh at Finn's protectiveness. "He just wants to catch up." I play dumb, knowing very well what his intentions are.

"This is literally booty call hour, Adeline." He doesn't even crack a smile.

I pretend to type. "You say it like it's a bad thing. It's been a while since my booty's been called." I lie and bite my cheeks to keep a serious face.

"Adeline." His eyes are pleading.

"What?" I question. "He's cute." A grin slowly spreads across my face.

I can tell he grinds his teeth by the micro movement of his jaw. "Listen, I can guarantee whoever this Earl is—"

"Eddie," I correct.

"Same thing. I'm not letting some douchbag drive you all alone in his car, to some bonfire with a bunch of other douchbags."

"You don't even know him," I protest.

"I know enough. Look at his text 'Sup, Ad' I mean who talks like that?" He rolls his eyes, air quoting. "Definitely not a deserving man of you, that's for sure." He opens his mouth like there's more to say, but I interrupt, breaking out into laughter.

He lets out a breath. "Just block him, okay?"

Suddenly I feel claustrophobic. If I want to block him, that's my decision to make, not Finn's. Granted, I was going to block him either way.

"No," I say defiantly, putting my phone in my pocket.

"Adeline, he's just going to—"

I stand, frustration building amongst the crankiness from sleep deprivation.

I throw away my ice cream, walking to Finn's car. I know I'm being unusually grouchy with Finn, but I'm tired and aggravated. I can't help but feel caged when someone tells me what to do. Even if it's as simple as this—Even if it's from Finn.

It feels too similar to the years I was raised by Jason.

"Adeline, slow down." Finn comes up behind me.

I inhale, knowing Finn means well. "I'm being ridiculous, I know I am." I blow out a breath. "I just don't want you to tell me what to do… It feels demeaning." I shrug, knowing he probably doesn't see it that way...knowing most people don't see it that way.

"I'm sorry. I know Jason was controlling and made you do things you didn't want to do. I know he also took away the things you *did* want to do." He doesn't realize it, but this moment is everything.

I didn't need to explain to him why this bothered me as much as it did, he just knew.

"I know you can make decisions for yourself. I was caught up in the heat of the moment, but I shouldn't have told you what to do. I know better than that." He looks at me like there's more he wants to say, but he hesitates.

"What is it?"

He clears his throat. "I'm also really sorry about the other night. If I made you...uncomfortable when I kissed you." He glances away. "Especially in front of all those people."

My heart jolts. I can't look into his eyes, so I focus on my sandals.

"I can't believe I did that. I know it was probably your first kiss and I ruined that for you." His eyes hold a world of sorrow, "I am *so* sorry."

My cheeks blossom in embarrassment. I wish he thought I'd kissed someone by now, but the truth is, I never wanted to kiss anyone...until now.

I've never had a boyfriend or the desire to kiss a random guy. My lack of experience has never bothered me until this moment. Honestly, I couldn't imagine a better person to share it with.

I rack my brain with how to respond. *I didn't mind the kiss.* But if I tell him that, he might realize I *enjoyed* the kiss.

But he certainly looks as if he didn't like it, and I can't handle that type of rejection from Finn of all people.

"It's okay," I whisper, already hating my answer.

He gives me a gentle smile, but it doesn't reach his eyes. His shoulders sag in what can only be regret, as he walks around the car, ready to get into the driver's seat.

I hesitate for a few moments, frozen in embarrassment and shame for liking the kiss he probably wishes never happened.

A part of me tears away with the realization of how much things have shifted. When Finn's lips were pressed into mine, I peaked. I mean, it doesn't go up from there. Finn is the best I could hope to achieve.

The amount of love I felt during those thirty seconds could last someone like me a lifetime.

I want those kisses every day.

I blink back into reality. It's a thought so incredibly out of reach, I'd have a better chance of witnessing an alien before Finn would ever want me that way. Before I would ever chance something like lust ruining what we have.

"Want to drive around for a little while?" he asks as I slide into the passenger seat.

I study the dash displaying the time. It's already four in the morning. My body screams to sleep, but I want to take in as much time with Finn as I can get.

I nod my head.

"Switch spots with me." He opens the door.

"What?" I ask. Panic sets in as I realize what he's insinuating. "I'm not driving your car. It's your *baby*."

He is already standing by my door, waiting for me to slide into the driver's seat. "There's no one on the road. It'd be really hard to hit something."

I point to a tree. "There's those."

He narrows his eyes with a bored expression like I'm not off the hook so easily.

I cave for those amber eyes, climbing over the center console and getting cozy in Finn's seat. I'll admit, his seats are very comfortable. I wiggle my bottom around, enjoying the cushiony leather.

"Dear lord." Finn groans, covering his eyes.

I raise an eyebrow.

"Stop doing that thing with your...*ass*." His voice lowers on that last word, like the discussion of my ass puts him in discomfort.

"What thing? This?" I do it again.

His breath hitches. "Drive the car, Adeline."

A chill travels down my spine at his biting voice.

"Or what?" I taunt.

He pinches the bridge of his nose. When he drops his hand, I squirm beneath the fiery amber. It's both mesmerizing as it is venomous.

He searches my face for something.

Everything is spinning; the world moves a million times faster while my breath feels fast and shallow. My breasts are moving with each inhale of the blistering air.

"Ad—" he whispers.

I've never been aroused by my own name. He makes the single syllable sound poetic.

"Yes?" I choke out the word. It doesn't sound nearly as beautiful as the way he said my name. My ears burn, and I'm sure Finn can see the blush filling my face and neck. I gasp when he draws closer.

Everything becomes foggy. I don't know if it's the quiet of the night or my exhaustion. The line between friendship and desire doesn't fade just a little——It becomes invisible.

I investigate his gaze, and I see a glimpse of something that looks an awful lot like attraction. My conscience doesn't even try to decipher whether it's the reflection of my own or if it's really his.

When Finn reaches for my cheek, my world falls off its axis. A sound of shock escapes my lips. Each cell burns beneath his touch and he's only touching my *cheek*.

A light tap on Finn's window humbles me back into reality. I'm mortified when I see the girl who served our ice cream holding my purse.

Finn rolls down the window.

"Hi guys, so sorry to bother you. I think you left this…" She hands Finn my purse.

Finn nods, taking my purse like she hasn't interrupted anything.

"Have a safe night," she says as she walks away.

"Adeline."

"Yeah?" I swallow.

"Drive."

It's nearing five in the morning when I get home.

I climb under the covers and make myself comfortable as my eyes fall heavy. A wave of slumber washes over me and a dream too good to be true fills my head.

Finn's other hand grabs the back of my head and brings me back to where we were. An inch of space separates our lips. I become greedy, taking a few centimeters away.

"Ad, you gotta stop me," he pleads with furrowed brows.

I shake my head no. The small gesture must put Finn over the edge. He finally closes the space between our lips.

He kisses me softly, gently tugging my hair. It's a sweet kiss, like the kind boy from my memories.

He pulls away for a moment to look at me, as if he wanted to make sure it was still me he was kissing.

Our lips meet again, only this time he kisses me deeper, no longer holding back. I forget about the gentle boy from the past and lose myself in this *Finn. The Finn I've only had a short taste of once. I make sure to bask in this ecstasy while it lasts.*

I climb over the center console and straddle his lap, something I've never done before now.

I like it.

His tongue finds mine; he tastes like the ice cream he ate only minutes ago. It makes me crave more of him.

My hips move against him, it comes so naturally.

His lips travel to the side of mine and make a trail along my jaw. One big hand grips my waist, the other holds my lower back. I find myself arching against him as his kisses my neck with so much starvation.

I sit up in bed. Sweat coats my skin as I try to inhale as much air as my lungs will allow.

If there is a God, he must enjoy torturing me. First with the psycho dad, then the addict mom, and now this? Falling for the one person I can't bear to lose.

And that's exactly what would happen if he knew.

I'd lose him.

It would complicate everything, and that's to say if he even feels a fraction of what I do. But if I sprung these feelings on him and he *didn't* feel the same I'd be mortified. Our easy bantering relationship would turn to a mush of awkwardness. He'd pity me for the feelings I have that he can't return.

So, I make a promise to myself from this point forward. Whatever you feel toward Finn Walker, swallow that shit right back down.

8

re we really allowing our daughter to have a boy in her room?" Jason's voice is always angry, but right now he's furious. The walls vibrate as he shouts at my mother.

I look at Finn and shrug with a small smile. "I warned you."

Finn's mom insisted we spend some time at my house since we are always at hers. "Your parents probably miss you," she'd said.

I couldn't argue with her, I mean I spend almost every day at their house after school. She has no idea what life is really like for me at home.

To the Walkers, I'm just an ordinary twelve-year-old girl.

I like that.

Finn sits crisscrossed on the floor, too nervous to sit on my bed and risk my dad walking in.

"This is why I need a fucking divorce." Jason curses,

throwing the word divorce around loosely like he's done for the past year.

Ever since the first time he announced he was divorcing my mom in a fit of rage, I've learned not to get excited.

Excitement leads to disappointment, and that's exactly how I've felt each time he wrapped my mother around his finger after threatening to divorce her.

It's always the same routine: Something enrages my dad. He storms off, probably to Erin's house—who I thankfully have not seen since I met her. He puts on a convincing façade that he's "so sorry" and "will make it up to you." Sometimes he even takes us all out for ice cream or the movies.

Repeat.

It's a cycle I've become used to and I fear will continue for eternity.

"Want to play *Would You Rather?*" Finn asks, slowly standing up and glancing at the closed door to my bedroom.

"Just sit," I command from my bed.

His eyes widen as he hesitates.

"We'll hear him coming," I reassure him. I know how to stay out of the way of Jason's wrath.

He sits uncomfortably on the corner of my bed, three feet away from me.

"Would you rather go to Miss Picket's house or eat the fish sticks at the fair?" he asks me.

I ponder this for a moment.

Miss Picket is the meanest woman in the entire town. She yells from her porch at any kid who gets too close to her yard. Legend has it, one time she yelled at a little boy and a lightning bolt struck the tree only fifty feet away.

On the other hand, one time a bunch of people threw

up at the annual fair after eating the fish sticks from the concession stand.

"Miss Picket's house."

His eyes widen like I've shocked him with my answer. "You're insane. She's so…*scary*. And mean."

I shrug. "Look at my dad. I'm used to mean. Food poisoning, on the other hand…"

"This sucks," Finn announces.

I raise a brow.

"You should come live with me," he whispers, as the shouting downstairs gets even louder.

"I'm not raising my daughter to be a little fucking slut like you!"

Finn winces. I blow out a steady breath.

What does he think we're doing up here anyway? We're only twelve.

"I can't live with you. I think my dad would blow a fuse." I joke to lighten the mood, but my smile quickly fades since Finn doesn't return one.

"It wouldn't hurt to ask," he says.

I picture my mom with another injury. Purple swelling around her eye, or maybe this time it will be a busted lip. "It would."

Finns face pales as he realizes what I mean. "It can't be that bad, right? You'll move out when you turn eighteen, we'll go to college together and leave this place behind." He smiles, full of hope.

Hope is a dangerous thing; I've learned from the many times my dad's mentioned divorce. Every time he does, I allow myself to dream just a little—my mom and I living on our own, never feeling such fear and pain. Just the two of us taking on the world.

Eighteen is so far away, it feels like I'll never reach it.

How will I survive this every day for the next six years of my life?

Six more school years… Six more summers.

I steal a glance from Finn, who smiles at me. The yelling in the background seems to go mute, along with the pressure from my chest.

That's how I'll survive.

"Want to escape?" I bounce up from the bed, a thrill of excitement shoots through me.

Finn looks like I've grown another head, with the way his eyes widen to saucers. "I'm not going down there!" he hisses.

"No, not through the front door," I say, walking toward my bedroom window.

"Isn't it too high up?" he asks, which is reasonable considering we are on the second floor.

"I do it all the time. Here, let me show you." I slide open the window slowly, not to make too much noise.

The tree branch that was once so far away grew taller, and so did I. I easily swing down from the branch, landing on two feet. I glance up at Finn, gesturing for him to follow me.

Finn looks like he might need to change his pants, but with a little courage, he follows suit, landing right next to me. He lets out a breath of relief.

I grab his hand, running as fast as possible, dragging him away from here.

He follows me, just like I hope he always will.

9

NOW

I walk as if I'm on a tight rope, on the edge of the elevated sidewalk. I hold my arms out on my side to keep my balance. Finn casually hums as he walks next to me.

I stumble and his arm suddenly wraps around my waist and easily lifts me off my feet. He sets me on the other side of him, so he's the one closest to the road.

Such a gentlemen… *How do you not have a girlfriend?*

Who says he doesn't?

"So…" I break the silence.

The sun starts to set, elongating our shadows along the asphalt.

I love Finn's neighborhood. The houses are all so unique in color. One is a light pink, the other a teal color, some white, some a faded yellow. There are boats in almost every white rock driveway.

"What's the love life like at FSU?" I ask casually, like there isn't an answer he could give that would burn me alive.

He raises a brow. "How's the love life here?" he counters.

"I asked you first," I spit out, way too fast.

He shrugs. "There's lots of girls at FSU." He kicks a pebble on the sidewalk.

My large intestine wraps around my stomach like a snake suffocating its prey, or at least that's how it feels.

I focus on the dolphin shaped mailbox we are about to pass.

"Some flirt or find a way to text me about an assignment," he says, unbothered by the idea.

"Sounds like you're quite the ladies man." I try to leave out any emotion attached to my words, but they threaten to slip out my eyes.

"But you know how it is. Dating in college is rarely anything memorable. Mainly a one-night stand followed by another."

I think I just died. I leave my body and watch the conversation that killed me from a bird's eye view.

"I have no interest in it." He stops dead in his tracks, giving me his full attention. "I want something meaningful, with somebody who *knows* me."

He's awfully close, much closer than he was a few seconds ago.

I take a step back to put some distance between us, my heel slipping off the edge of the sidewalk.

Everything happens in a matter of a second. A car honks, and its brakes squeal.

I squeeze my eyes, accepting my fate.

The front of my body slams against something hard.

"Shit. You, okay?"

I blink my eyes open. I'm not dead.

Finn caught me before I could fall and get hit by a car.

My heart drums in my chest, both from the close call and from the close *Finn,* who holds me tight.

"Miller?"

"Yeah?"

"You're clearly incapable of walking yourself. You leave me no choice."

"Wha—" The air rushes out of my lungs as Finn sweeps me into his arms, taking me by surprise and sending weird signals throughout my body that make me blush.

"Put your arms around my neck," he says in a low voice.

I hesitate for a moment. His face is so close to mine that I can feel his breath against my skin. He smells like mint. I slowly wrap my arms around him like he ordered. His face remains the same but the corner of his lip twitches for a short moment. If I had blinked any sooner, I would've missed it.

He walks staring straight ahead for several steps and then asks, "And you?"

I look at him with confusion.

"Are *you* breaking any hearts down here, Adeline?"

I gawk at him. "I lost Pete's favorite pen... Does that count?"

He smiles easily, shaking his head. "I mean it, are you... seeing anyone?"

I wait for him to laugh, since this conversation is surely a joke, but he doesn't, he just waits for my answer.

"Um, no. I'm not." Why is he even asking? He's the one who assumed I'd never even kissed a guy until him.

"But there's someone you're getting to know..." He trails off his sentence like it's a question.

I let out a laugh. "Definitely not getting to know anyone."

"So, there's no guy in your life then."

"Just you."

His features show no reaction to this, but he lets out a quiet breath. "Good."

"Good?"

"I just wasn't sure if I was going to have to knock someone's teeth out while I was in town."

I laugh. "If I was seeing someone," I mock his choice of wording, "I'd like to think he wouldn't be the type of person who would require your protectiveness," I say quietly since I'm so close to his ear.

He watches me now. "I'd like to think so too."

I search his face, it's honest. He wants me to be with someone respectful, someone he would feel I'm safe with. Someone unlike my dad.

I've never thought of how Finn must've worried for me when we were kids, how that worry must've transferred to who I'd date now that we're older. Now I know he fears I'll end up in a relationship close to my parent's. I never will, and I realize he needs to know this.

"If I were to ever be with someone, it would be a man like you, Finn." He doesn't seem any less tense, so I elaborate. "Someone who treats me as their equal and respects me as a person."

His eyes sparkle as he gives me a curt nod. "That's the bare minimum you deserve, Adeline. Don't ever thank someone for treating you like a *person*. You can thank them when they treat you like their world will end if you're unhappy. Even the slightest frown from you should have them on their feet, doing everything to bring back your smile." His eyes rest on my lips that hold the slightest grin. "Please let that be the standard you set for yourself."

His words electrify me. That's what we all deserve, and I

think a lot of us forget this. "I'll never settle for less," I promise.

He smiles. "Good. Any less and they are losing some teeth."

I realize as my laughter fills the air that I'm always smiling when I'm with Finn. More than I ever am when we're not together.

10

SIX YEARS AGO

L et's go on the roof." Finn's cracking voice interrupts the silence of his bedroom. I fold the page at the corner of my book and set it down. Goosebumps line my arms, and I attempt not to shiver beneath Finn's comforter plus the extra blanket he gave me. His parents set the temperature so low compared to what my parents leave it at.

"Yeah, okay," I say sarcastically, followed by a yawn. His parents would kill us if they found us on the roof, and Finn's not the kind of fourteen-year-old to disobey. Although, I don't think they'd be too fond of finding us lying in bed together either. But it's not like that.

At all.

I jump when Finn's hands suddenly grasp mine, pulling me up from his bed. He leads the way to his closet, grabbing one of his sweatshirts. He tosses it at my face. *Key Largo, FL* is printed on the front.

"Who buys a tourist shirt of the place they live?" I ask.

"My dad. He thought it would be a funny Christmas gift." He shrugs. "Put it on. You're cold."

I throw on the sweatshirt and Finn grabs me by the waist and hoists me over his shoulder like a sack of potatoes. As soon as I shriek, my hand shoots up to cover my mouth.

"Keep quiet, my parents are sleeping."

My voice comes out muffled. "Then don't pick me up in the first place!" The thrill of excitement runs through me, spontaneity is one of the only things that make me feel alive.

"Up to the roof we go," he says, definitively.

Blood rushes to my head, my long hair sweeping the floor as Finn walks to his bedroom window.

He sets me back on my feet and lifts open the window. It squeaks loudly and I cringe at the sound contrasting the dead of night. He steps out the window first, then holds a hand out for me.

I roll my eyes and grab his hand, climbing out the window and stumbling over my own two feet. Finn catches me before I slip, holding me tight. I glance up and realize our faces are really close. He looks at my mouth, and I duck my head into his chest, feeling insecure. *Do I have something in my teeth?*

Finn takes a deep breath and clears his throat. A salty breeze messes up my hair. I walk to the edge of the roof and sit with my legs crossed. I fidget, trying to get comfortable, eventually I settle and let my legs dangle off the edge.

The full moon illuminates Finn's neighborhood. Palm trees sway in the soft wind. I feel Finn's eyes on me, when I turn around, he peers down quickly.

I pat the roof, right next to me. "Sit," I demand.

He walks over to the spot, sits, and dangles his legs like mine. His are much longer. He's starting to go through a growth spurt. His body is getting longer but his weight remains the same. His hair is in desperate need of a haircut. I always pick on him for the long pieces that never know how to lay properly.

"Are you nervous?" He turns to me. The moonlight reflects in his eyes.

"For what?"

He nudges my side. "If you're nervous about tomorrow, you can talk about it."

Tomorrow is our first day of high school, also the first time we will be attending the same school. I am anything *but* nervous. I'm elated.

"You seem like the one who should be nervous," I state.

"Oh yeah? Why's that?"

"You've never gone to school with me before. For all you know, I could be a completely different person in high school society."

"You couldn't be any different if you tried."

"What does that mean?"

"You're you," he starts. "You're kind and selfless, and I'm sure you're going to be very popular, but in a good way. A nice way."

My heart flip flops in my chest because that is the nicest thing anyone's said to me. I can't even think of a playful comeback or snarky comment, so I just rest my head on his shoulder and whisper, "Thank you."

"Four *whole* years," he eventually says out loud. "I don't know how I'll survive *that* much of Adeline Miller."

I smile and go along with it because I love bantering with him. "I can't stand that girl. I mean, come on! And don't even get me started on that *hair*, what a catastrophe."

"Hey, hey now lady, don't go talking about my best

friend's hair." He looks at me like I'm someone else. "It's way prettier than yours."

There he goes again making my heart flutter, he laces a compliment in every witty remark.

"So much is going to happen over the next four years," he says, staring off into space, as if he's picturing a million different possibilities.

I smile, tucking a knotted piece of hair behind my ear. "Maybe I'll lose my virginity in these next four years."

Finn swallows hard, and his eyebrows pinch together. A line forms between them, and I want to rub it away.

"What?" I frown.

"Hm?" He acts clueless.

Finn and I have such a tight bond, unlike anyone else, especially at our age. We've spent every day together and we know everything about one another. He's never judged me a day in my life.

It's unspoken, but no one we date will ever come close to what we have, and maybe the idea of me spending time with another guy instead of him makes him a little jealous. I know I feel that way when I picture him having a girlfriend.

I just don't want things to ever change. I want to be in a tiny world where only Finn and I exist.

"The serious face," I say.

"I don't have a serious face," he says, and then crosses his eyes.

I giggle a little, sighing as I fall back onto the cool roof. I stare at the moon, smiling at the face the craters formed over the centuries. "What happens next?" I wonder out loud.

"What do you mean?" Finn lays back like me.

"When we finish high school. Then what?"

"Well, I'm sure we will be packing our stuff to go to

college. Saying bye to our families." He turns his head toward me. "Maybe even each other."

My stomach sinks and fear creeps in. I turn to him. "That will never happen," I say to convince myself. "We're going to the same college." I roll onto my stomach, glancing down at him. "Well, that is if you can get into Harvard," I joke. Neither of us are getting into any Ivy League; he knows it, and so do I.

He breaks out into dramatic laughter. I cover his mouth with my hand. "Your parents are sleeping," I whisper.

He mumbles something beneath my hand. I slowly move it away and widen my eyes in warning.

"We have four years to worry about it. A lot can happen in that much time. We could fall into different cliques and become total strangers."

I flick his forehead. "That would never happen." I shake my head. "Who's going to accept you into their clique?"

He rolls his eyes, but his dimple peeks through his irritated expression.

A new light illuminates the roof, coming from his parents' bedroom.

"Don't worry, I'll start my own clique so you have somewhere to go." I push off the roof, glancing at the ground.

I bet I could make it down there if I swung from the edge of the roof and landed in the bed of Burt's truck—

"You will one thousand percent break your fucking legs," Finn warns from behind me as if he can read my mind.

A smile breaks out across my face. He knows me too well.

∽

"It's eleven o clock," my mom calls from the couch as I walk through the front door. "Hurry up and get to bed before your father sees you." She holds a glass of red wine, gesturing toward the stairs with it.

I've been sneaking out and walking to Finn's house every day for years, and still, my negligent dad has never noticed. My mom, on the other hand, encourages it. It's an unspoken agreement between the two of us.

She wants me out of the house, protected from the chaos.

She also wants me happy, and being with Finn makes me happy.

So, instead of locking my window and keeping me here to listen to the constant yelling, she keeps my dad out of my room and looks the other way when I sneak out. Despite all the shit she deals with, she's a good mom. In an unconventional way.

"I love you." I give her a tight-lipped smile before walking up the stairs.

She takes a breath, almost as if she's relieved to hear the words. "I love you too, puffin. Have a good first day tomorrow."

As much as I wish things were different, I know my mom would protect me. No matter what. If Jason ever hurt me the way he does her, we'd be out of here.

I just wish she had the same courtesy for herself.

II

NOW

Waking up from a nap in the middle of the afternoon is always so disorienting. I blink my eyes several times, urging myself to fully wake up. I dig around my sheets, searching for my phone—found it.

I rub the sleep from my eyes, the brightness from the screen causes them to ache. I have three missed calls and a single text message from Finn that reads, *I'm coming over.*

I look at the time the text was sent—over an hour ago.

Shit.

Static buzzes through my head as I sit up, panic consumes me as I check his location.

He never comes to my house, what if there's an emergency?

If he made it here, he would've woken me up.

What if he got in a car accid—will this stupid thing load already?!

I throw my phone across the room, my thoughts all over

the place. I push off the bed and barge into the hallway, but I don't get more than three feet before I pause.

My hand flies up to my chest in relief as I overlook the living room. Their voices ease my worry.

"Mom… Finn?" I ask, slowly creeping down the stairs.

"Hey, puffin, you're awake!" My mom sips something from a mug.

I immediately imagine my appearance, not having the chance to look in a mirror. I self-consciously bring my hand to my face, pretending to scratch my cheek.

"We figured we'd let you sleep," Finn says, smiling up at me from the sofa. He holds a mug in his hand too.

Fury builds rapidly in my chest, burning me from the inside out. My eyes ping pong between the mug in Finn's hand and the mug in my mother's. Why the hell would Finn think drinking with my mom would be a good idea?

"Would you like some tea?" My mother stands, setting her mug on the coffee table and walking into the kitchen.

Oh.

I follow her, rounding the corner and audibly gasping at the difference.

My kitchen is *clean.*

Like…spotless.

I slowly turn my head, watching Finn mindlessly sip tea in my living room. Did he do all of this?

I lower my voice, so only my mom can hear, "What happened in here?"

My mom gives me a confused look. She laughs under her breath. "Finn brought some groceries over for us." She lowers her voice like mine. She grins, pulling a bag of Hershey Kisses out from a grocery bag. "Look!"

I swallow.

My favorite candy.

"What else did he bring?" I ask, a little stunned from the last three minutes of waking up.

She jumps a little on her toes. It's a strange sight, seeing my mom excited. She pulls out a raw fish fillet.

I cock my head, frowning. I don't understand. My mom and I don't know how to cook, why would he bring over raw fish?

"I know, right? I was confused too when he showed me. He's making dinner for us, I guess. Hope he's a good cook," she teases.

"And the kitchen?" I ask.

"We cleaned it." She smiles, nodding her head like she's proud of herself.

Wow. "So, you and Finn have just been, like...what? Hanging out?" I don't know why this is so hard to wrap my mind around.

"He's such a nice boy. They didn't make them like that when I was your age." She squeezes my cheek with a knowing expression, turning around to grab the kettle of tea and a mug for me. "Just look at your father," she mumbles.

My mom continues to fawn over Finn, like she has a crush of her own on him. I try to ignore the several swigs she takes from a bottle of vodka... She even pours some into her mug.

"You know what, I'm okay for now." I gesture to the tea she just poured me. "Finn—" I call out, walking back to the living room and grabbing his hand. "Let's watch a movie." I widen my eyes at him. "Upstairs."

He shifts uncomfortably as he stands up, following my lead as I march up the stairs with purpose.

Once we are enclosed in the privacy of my bedroom, all the questions pour out of me. "Why are you here? Did something bad happen? Why did you bring raw fish and why are you drinking tea with my mom? What did you talk about for the past—" I check my phone for the time, "Hour and a half. Thanks for the kisses, by the way." I catch my breath, about to open my mouth before Finn stops me.

"Calm down, love." His hands gently slide from my shoulders to my hands, causing me to break out into a chill. He releases them at my sides, running a hand through his hair while the other one remains unoccupied.

Grab my hand again.

"I know you're having a hard time. You know, with your mom and all. I figured I'd feed the Miller ladies and help them out a little." He shrugs. "Is that all right with you?" he asks sarcastically.

"Only if you hand feed me and wipe my mouth after each bite," I tease back.

"Sure, love. Oh, and you can have kisses any time you want. All you have to do is ask." He casually walks to my bed, collapsing onto the unmade mess of pillows and my comforter.

I stand unmoving, while all the blood in my body drains. I choke, "W-what?"

He leans against my headboard, a grin spreading across his face as he lifts the comforter up to his chest. He doesn't say anything, he just watches me turn red.

"Um, well…" I play with my fingers, staring too intently at my cuticles.

He breaks my awkward silence with ease. "*Hershey* Kisses," he elaborates.

I inwardly kick myself. "I know," I say with too much confidence, hoping he'll believe it as I climb into bed with him. A bolt of electricity shoots into my core as my leg grazes his, hidden beneath the covers.

Neither of us move, our legs touch in secret and tingle

every nerve ending within my body. I let my toe softly run over his shin like a whisper.

He tenses next to me.

The heat I felt a second ago darkens. It sits heavy on my chest.

"Ad." His sharp voice touches my entire body.

I swallow. An unfamiliar fear creeps in, speeding the beat of my heart. *Please don't break it.* My voice comes out small, "Yeah?"

"You look really pretty today," he says.

Who knew such simple words could become my favorite?

You *and* look *and* really *and* pretty *and* today.

They burn inside my chest, melting my heart to goo. I smile. "So do you." I quickly shut my eyes. "I mean, handsome. You look *handsome* today. Well, not just today—"

"Adeline." He cuts me off, rolling over until he's directly on top of me, gazing directly into my eyes.

His weight doesn't ease the ache I feel, it only makes it stronger.

"Have I ever told you how cute you get when you're embarrassed?" His lips hardly feather mine.

My heart beats so loudly in my chest, if he doesn't hear it, he definitely feels it.

No, I mouth.

"How's the moment promised?"

He smells like tea. I want to drink him up. Before I can ponder how to respond, his lips press into mine. I gasp from the unexpectedness of it all, taking no time to reciprocate.

It ends faster than it started because something loud thumps downstairs. Finn is in action faster than my brain can catch up. His pushes off me and bolts down the stairs.

I'm right on his heals, gasping for air as it seems to escape the room.

The shattered pieces of glass don't stop him as he sweeps up my mother's body, ignoring the shards that must dig into his feet. He leaves a trail of blood, mixing with the last remains of vodka from the broken bottle.

The room spins, and my mother's life flashes before my eyes as she lays limp in Finn's arms.

I can hardly comprehend Finn telling me to open the front door, my ears ringing like shots have been fired. Somehow, I do as I'm told in a daze, opening the door to my house and the one to his car.

He sets my mother in the backseat where she collapses unconscious against the door.

"Mom," I whisper, sliding in next to her and caging her hand in mine, trying to hold onto her for dear life when she can slip away at any moment.

I bring her lifeless body over my lap, resting her on her side in case she throws up. Her skin is cold and clammy. I watch her chest rise and fall only so often... Not nearly often enough. Between each breath I feel her slipping away, like the next may never come.

Finn speeds through my neighborhood, onto the main road.

Time feels infinite, like we've been driving for eternity, when only minutes have passed.

"Please don't die," I whisper. "I love you, Mom." My voice cracks, but I imprison my emotions for now.

We just need to make it to the hospital. Then I can cry. Then I can break.

After what feels like hours, Finn finally says, "We're here." He wastes no time getting out of the car, he rushes into the ER, probably alerting someone to help us.

In seconds, a team of nurses rush out with a stretcher, Finn swings my door open. He lifts my mom out of the car, placing her on the stretcher. She looks so fragile.

They rush her into the back, but one nurse stays behind with a clipboard. "What's the patient's name?" she asks as we enter through the automatic doors.

Cold sterile air slaps me in the face, making this so very real.

Finn is right next to me, squeezing my hand and letting me talk.

"Um, Marsha Miller." I hardly recognize my own voice. This one belongs to someone broken, much weaker than me.

I answer more questions, like my mom's date of birth, if she has any allergies...the easy ones.

"Has she been taking any medications you are aware of?" she asks, giving me respectful eye contact, unaware of the hurricane wreaking havoc throughout my body.

This is a hard one. "She takes pain killers." I swallow. "She takes them every day, way too much. And when she passed out, she was holding a bottle of vodka." I state the facts, trying not to feel the weight of my sentence.

"Do you know the specific opioid?" She jots things down on the paper.

I panic. "I think it started with Vicodin, but it was prescribed to her years ago when she broke her foot. I don't know if she takes a different one now." How do I not know this? What if this is the one piece of information they need to save her life? If only I had read the bottle—

"That's okay. We will administer Narcan to reverse the opioid effects." She writes so fast, I try to hone in on the way the pen moves in her hand, but she throws more information at me.

92

"We'll probably pump her stomach and give her an IV with fluids. She's in great hands. You did the right thing bringing her when you did." She smiles, glancing between Finn and I, and then widening her eyes. "Sit down, sir. We need a wheelchair over here!" she calls over her shoulder.

I frown, looking at her puzzled and then following her line of sight to Finn's feet—They are shoeless, covered in blood.

"Oh my god, Finn!" Tears blur my vision.

"I'm okay, Ad. It looks worse than it is." He somehow comforts me when I should be the one comforting him.

The nurse quickly places a wheelchair behind him, and he sits down and gets wheeled to the back.

I follow him, pausing at the room they took my mom into.

"Come with us, dear. You don't want to see your mom like that." She gestures to follow her.

"What if she dies?" I ask, going down a long hallway.

She takes a deep breath, walking us into a room sectioned off by a curtain. "Your mom is at very high risk. I won't sugar coat it." She gives me a sad smile.

Finn reaches up, squeezing my hand and rubbing circles on them as my spirit dies and eyes leak.

"Alcohol overdose *alone* is very dangerous. The area of the brain that controls things like her breathing and heartrate can't function correctly with that much alcohol in her blood stream." She grabs a pair of gloves, putting them on. "If you didn't bring her here when you did, there's a high chance she would've died. But she's here with the best team of nurses and doctors, and we are going to do everything we can to help her."

I nod a few times, blinking away tears that keep falling.

"Ad—" Finn starts.

I stop him. "I'm okay." I smile through fallen tears.

The nurse kneels, using a pair of medical tweezers to pull small shards of glass from the bottom of his foot.

He doesn't flinch, he just stares at me with a world of worry in his eyes.

Instead of me comforting him, he does the opposite, rubbing up and down my arm.

Finn hands me my second cup of coffee for the night. It's nearing midnight, my eyes falling heavy.

"You can go. Thanks for driving us," I say as I take the Styrofoam cup from him.

He rolls his eyes as he sits next to me on the blue chair.

"I mean it. It's late and you have no reason to be here." I try to dismiss him, feeling bad he has to sit in this depressingly cold waiting room any longer.

He looks me head on. "I have every reason to be here, Adeline. Now stop, because we both know I'm not leaving."

Despite this making me feel more guilty, it means everything to me, so I just nod and take a sip of coffee.

We haven't heard anything about my mom. I'm hoping that's a good thing, rather than a bad thing.

Finn's feet are bandaged underneath the hospital bootie, and the nurse predicts they will heal rather quickly. He needs to keep them clean and wrapped for a few days and should be as good as new. It's not a lot, but that news felt like a miracle given the situation.

"What if it's my fault?" I whisper, like the reality of my statement shouldn't be proclaimed at full volume.

Finn looks at me like I couldn't be more wrong. "How could this be your fault?"

I decided to push her to rock bottom. I just never antic-
ipated *this* would be rock bottom. What if she never wakes
up? After a few Google searches, I found out she could fall
into a coma.

A freaking coma.

Maybe there was a different approach to help her,
maybe if I had talked to her—

"You have no control over what your mom does." He
turns his entire body to me, his knees touching mine.

"If I had been there—"

"You were," he says with so much conviction. "You've
been there every single day. You stayed with her instead of
going to college. You think about her in every decision you
make. You were *here.*"

"I know but—"

"You can't sit on top of her every single second, Adeline.
That's not a life."

"Adeline Miller?" an older nurse calls into the waiting
room.

I stand with a marching band drumming inside my
chest. "That's me." I squeeze my hands at my sides to keep
them from shaking.

"Your mom is awake and asking to see you." She smiles,
waving me to follow her.

I gaze up to the ceiling, intense relief washing over me. I
glance at Finn, making sure he's okay.

"I'll be right here waiting for you, love." He smiles reas-
suringly.

The nurse speaks as we walk down the hall, toward my
mother. "We were able to flush most of the alcohol and
drugs out of her system, but I can't promise we will be able
to do the same next time." She speaks so fast, it's hard to
keep up. "Her liver is in horrible condition, and if she

doesn't make lifestyle changes, we don't see her making it to the next five years." She opens the door, allowing me to walk through. She spits heavy information out, giving no time to process before the next. "Since your mom is an alcohol user, she wouldn't qualify for the transplant list, so her only chance at living is getting sober."

The room is filled with beeping machines, my mother lays in a hospital bed, wearing a paper gown with purple under her eyes.

"Your mother has all the information she needs, and if she agrees, we can get her into a substance abuse rehabilitation center within the week. She has great insurance; it shouldn't be a problem getting coverage."

She leaves with a tight-lipped nod, leaving me alone with her.

"Hi." I smile, sitting in the chair next to her bed.

"Hi, puffin." Her voice comes out raspy.

We just sit there in silence. I take in the miracle it is she's awake and in my presence. Judging by her expression, I have a feeling she feels the same.

"Mom," I say.

Her eyes squeeze shut, like she's already heard what I want to say.

"I need you to live." I laugh through a turmoil of emotion, while tears pool in my eyes for the thousandth time today.

"Adeline—"

"Who else is going to walk me down the aisle at my wedding?" I sniffle. "I want you to meet my children… I still need my mom."

"I know." She sobs, crying and breaking with me.

I stand to hug her, feeling like she'll slip away sooner than I can handle.

She hugs me back. Crying into my hair, she whispers, "I'll be better. I'm going to rehab."

She drops this proclamation onto me, and it's so heavy I don't think I can carry the weight of it. "Oh my god." I reel back, searching her face to make sure she means it. I see more strength than expected in her green eyes.

12

I'm free.

For the first time in nineteen years, I can say from the pit of my soul *I am free.*

The withdrawal started immediately, and by some miracle we were able to get my mom into the best rehab in all of Florida. Finn and I drove her the few hours away. I said goodbye and told her I was proud of her.

She said she was proud of *me.*

I felt so seen in that moment, but now that I know she is in great hands, I can revel in the fact I'm not responsible for her anymore.

For now, at least.

I deflect from the thoughts of what would happen if she wasn't able to get sober, how they told me she wouldn't make it to the next five years. I cannot think of those things because right now, I'm all my mom has. And what she needs is hope, so hopeful is what I'll be.

"Your shower has horrible water pressure." Finn enters

my bedroom with dampened hair and a towel wrapped around his waist. My gaze automatically follows the water droplet that slowly trails down his toned stomach, gliding along V lines and disappearing beneath his towel.

I blink a few times, realizing exactly where I am staring. I lay flat on my bed, putting my book on my bedside table to give Finn my full attention. "You could shower at your own house, you know." To an outside perspective, it would seem like Finn and I are a couple.

We've been playing house the past two days while my mom's been away. They said she could be in rehab for at least a month. A month of freedom. A month of not worrying. A month of living for only myself.

It's perfect.

The moment promised is *perfect*.

"I can't leave you here by yourself. What if you leave the dryer on and your house catches fire while you're sleeping? I'd feel shitty for the rest of my life thinking, 'If I stayed, she would still be alive to banter with me.'"

I bark out laughing.

"And what if someone breaks in? What if you fall down the stairs and no one is there to help you back up?"

I say with humor, "I won't start the dryer before going to bed, I'll put up a good fight, and I can help myself up."

"I'm still staying."

I roll my eyes. "I'm no damsel in distress." I don't care why he's here. I'm just glad he is. I get to play a new game in my head, where I pretend this is our house, he is my boyfriend, and it is our love that brought us here.

"I know you would be just fine, love. You've been taking care of yourself your whole life. I just feel better knowing you're okay and happy. Plus, I like being here with you."

I ponder that for only a moment before his muscles pull me from my thoughts. "Who wouldn't be happy with *this* view." I roll onto my stomach, propping my chin up with my hands to admire.

He raises his eyebrows, used to my sarcasm. But this isn't sarcasm.

I don't know what comes over me, maybe it's because for the first time in my life I have nothing to worry about other than what's right in front of me, but I feel confident. And maybe even a little flirty.

Finn grabs some clothes from his bag, then returns to the bathroom to get dressed.

"That's no fun," I murmur.

After everything that happened in the ER, we never once spoke of our kiss. How there was so much tension pulling us toward one another it was impossible to ignore.

But now it's been two days. Surely the time frame in which it should've been discussed has expired. I certainly cannot be the one to bring it up, and since Finn hasn't, I'm sure he concluded it was a mistake.

The thought alone hurts, but I try to ignore it for now.

If a few weeks ago someone would've told me Finn would be home from college, or he'd be basically living at my house, or my mom was getting the help she needed in rehab, I would've laughed in their face.

Happy endings aren't handed to girls from broken homes. We don't expect it, and we certainly don't believe in it.

But right here, right now, I'm happy, even if I have a feeling that I haven't reached The End.

I pop up on my elbows, a sudden bolt of excitement shoots through me. "Let's leave." A bright smile overtakes me face.

Finn mindlessly stares off into space. "What?"

"Let's throw some stuff into bags and *leave*." I push myself up, standing on the bed.

Finn cocks his head with a raised brow.

"Finn." I bounce a little, shaking the mattress. "Don't you realize we've been given a gift."

He just stares at me to continue.

"You're home from college for the summer, and my mother is in rehab for at *least* a month. What are the odds these occurrences happen at once?" I pull my legs in, falling on my bottom, causing the bed to bounce and squeak. "Wow, this bed is loud."

Finn's eyes sweep over my bare legs, landing on my eyes with a smirk.

"Anyway," I say, getting back on track, "we've been granted this time to do *something, anything*. We would be doing a disservice to ourselves if we didn't make something out of it." I take in a breath after talking way too fast.

Finn sits up, pulling me onto his lap and cupping my jaw in one hand. "Now, love, you're talking *fun*." A wide smile slowly spreads across his face.

My skin breaks out into goosebumps and a giddy energy begs to escape, banging on the walls of my stomach. I giggle, pushing off Finn and moving into action.

"I've never left Florida," I remind him, pulling open my closet and finding the only suitcase I own.

It's sparkly and has hearts printed on the zippers, only used once during a short trip to Orlando when I was five. My dad was too stubborn to take my mom and I to one of the theme parks, so instead we spent the weekend at a hotel. It had a big pool though.

"Oh my god, maybe we will see snow!" I throw everything from my dresser into the small suitcase, it overflows onto the floor.

Finn watches me amused, chuckling under his breath. "It's July, love."

"It doesn't snow in July?" I act clueless, trying to zip my bulging suitcase.

I gasp at Finn's sudden presence next to me. He stills my hands, pushing me aside as he opens the suitcase and sorts through my clothes. I watch as he makes a large pile of useless clothes, while neatly folding the clothes that makes sense, placing them nicely in the suitcase. He fills it with short sleeved shirts, and a few light jackets. Shorts, leggings, he even goes into my closet to pick out some bathing suits. I blush at his choices, picking the ones that flatter my body and skin tone the best. After a few minutes of him packing, he reaches up to open my underwear drawer.

"I'll do that!" I say quickly.

He rolls his eyes, standing and grabbing the bag he brought to stay at my house. "Finish packing everything else you need. I'm going to pack my stuff at home. I'll pick you up in an hour," he says with confidence, leaving me alone in my room.

Everything barrels into me. I smile wide. It feels almost like a sugar rush, how jittery and excited I am. Once I hear the front door shut, I squeal.

We are really doing this.

I have a feeling this moment is going to be monumental.

"I love road trips!" I sing. The thrill of spontaneity courses through my veins. We already passed the *Thanks for visiting*

the Florida Keys sign, and a heavy weight I've felt lying on my shoulders for as long as I can remember went with it. My smile is so wide, my cheeks hurt.

"It's been forty-five minutes, love." Finn lets out a laugh, his hand moves toward me, but twitches back into place.

"Woo-hoo!" I shout out the window. I've never done anything remotely close to this in my entire life, and I never knew how much I would enjoy the thrill of leaving my life behind, bringing the only good thing in it: Finn Walker.

I click a button, and the sunroof opens. I give Finn a mischievous grin, and quickly unbuckle my seat belt. Elton John's *Goodbye Yellow Brick Road* is playing on the radio, which electrifies this moment. I stand on the center console and lift my head out the roof.

Finn grips onto my ankles, anchoring me into place. My legs go up into flames, and my stomach flips.

Tangled waves of auburn hair float around me; the wind makes my face reverberate like in the cartoons. I let out a genuine laugh, perhaps the most joyful filled one of my entire life. It gets lost on this empty highway.

I feel something I've hardly ever felt before.

Freedom.

I lift my face into the sun, the rays kissing my skin. I breathe in, smelling the last remains of salt water. Florida pine trees surround us, a few palm trees sway with the breeze.

In this moment, I am whole.

"Love," Finn's voice wakes me up. I glance around and remember where I am.

Finn's car. The sun is soon to set.

"I'm getting gas, do you want to go grab a snack and use the bathroom?"

I rub my eyes and break out into a smile. "Yes!"

Finn follows me into the convenient store. I take in all the mouse shaped trademarks, knowing exactly where we are. Orlando. I walk over to the sunglass section and grab a heart shaped pair.

"Try these on." I hand him the sunglasses.

He rolls his eyes, but for some reason does as he's told. I smile wide at his appearance. I grab a mouse shaped pair for myself and put them on.

I hear a little voice from below me say, "Mommy, mommy! I want those sunglasses!"

I glance down, and the little girl gasps. She can't be more than three. "A-are you…a princess?"

A giggle catches in my throat, I'm about to tell her I'm not when Finn interrupts.

"Shh." He brings his index finger over his mouth. "She is, but she's an undercover princess. No one is supposed to know…actually—" He appears thoughtful for a moment. "How did you figure it out?"

The little girl's eyes are two big circles staring up at me like I'm the coolest thing she's ever seen. "She's really pretty. And has princess hair," she says.

Finn pulls the sunglasses right off my face, crouches down to hand them to her. "I know, right. A face shouldn't be that pretty."

"Maddy! Get over here!" the girl's mother calls, realizing her daughter is talking to some strangers at a gas station. I back up a little, knocking into the sunglass display.

The girl glances at me one last time before following her mom out of the small store.

I flick Finn's forehead.

"Hey!"

"An undercover princess?" I laugh. "What even is that?"

"I was put on the spot, okay?" He rolls his eyes. "What else was I supposed to say?"

"Hmm, maybe that I wasn't a princess?"

"Yeah, okay, love. I also could've told her the tooth fairy isn't real."

I shake my head with a smile. "So…you think I have a pretty face," I tease.

He reaches past me, grabbing another pair of sunglasses, slowly putting them on my face. "That, Adeline, was never a secret."

I can see my reflection in his sunglasses turn red. The closer I look, the more I realize there's a button on the frame. I reach up and press it, and suddenly the heart shaped glasses are glowing, and I break out into laughter.

His lips lift at the corner as he watches me intently. I can still make out his eyes through the glasses, they wrinkle at the sides in an easy-going smile.

I pull out my phone, snapping a picture to remember this moment.

Finn and I grab some candy, and a magnet from the souvenir section. He checks out while I use the ladies' room, and then we are back on our way.

After an hour or so of listening to the radio, Finn disturbs the silence. "What do you love the most?"

You.

I gasp out loud by how fast my brain answered his question. Everything crashes into me at once, making it so very clear how undeniable my love for Finn Walker really is.

Oh my…

I am *in love* with him.

My cheeks flush, and a new fear creeps in, like the confession of this could rock my entire world. In the worst way possible.

I feel embarrassed all of a sudden, even though he can't read my thoughts. His eyes reflect the taillights before us, illuminating his perfect features. He notices me staring, the dimple on his cheek deepens.

"People? Or material things?" I ask, making sure I answer this right.

"Anything, both. I don't care. Name a hundred things if you want."

Ok. I close my eyes and think of anything other than the man next to me. "I love…the ocean. Swimming in it." I smile, already missing the way the waves brushed over my skin.

"Why?" he asks.

"Because it's the ocean. Everyone loves the ocean," I say like it's obvious.

"With you, love, there is always a deeper meaning."

There's a stretch of silence before I say. "I love the ocean because it makes me feel small." Most people fear being insignificant, but to me, it's a relief. "My problems don't matter at the end of the day, because all of this," I wave my arm around, "exists too."

When I feel the waves roll over my shoulders, it feels like it's repairing my heart. I roll down the window and let my arm sway with the wind. "Sometimes it feels like a peace offering from the world. A little, 'I'm sorry for what we put you through, but hey look over there. It's a dolphin!'"

Finn reaches out and grabs my hand. His thumb rubs circles over my skin, igniting every cell he touches.

"What else?" he asks.

"Pizza. I love pizza. And yes, there is a reason. It's cheesy and delicious and reminds me of the good in my child-hood." I smile at him, and he returns it. I think of tiny Finn and Adeline sitting in a booth at Pete's for hours in their own little world.

"Tell me more." He squeezes my hand.

"I love your parents. They gave me something I never thought I would experience—the feeling of *family*."

He squeezes my hand, like he gets me.

"There's nothing like it. The playfulness, the under-standing, the unconditional love. Unity and loyalty. It's unlike anything my parents could've given me, but some-how, by some God-given miracle, I was in the right place at the right time and met *you*."

"You're my family, Ad." His voice is lush with emotion.

I bring my arm back inside the car and roll up the window. The road is silent. An occasional car will pass by but other than that, we are alone. "What about you? What do you love?"

He smiles, pondering this for a few beats. I almost think he won't answer, but he finally speaks. "How close we are." He's quiet for a little longer, but his mouth opens like there's more to say.

"Keep going," I whisper, needing to hear the rest.

He wastes no more time. "I've never felt like I'm alone in the presence of another person, except you for when I'm with you."

I frown.

"Not in a lonely way though. In a way that I feel the most comfortable and at ease. It doesn't matter what I say or how I act around you, you'd never judge me." He squeezes my hand with a coy smile. "Don't laugh, but I like to think you and I share one soul. I'm made of half, and the rest of me belongs to you. Together, we make a whole and so it's like I'm alone with myself when I'm with you."

His words are like fishing net, casting around my heart and drawing me in.

My eyes go misty, I pretend to take interest in gazing out the window.

Finn eventually says, "I love that I am the one you choose to spend your time with. That I get to be your best friend." He puts on his turn signal, pulling off into the exit lane.

Stone cold realization plummets into me, and I breathe it in, swishing it around my mouth, testing the way it feels on my tongue.

Finn and I will never be *more* than this—friends.

We have everything. Trust, belonging, companionship, *love*. We might not share romantic love, but there is love here none the less. Altering with our perfectly established ecosystem will throw everything off balance. We won't make sense, things will change. We'll lose more than we will gain. We can never be more because we've already got it all. We weren't meant to be romantic partners. We are *more* than just that. He's my person and I am his.

Becoming anything but friends will put all of that at risk. I can't chance sinking my lifeboat.

I think about my mom and dad, the fighting, the tears, how complicated it all was. With Finn, it's as easy as inhaling.

I ease into this newfound peace and let out a breath, one I have been holding in since I was nine years old. I never realized until now, I spent every day falling a little bit in love with him. It wasn't obvious back then, but right here, right now, with ten years of built-up love, I feel it in every cell of my body.

"I love being your best friend too." It's for the best to keep things between us as they are, and I always knew we'd never actually be anything but friends. And yet it feels like a dream has been ripped away from me.

I always knew love hurt, but I never imagined it hurting like this.

13

There's one, turn right!" I say quickly, clutching Finn's phone in my hand and staring at the GPS. My phone stays plugged into the charger since I used up its battery reading an eBook for the past two hours.

"Jeez lady, you couldn't have told me a few yards before we got to it?" he jokes, making a U-turn so he can make the turn I made him miss. Oops.

We go down a dark, narrow road until we reach the neon sign that reads *otel*.

"I think someone stole the M," I joke, trying to lighten up the very eerie mood.

"This is the only hotel in the area?" Finn asks, a yawn breaking up his voice.

I pinch the digital map on my phone to get a wider view, the next hotel is an hour away. There is no way Finn, or I could drive for another hour; we're both beat. I tell Finn this and he sighs.

We pull into the parking lot, and I let out an exhausted laugh. There is only one other car, probably the person working the front desk. The only source of light is a street-lamp that flickers on and off. Swarms of moths flutter around the light, only to be disappointed every few beats when it goes completely dark.

Finn puts an arm out in front of me, stilling me while he gets out first. I unbuckle my seat belt and jump out anyway.

"You are one stubborn lady, you know that?" he whispers, popping open the truck.

I round the car until I reach the back where he is. I smile a wide, innocent smile.

He rolls his eyes and reaches for my bag. My eyes make the journey up and around the curves of his muscles. His skin pulls taught with each movement, accentuating his biceps and triceps. *Best friends, Adeline. Nothing else.*

I clear my throat and offer a helping hand.

"You can grab the pepper spray in the glove compartment," he says, easily grabbing his heavy bag.

I go to reach for my bag that sits on the ground, and he swats my hand away. "A pretty lady shouldn't have to carry her own bag." He gives me a sarcastic smile.

I give up and grab the can of pepper spray, despite there being only one other car. I tuck it into my bra, creating an obvious bulge.

A chill runs down my spine at the ghostly silence. The buzzing of the streetlamp and our footsteps are the only sounds to disrupt it. Even so, I can't shake the creepy feeling. I grab ahold of Finn's belt loop, hiding behind my best friend.

Quick footsteps get closer, and something bolts in front of us—*Ah!* I shriek, climbing up Finn's back. My heart beats out of my chest.

"Aw." I smile, letting out a relieved breath when I realize

the thing running was just a black cat who is now eating from a bowl to my right.

"Holy shit, Adeline, I thought you saw a fucking ghost." He brings his now empty hand to his chest. I laugh at the way he dropped the bags from me startling him.

"You were scared!" I jump down, pointing an accusing finger at his chest.

He shakes his head. "No"

"Oh, you *so* were. I bet there's even a wet spot in your jeans." I laugh so much.

I gasp when Finn grabs ahold of my sides. "No-no-no," I plead, and he gives me a look that says *I win* and starts tickling me.

I wiggle in his arms, laughing despite the fact that I want to pull his hair out one by one. I *hate* being tickled.

"Okay, okay," I say, breathlessly. "You weren't scared." I raise my arms in surrender.

He releases me and picks up our bags.

The front door might be the creepiest part. I take a deep breath, slowly opening the door, not able to see what's inside.

"This isn't getting any lighter, love."

Right. "Okay, okay." I inhale a deep breath and open the door, squinting my eyes anticipating a jump scare.

"Well, hello there!" a lady with a country accent pipes up from behind the desk that sits only three feet away. I take in the small lobby. The bookcase to my left holds travel pamphlets. The alligator mascot appears on some. We must be in Gainesville, Florida. Only a few more hours until we reach Georgia, and I will have officially left this state for the first time in my life.

I breathe in the welcoming scent of cinnamon. Finn

walks up to the desk first. I follow suit. This is not what I expected.

"Y'all need a room?"

Finn nods politely.

I grab a mint from the tray sitting on the front desk, and pop it in my mouth. The woman opens a drawer and hands Finn a key that has the number 5 attached to it. "Since you all looked so darn cute together out there on my security camera, I'll let you have the couple's suite for the price of a normal room." She winks.

I open my mouth to correct her assumption, but Finn chimes in before I get the chance. "That would be great, thanks." He grabs the key and puts it in his pocket, handing her a fifty-dollar bill. I open the door for him while he picks up our bags.

"Have a nice stay!" the woman says while we leave through the creepy door. I lead the way to room five and pull the key out of Finn's front pocket. A blush covers me, and I am relieved the streetlamp flickered out again.

I push the key into the hole and turn it. When we walk inside, Finn lets out a deep bellied laugh. "No way this is real life." We step into the room, and I take it all in.

A neon sign of a phallic shaped palm tree hangs above the bed. Red, wilted, roses cover the white fabric. I walk over to the nightstand. A bowl of condoms are sitting there.

"Strawberry banana?" his voice startles me, suddenly much closer than I expected.

"W-what?"

He reaches a hand in front of me, picking up one of the condoms. "It's flavored."

Finn puts it back in the bowl and I duck beneath his arm, grabbing my bag and locking myself in the bathroom.

The mirror is warped, and as I walk further into the

bathroom, the reflection of my head distorts. I breathe in slowly and hold it, then slowly blow it out. I remind myself again of my realization in the car.

I turn on the cold faucet to the sink and cup my hand under the running water. "Shit!" I hiss. The water is boiling hot. I turn off the cold faucet and twist the one labeled *hot*. Cold water comes out.

Of course.

"Everything okay?" Finn asks, knocking.

"Yeah." My voice comes out louder than I wanted it to. "The faucets are labeled wrong. I burnt my hand." *And I'm in the midst of a mental breakdown because I realized I'm in love with you but don't want to ruin our friendship by doing anything about it.*

"That's the fun of sleeping on the road," he says with ease, and I hear the bed squeak. He must've just sat down.

I splash some cool water on my face and change into a pair of spandex shorts and a light pink tank top.

When I open the door, the cool air hits me in the face. Finn's house is always cold, no doubt he set the air to sixty degrees.

Finn lays comfortably on the bed, legs crossed, with a travel pamphlet in hand. When he hears the bathroom door open, his eyes slowly lift to mine. They widen for a millisecond, but I didn't miss the way they traveled up the length of my legs…and then to my chest. I glance down, realizing the cool air and no bra combo happening to my breasts. Instinctively, I shift my arms to cover up, and respectfully, Finn pretends he didn't see.

"I'm going to grab a quick shower," he says while getting up from the bed.

I get under the covers and try to bundle up for warmth. I browse through the pamphlet while Finn is in the bathroom. There's not much to do here, other than tour colleges. I toss and turn, realizing how much energy I have stored up from sitting all day.

I pull open the nightstand drawer and find the remote to the small TV. I turn it on, the local news starts playing. I click the button to go to the next channel, it's a cooking show. I go to the next one and the news plays again.

There are only two channels, so cooking it is.

I hear the bathroom door open and peek up. I have to take a deep breath to keep from drooling.

Finn is wearing joggers that stop right at his hips, and a pair of black socks. That's it. His muscles curve and twist around his arms, moving while he rubs a towel over his tousled, wet hair. My eyes move all around his body. I turn my attention back to the TV.

For fuck's sake, Adeline, get a hobby or something.

Finn finally settles in for the night, going under the covers. My leg accidentally brushes against his. I mumble a quick apology and roll over, facing the stupid bowl of condoms.

A half hour goes by, I hear pages turning so I'm assuming Finn is reading a book or something. I make a distinct effort not to look, because he is still shirtless and still as hot as ever.

"Do you need the light?" Finn's hand touches my shoulder as he peers over me, seeing if I'm awake.

"No." I yawn, turning around to face him again.

He reaches over to the lamp on the side of the bed, pulling the string to turn it off. He lays down. The dim glow from the moon helps me make out his features. He gives me a lopsided smile. "I'm really happy we're doing this."

Now I'm smiling. Despite the circumstances with my

mother right now, I am happy. "Me too. Thank you for this."

"Wherever you go, I'll be right there. Always." The mattress dips when he scoots in closer.

My knee meets his thigh. He doesn't do anything to correct it. I stay still.

So does he.

He leans forward, placing a barely there kiss to my forehead. "Sleep well, love."

Pesky insects swarm my stomach.

"Night."

I squint my eyes at the brightness of my phone and sigh. It's only one in the morning. I look to my right, Finn lays with his hand under his face. His mouth hangs slightly open, his closed eyes hold a peacefulness to them. I can watch Finn sleep all night long, never once tiring. His slow inhale and exhale move the comforter up and down. Its mesmerizing, watching the person you love simply *breathe*.

How did I become such a cliché?

I slowly lift the blanket off my body and tip toe to the bathroom. I comb my hair and put on some lip balm. I have so much energy, I wish it was the morning. I stare at myself in the mirror for what feels like a vain amount of time and quietly settle back into bed, trying not to wake Finn.

"What's with all the noise, Sleeping Beauty?" Finn's raspy voice settles into the night.

I gasp. Guess I wasn't as discrete as I thought. "Sorry," I whisper.

"No, thank you, actually. You pulled me out of the most boring dream."

I cover my mouth to stifle a giddy laugh. Partly because I am thankful to be able to talk to Finn right now to ease the boredom. "If you're having boring dreams then what does that say about you?"

My eyes adjust to the darkness, I can make out a dimpled smile. Finn turns on his side, so he's facing me, our knees knock together again but neither of us move.

"That a crazy girl kidnapped me and forced me to drive her across the state, and now all I dream about is the road." He says, "She's hot though."

My eyes widen, and that flirty energy twirls back in, dancing and parading around my heart. "What would this hot girl want with you?"

He shrugs, inching in closer, his knee grazes my inner thigh. "I've been wondering that all my life."

My voice comes out sensually low, "Maybe she thinks you're special."

His eyes fall, no longer looking at mine. "I'm just a guy who happened to be at the right place at the right time."

His sentence holds so much weight. Is he talking about when we met or when I allegedly kidnapped him?

"Or maybe it was her who was at the right place, right time," I say. My stomach drops when his eyes flicker from my lips to my eyes.

This unspoken push and pull we've been teetering on ends now. I don't know what it means on his end. Those two kisses we've shared, and his compliments embedded into our usual banter… It cannot go on.

My heart aches like grief, but I'm grieving something that was never mine to begin with.

I've played out every scenario in my head and there's a

ninety-nine percent chance of failure...heartbreak...loss. With my track record, who says I'll be the exception, that one percent? I would be kidding myself to think I could achieve anything near happily ever after. I know how this really ends. I'll always be the best friend, a bridesmaid at his wedding, the Aunt Adeline to his children. But if I risk something more than friends happening, I might even lose *that* future.

I can either give in and let this spark—that I think is between us—ignite, risking all the good in my life now, or I can smother it before it becomes a wildfire and burns my happy life with him to the ground.

What we have now is a perfectly built home. My only home.

My heart tells me to let him pull me close. Instead, I roll over and say easily, "I just got really tired all of a sudden."

Neither of us say anything the rest of the night, and before I know it, the morning sun lights up the motel room.

Someone bangs aggressively on the door, instinctually I scoot next to Finn. He startles awake and holds on to me, looking around the room. Probably feeling the confusion of waking up in a new place other than his own bed.

The banging continues, and Finn jumps out of bed, glancing around. He grabs the lamp, unplugs it, and then opens the door.

"Rise and shine—what's the lamp for?"

I rub my eyes and peek around Finn, at the lady from the front desk. She holds a basket full of pastries.

"It's six a.m. I could've seriously hurt you with this," Finn says, coming down from the adrenaline I assume. He turns to face me, and my eyes zero in on the bulge in his pants. My face swells in a deep red no doubt. I look away and squeeze my eyes shut.

The lady lets out a deep laugh. "You're one funny fella." She peeps her head in. "I see why yah like him." And then she uses her hands to gesture measuring out something very big.

Oh my gosh.

Finn catches on and looks down. "Fuck," he mutters, using the lamp to cover himself up. He grabs something out of his suitcase and rushes into the bathroom. I roll out of bed to retrieve the basket.

"Hey, hey, hey, leave some for the rest of us," the lady says.

I thought she was giving us the whole basket. I blush and grab two bagels and blueberry muffins.

"You two have a good morning." She gives me a knowing smile.

I muster up a smile and shut the door.

Welcome to Georgia. I snap a quick photo of the sign. We stop to fill up the gas tank. The air feels dryer here. I look around at the nothingness that surrounds us. There is one other car here, a copper-colored Volvo, and other than that it feels like we are in the middle of nowhere.

It's terrifying, like if I scream right now it would get lost in the trees.

The gas station looks the same as the ones in Florida. I think knowing I'm in a different state than my mom is freaking me out a little. I'm so used to being always a five-minute drive from her.

The smell of gasoline gives me a headache, my breath

becomes short, and I feel a minor panic attack coming on. Finn finishes filling up his car, docking the gas pump. He walks over to me and places a gentle hand to my cheek. "You okay?"

No. "Yeah, I'm fine."

He pulls me toward him, hugging me tight and whispering against my ear, "You're a terrible liar."

I breathe him in, smelling a hint of the cinnamon and clove soap he's been using since we were kids. You can only catch the scent if your nose is pressed into his skin.

"If you want to go back, say the word and I'll turn around," he says.

I picture my mom, detoxing and surrounded by nurses and psychologists. Safe and sound. The photo I took only ten minutes ago of Georgia's welcome sign flashes across my memory, a significant moment, because I'm the farthest I've gone into the world, right here with Finn by my side. It only makes me want to go further. "No, let's drive." I breathe him in one last time, before pulling away and climbing into the driver's seat.

Finn looks at me like he's kind of scared but gets into the passenger seat anyway.

I shift gears, accidentally switching to sport mode and accelerating all too fast, immediately slamming on the brakes and jolting Finn and I forward. I smile hard. "Oops."

Finn slowly inhales with tight lips, turns toward me, and calmly shifts the car back out of sport mode.

I pull onto the highway, driving as fast as Finn allows without him clutching his seat for dear life, which is a solid eighty-five miles per hour. I turn the radio up, letting the music wash over me, electrifying my pulse and bringing a wide smile to my face.

Finn eventually screams over the music, "Having fun over there, Miller?"

I grin at him. "The funnest!" I shout, remembering him telling me how we are going to have the "funnest summer yet."

Using the word that doesn't exist makes it all the more fun.

∾

"Adeline, you're going to hate me," Finn says.

"Is it just me or is the road starting to look like space?" I ask, tiredly.

Finn yawns, a very obnoxious loud one. "I was thinking more like the circus." He points to the road before us.

"Circus? Where do you see bright colorful lights and elephants doing backflips?" I ask.

He laughs. "Have you ever been to the circus, love?"

"No. Are there no backflipping elephants? Because if so, you might as well just tell a little kid Santa isn't real."

"Then yes, they do backflips," he says.

I change the subject to a more productive one. "Just let me know when to take an exit." I yawn, in need of a cozy hotel bed.

"That's the thing…there aren't any hotels nearby."

I take a deep breath. My white knuckles grip the steering wheel. "One job!" I say, "You had one job!"

"If you get off on the next exit, I can direct you to a campground."

I give him my evilest death glare. He looks down, like a wolf surrendering to the alpha. At least he knows who's boss.

"In the moment promised, I hate you." I turn into the exit lane and Finn tells me how to get to the camp site.

"Voila," Finn chimes, attempting and failing to lighten the mood.

"How exciting, we get to sleep in the car we've been sitting in *all day*," I say wryly.

"That's the fun of road tripping." Finn reclines his seat.

"No, that's the fun of having a friend who doesn't know how to use a GPS," I huff.

"Ouch." He touches his chest. "I'm just your friend, now, Adeline?"

He doesn't realize the weight of the sentence, but it becomes a chainsaw tearing my heart to shreds. "You're my best friend, but I'm tired and hungry so for now, you're the friend getting in the way of a good night's sleep."

I peer into the back seat and grab a bag of sour gummies. I plop one into my mouth and say between bites, "Most delicious four course meal I've had in a while." I hand one to Finn. I chew as loud as I can.

Finn laughs, grabbing at the bag of gummies while I tighten my grip. I don't give up my snacks that easily, especially to Finn who eats handfuls at a time. He pulls even harder.

"Finn you're going to—" *Break it.* Gummies go everywhere. Finn's laugh echoes in the forest surrounding us.

A screech escapes my throat when he leans over me to grab my arms, pulling me onto his lap. He's still laughing as he hugs me to his chest. My heart stops, wait no, maybe it's beating so fast I can't feel it anymore. Finn's touch is everywhere on my body as he tickles me.

I laugh so hard, begging him to stop but I can't get the words out, so I do the only thing I can. I bite his neck.

Finn's laughter immediately stills, silence drowns the air.

I am suddenly very aware that my action could've come across as sexual.

"That was not meant to turn you on!" I blurt out. I shake my head immediately, stomach sinking. "I mean, not that you *are* turned on." I keep on rambling, not knowing when to shut up, "Or that I could turn you on in the first place, I mean—"

My tangent is interrupted by Finn's palm covering my mouth. "Adeline." He slowly takes his hand off my mouth. He pulls the seat up into the normal sitting position. I adjust myself in the only way I know how. I must be fifty shades of red as I straddle him.

"It's cute that you get embarrassed so easily, you know that? Help me clean this up, love." He picks up a gummy and plops it into his mouth, while I resist the pull behind my eyes begging to watch the way his dimple appears as he chews.

I lift myself up to climb back to my own seat, but Finn grabs my hips, pushing me back to where I was.

My eyes widen. I tuck a piece of hair behind my ear to seem at ease with our seating arrangement. I nonchalantly plop gummies into my mouth and shift my body so I no longer straddle Finn, and face forward like a child sitting in their parent's lap.

I open Netflix on my phone and pick out a romance movie, resting it on the dashboard.

When Finn starts to protest, I connect the Bluetooth and put the volume all the way up. Instead of fighting me on my movie choice, he wraps two arms around my waist and rests his chin on my shoulder.

The way he holds me shocks my system.

I try to focus on the movie, I really do. But instead, I sit in Finn's lap, hyper fixating on the circles he rubs into my side. His body is warmer than mine, his inhale and exhale breathe life into the insect swarm in my stomach.

I shouldn't feel this way, not anymore. I thought I cut the line to my feelings for Finn at the beginning of this trip, but we aren't back home. We're someplace far away. Everything that tells me this shouldn't happen melts away. This place is like an alternate dimension where nothing that occurs truly exists anywhere else.

Maybe what I've been craving is allowed here, hidden away in the forest.

My breaths become heavy. Instinctually I push my bottom against his pelvis. It's a micromovement. Finn could've easily brushed it off as an accident. I consider doing it again, weighing the pros and cons, dreaming of what could be, when rain drops suddenly pound at the car. It picks up quickly, falling so loud I can hardly hear the movie anymore.

"That came out of nowhere." Finn's breath trickles against my ear, sending a chill down my neck.

So much restless energy buzzes within me. "There's no good in wasting perfectly clean water," I say, loud enough so he can hear me.

I turn around to grab my bag from the back seat. Finn's face is so close to mine, I can smell the gummies on his breath. His features reflect his confusion.

I dig through my bag until I find what I am searching for and push open the door.

I gasp as the rainfall chills my skin and steals my breath. Despite there being about a million trees in the campsite, rain still manages to soak my clothes. I let out a laugh, each droplet cleansing me further.

"What in God's name are you doing?" I hear Finn call from the car as I walk further from it.

I blink away the water that gathers on my eyelashes, turning my head to peer beneath them to see Finn. He has the expression of someone who's witnessed a friend losing their mind. I smirk at him before turning my attention back in front of me.

I pull my shirt over my head, throwing it at the car. I can't look at him anymore. My insecurities draw pictures in my head of his face scrunched up in disgust.

I kick off my shoes and peel off my leggings.

I'm left bare, with only my dark purple bra and underwear covering the intimate parts of me. I say a mental thank you to the Adeline twelve hours ago who put on a matching set, as opposed to the beige granny panties I packed. I bend down to grab the bottle of soap. I peek up when I hear the car door being slammed shut.

With the rain dripping down his forehead and the storm surrounding him, he's unbelievably desirable. He walks with purpose until he reaches me, taking no time when he lifts me over his shoulder. His hand rests on my bottom to support me, making me ache for him.

The world is upside down as he walks back toward the car.

I pound at his back. "What are you doing? I didn't get to wash my hair!" The blood rushes to my face.

"I don't want some sick fucks watching you like this."

I suddenly picture all my deepest insecurities. "Like what?"

He sighs, stopping in his tracks. "With water dripping down your half naked body, Adeline. It's every guy's fucking dream."

My eyes are saucers, and I strain my ears to make sure I heard him correctly.

He bends and sets me down. Amber eyes wander and

his lip twitches. "Damnit, Adeline. If this is your idea of fun, then go shampoo your hair." He holds up a finger. "But if I catch anyone hidden in the bushes with a pair of fucking binoculars, someone's dying."

I gasp. "*Fucking* binoculars…the horror," I tease, spinning around to retrieve my soap.

I walk a distance back to where I was before Finn picked me up. I twist the bottle, pouring some into my hand and rubbing suds against my skin. The rain rinses it away almost the second it touches me. I scrub some in my scalp, trying to slow my breathing as I recall the last minute of my life.

It's awfully quiet coming from where I left Finn, and I turn around to see where he went.

"Ah!" I touch my chest instantly, startled by Finn who stands only two feet from me, expressionless. "I didn't know you were there."

He stays unmoving.

"You can wait in the car. I'm almost done." My words linger in the air, an uncomfortable amount of time goes by before he speaks.

He shakes his head. "I'm not going to make you stand out in the freezing rain by yourself." His hair appears black from water. A single droplet runs across his jawline, gathering beneath his chin and finally falling to the ground.

Soap starts to drip close to my eyes. I tilt my head back and use my hands to rinse it away. I put some more soap into my hand and reach for Finn, slapping some onto the top of his head. "Might as well clean up while you're here then." I'm completely giddy, and even closer to the man than before.

The corners of Finn's lips slightly lift …he almost smiles. I massage the soap into his hair, loving the feel of the strands slipping between my fingers. As the shampoo rinses from his hair and travels the length of his body, I wonder what the rest of him feels like wet and soapy. The fabric covering my breasts graze his chest.

He studies me, and the amber is nowhere to be found behind his dilated pupils.

The only air between us is our breath.

I still completely, warmth erupts in my belly. His lips are hardly feathering mine. I breathe him in, tasting the remains of gummies. Every sense of reasoning goes out the window.

I want him.

I forget about the boundaries being best friends with someone implies and let an almost inaudible moan break free.

A sound comes deep from his chest as if answering me. He cups my face in his hands, staring into my eyes, unhurried to move.

I can't take it anymore, but before I can even blink his lips devour mine. They feel different than before, lubricated from the rain.

"Fuck," he mutters, gazing so deeply into my eyes. It feels as if he sees through them, studying the deepest parts of my soul. "I'm sorry." He breaks away.

No.

"For what?" I shiver, not from the cold.

He is three paces away from me now. "I keep messing up. God, you're just—" He pulls at his hair. "You make it so difficult to resist sometimes." He laughs without humor. "I don't know why I can't stop myself from kissing you."

"I don't want you to stop," I whisper.

Do you want me just as much as I want you?

"I can't do this, Adeline," he whispers at the ground.

I shatter.

"Look at me." He's closer now, gently raising my chin. "I want to kiss you so badly. Hell, I want to kiss every inch of your body and do things to you that you've only read about in the filthiest book."

Every cell I'm made of burns to discover the things he desires. *What's stopping you?* Is on the tip of my tongue.

"I won't risk our friendship and your happiness out of selfish desires. So yes, I do want this, but I can't have it." he says so low I almost don't hear it.

"But this *would* make me happy."

He shakes his head, says in a pleading voice, "You deserve the whole wide world. I'm in college, hours away, for another three years. That's not enough for you. I *know* that's not enough, and I'm not doing anything halfway when it comes to you." He pauses. "Us kissing won't do anything aside from temporarily relieving ourselves and complicating things."

"It doesn't have to complicate things." I say something I never imagined I'd say to him, "I-I want you, Finn." I shake my head because that's wrong. "I *need* you," I say like my survival depends on it.

His eyes hold hope for a moment before something slaughters it. "If we crossed this line and it didn't work out, I'd just be another man who hurt you. I can't risk that happening and I can't lose you."

"But—"

"You'll thank me one day." He releases his hold on my face and walks back to the car without glancing back.

I stand nearly naked in the rain, shivering from the rejection of the man I love.

Perhaps love only ends well in the novels, and maybe this is his way of preserving the closest thing to happiness as we could get: by withholding ourselves from the flame that begs to ignite.

But I know I'd be happy doing this with Finn, surpassing any level of the emotion I could've experienced before. I want to let this passion free, let it take us somewhere I've never been.

Even if we never blossom into something worth reading about... I still want Finn. In every way.

I glance around this empty forest, noting it's something out of a fairy tale. This place, it's almost as if it doesn't exist. Like whatever happens here doesn't happen in the real world.

Like a dream.

I can already feel myself grieving him after this, experiencing a worse pain than if we smother the flame right now.

But I think in the end, if I don't get him at all, maybe I've lost more than I gained by being careful.

I pull my shoulders back and walk briskly to him. I open the passenger door, the one Finn escaped to. He stares at me, saying nothing. His expression is thin ice, like one little thing will shatter the guard he holds up. I feel my skin burning for his touch.

I climb onto his lap and pull the door closed, in need of what he can give me. His lips are still swollen from mine only a few moments ago. "Just for tonight." I say three simple words, hoping they convey everything I feel.

His eyes skim the length of my body.

I gasp at his cold hands that start at my lower back and slowly caress upwards. He's careful, eyelids heavy as he looks up through wet eyelashes.

I focus on pulling air into my lungs. I'm afraid if I don't, I will pass out on the spot.

"We shouldn't." His gaze is like honey dripping down my skin.

I rake my fingers through his dampened hair. "But can't we have this, just this once? We can leave it right here in the forest."

He fights something within himself, his eyes no longer on me but someplace else entirely. "Ad, we can't—"

"What if we never do this?" I try to bring him back, right here with me. "I don't know about you, but I will always wonder what it would have been like." My entire body feels as fragile as glass, and I realize I am already in too deep to be strong enough to resist Finn or what might come after this.

This might break me, but I'd rather live as Finn's shattered remains than never experience him. All of him.

I must've said the right thing, because his fingers tighten around the side of my hips, something ticks in his jaw. There is so much energy passing between us, I feel the slight tingle in the air separating us. It's almost as if it's silently pleading with us to close the space. To become one.

It's like we share one soul. I remember him saying those words.

"You're not someone I can just leave behind in a mossy forest." His face angles up to mine. Our lips catching with heavy breaths.

My mind goes still, the millions of thoughts I once had completely go out the car window. Like I was caught in a tornado and Finn grabbed onto me, pulling me out of the chaos.

He clings onto my bare skin while his tongue parts my lips.

All the doubts that once plagued my mind, that set up a barrier between us and this moment, they all just melt away.

All that exists is Finn. His groans and his touch and his breath.

His hand leaves my skin, I'm covered in goosebumps from the lack of warmth. A dull buzz rings in my ears as the seat reclines beneath us.

Finn is completely laying down, until he grips me with firm hands and shimmies us around so I'm the one laying down and he's on top of me.

His long legs settle between my short ones, and his face hovers above mine. I drink him in.

The feel of his body between my thighs sends waves of passion coursing through me. The way his eyes peer into mine, I know he sees me.

All of me.

He gets me on levels no one else ever could.

"You are perfect," he breathes, before kissing me deeper than he ever has before. He feels around my body, sending shivers along my spine. He finds the string of lace hanging on my hips.

I gasp, cold air meeting me when he slowly moves the cloth down my legs, sending out in involuntary moan.

"Your sounds are so beautiful."

His warm lips tease me, moving so slowly down my neck, over my collarbone, down the center of my chest.

I let out a ragged breath. I cannot tell up from down, like I'm in the center of the ocean and everything around me is blue. I have no idea which way leads to the surface.

I'm drowning in Finn Walker, and I never want to breathe again.

He cups my breasts, lightly massaging the soaked purple that covers them. He reels back to observe. "I've reached a wall."

"A-a wall?" I sound out of breath.

"Yes, love," he whispers so carefully. "Do I want this on or off?" He inspects the bra closely. He reaches underneath my back and unclips it, slowly sliding the straps down my arms. "*Off.*"

My nipples peak, meeting the cool air.

Suddenly he's drawing my breast into his mouth.

I stifle a moan from the pleasure. He sucks on the sensitive bud, then leaves a trail of kisses on his way to my other breast. Each spot he meets ignites a new heat that seeps into my skin. It all builds up in my core, so much so that I blurt out, "You're *insanely* hot."

My eyes go wide, I hide behind my hands, suddenly embarrassed to admit that to my best friend. My hope that he didn't hear me disintegrates the moment he pauses, completely stilling.

"What did you say?" he asks in a teasing voice, still only an inch from my chest that concaves deeply with each heavy breath, building on my arousal and embarrassment.

"I didn't say anything," I lie.

He grabs ahold of my hips and yanks me down to his level, meeting eye to eye. "I think you did." His eyes are stern. "You think I'm *insanely hot.*" He raises his brows, not letting me live this down.

I roll my eyes and say, "Fine. Yes, I think you're insanely hot, now can we get back to business?"

He laughs. "Listen to you trying to take advantage of me."

"I hope you realize you're ruining the moment—"

"Wait, stop." He covers my mouth with his large hand. "Did you hear that?" he asks roughly.

I must've tuned out my surroundings, but the moment I tap back in, I hear it. Something booms in the distance. Pops of sound trail shortly after it.

Finn rolls down the window, and I instinctively cover my chest and squeeze my legs together. There is no one around, but I suddenly feel so exposed.

Finn quickly pulls a T-shirt out of his bag in the back seat and hands it to me.

I pull on my panties that are soaked from the rain and my neediness.

Finn is by some miracle fully dressed, and he opens the car door to find out what the sound is. I follow close by, holding onto the hem of his wet T-shirt. The cold drizzle coats my skin, but after what just happened, I am still warm from the ghost of Finn's touch.

My bare feet sink into the mud, each footstep making a squashing sound.

After a few beats, the rain stops all together.

We finally meet an opening. It looks like the group of trees were struck by lightning. I start to conclude that's what the noise was, until I hear it again. I jump from the sudden boom, and I look up and watch the fireworks explode in the distant sky. It all adds up now, and I kick myself for not realizing what today was sooner.

"It's the Fourth of July," Finn and I say in unison.

Excitement shoots down my body, mimicking the fireworks in the sky above us when Finn takes one large step toward me. He grabs my hands and stares into my eyes.

I don't want this night to be the last time we're like this. Now that I've had a taste, I will forever be starved of him. He leans in to kiss my lips.

"I know we can't do this back home," I blurt out.

His face pulls away from mine.

I don't think I even know what is going to come out of my mouth until the moment it does. "Because when we go home, you'll be packing up for college. But we aren't home.

We don't have to be home for at least a month." I smile as the gears turn in my head and I picture doing this every day we are away from Key Largo. "Let's just let whatever this is run its course, at least until we get home."

He raises a brow, "You mean like…" He struggles, like he doesn't want to offend me, so I answer for him.

"A summer fling."

"Let me get this straight." He holds up a hand, eyes narrowed, half smirk playing on his lips. "You're telling me you want to like, what? Be in a relationship?" He clears his throat. "And when we go home, and I go back to college… everything will be how it was before?"

I try not to think that far ahead, to whatever lies after this trip. It might be my worst mistake, but in the moment promised I'm a desperate fool. "Yes." The word falls off my tongue before I can give another thought to the future, like it's a faraway land we'll never reach.

His expression shifts to something unreadable, but only for the blink of an eye. He rushes to me, sweeping me off my feet and wrapping my thighs around his hips.

He kisses me so deeply. The world spins and I feel like I'm going to fall. But Finn holds me so close to him that I couldn't.

He owns my heart and has no clue.

I let out a guilt-free moan. For the first time, this isn't happening by mistake. His lips are intentional, along with my reaction to them. Warmth piles up in my core.

"Adeline," he says, gripping my rear. "We should've been doing this since the moment we met." His voice comes out ragged, and it sends a heatwave down my body.

I try to laugh but I'm too overwhelmed with emotions I never knew existed. "You mean when we were nine?"

"Well, when you put it that way..." Everywhere he kisses catches fire, and right now my neck is his victim. "No."

I finally let myself feel beneath his shirt. His damp skin raises in goosebumps. I picture the way his muscles curve and dip as he tenses from the cold. But I want to see him with my own eyes, not my imagination.

His arousal grows against me, and my hand anxiously descends to grip him over his soaked clothes. His breath hitches and he grabs my hand, stilling it and pulling it up to his lips, placing a gentle kiss on my palm.

"Oh, sorry." I cringe at myself and my inexperience. What am I even doing?

"Believe me, I want you to grab me," he admits. "I just —" He sighs. "I don't think we should get carried away with this. We've been driving all day and have been confined in my car. Maybe we should sleep on it...besides, I'm not making love to you for the first time in the back seat of my car."

I don't want him to sleep on it, after a good night's rest what if he decides this was the worst mistake of his life? Sitting up in a coat of sweat, gasping for air like he's woken from a nightmare, only to find out it was real. He really did kiss me, and he has to run to the bushes to expel the remains of me from his mouth.

But before I can say anything, he starts walking back to the car with me in tow. He buckles in and starts driving. I don't ask where we are going, I just close my eyes and dream of a fling with Finn that has no expiration date.

14

W e're here." I feel a hand rub my arm.

I open my eyes and scan the length of the building beyond the window. It seems to be at least twenty stories tall. In a sleepy daze, I rub my eyes and get out of the car, immediately stopping when I realize I'm not wearing anything but panties and a moist T-shirt. I rush back into the car.

Finn tosses me a pair of shorts from my suitcase.

He carries both our bags. Despite my offering to help, he insists I only carry my purse.

I step around the car to see my surroundings. Mountains line the horizon, it's hard to make them out in the dark, but the dark purple hue is captivating. "I've never seen a mountain in real life before." I take in the shape of them, too far in the distance to see any grain of detail.

"Where are we?" This is what I imagine New York city to be like. There are a few cars driving on the streets and it's only two in the morning. I can only imagine how busy these streets are during the day.

"Atlanta, Georgia," Finn answers, coming up from behind me. His breath is warm on the back of my neck. His body radiates so much heat. He isn't touching me, but I can feel every inch of him.

I hope the hour or two he spent alone with his thoughts didn't make him change his mind about the fling I proposed.

"Let's check in, love," he says, putting a hand on the small of my back to lead me forward. We walk into the hotel lobby, the cool air against my damp clothes makes my teeth chatter. It is much different than the motel in Gainesville.

The lobby is the size of my house. My mouth waters at the smell of cookies. Finn gets behind the two people in line checking in, so I follow the smell and find a table with complimentary chocolate chip cookies. There are only a couple left, I grab the last two and make my way back to Finn.

He's talking to the man at the front desk, and I silently hand Finn a cookie. He gives me a smile that causes my heart to somersault. We get the room key and head to the elevators. I press the up arrow and the doors open immediately. I lean against the wall of the elevator, licking the last remains of my cookie off my thumb.

Finn plants himself between my legs, standing several inches taller than me. "You're sexy, Miller. You know that?" he whispers.

I let out a relieved sigh. *He didn't change his mind.*

He chuckles. "I love…" he begins, moving a strand of hair away from my face, "how effortlessly beautiful you are."

I bring my hand to the top of my head. The wild strands form a knot from drying without having combed through it after my rain shower. "Finn, I'm absolutely disgusting right now."

"Oh please. I love your wild hair. It reflects your personality." He rubs the top of my head, making the strands stick up and out even more.

It's weird, Finn openly flirting with me. We always tease each other back and forth, but we are hardly forward with compliments or kind sentiments. I think I love this new shift.

I don't know what's going to happen in the hotel room. I hope we're still on the same page with the summer fling idea.

He stares down at me, his eyebrows form a straight line. He closes the gap between our lips. He kisses me passionately, it's slow and romantic, and we both seem to lose our breaths.

The elevator dings and someone anxiously clears their throat to get our attention.

Finn turns around, and I peek beneath his tricep. An old lady stands in the doorway of the elevator, tapping her foot wearing an expression of disgust and inconvenience.

"Sorry about that. We're on our honeymoon," Finn says, grabbing my hand and leading me out of the elevator.

I hide behind him, a blush erupting along my entire body. Why is she even awake this early in the morning anyway? Once the elevator closes, taking the old lady away, Finn breaks out into laughter.

I slap him on the shoulder. "You're like that annoying dad who chaperones every school field trip and embarrasses the hell out of his kid."

"That's oddly specific." He brushes me off. "Let's go see our room," he says, holding up the key card and wiggling his eyebrows.

We push open our hotel room door, it looks like any other hotel room but this one is special. It's *ours*. The bathroom is immediately to the left, and after walking further in, I see the king-sized bed.

I've slept with Finn hundreds of times—when we were kids innocently having sleepovers, and the other night in the motel—but this feels different. The anticipation is slowly eating away my patience. Because I know what happens next. Or at least I hope I know.

I spin around, face planting into Finn's chest. I lift my gaze, and he peers down at me in amusement.

What is happening to my body contrasts his demeanor. My palms are slick with a layer of sweat, my heart drums so loudly in my chest I'm almost afraid Finn can hear it, and most of all…the annoyingly stubborn butterflies make their way down south, right between my legs. But Finn is completely at ease.

He leans down, feathering his lips against mine. I breathe him in, feeling the comfort of home.

He is the closest thing to family I have ever known.

I've never felt safe or unconditionally loved from my dad. I know my mom loves me, but I've been the only person I could rely on for as long as I remember. I don't blame her for her absence or addictions. Even though I witnessed the abuse she took from my dad, it will never be the same as her having to survive it. I can acknowledge now that she neglected me, but I will never resent her for it. It sucked. I deserved better. But so did she.

So many people probably looked at my mother's situation and wondered why she didn't just leave him and take me with her.

Life isn't that simple.

Yes, she had free will, but when you're being physically

and emotionally abused, the free will to leave gets further and further out of reach, until you are blind to it altogether. Until you forget what it was like to be in the driver's seat of your own life.

I've promised myself for as long as I can remember, to strive for something *more*. I never knew what it would look like, I didn't know what it would feel like to touch it. I just knew it was out there, and it was *mine*. Standing here, in Finn's embrace, I know I've found it, and never want to let it go.

This fling is the closest thing I'll have to a happily ever after, so I'll soak it all in before my time runs out.

There's no one I trust more than Finn.

He is beautiful. I never noticed the guard of steel he held up until this moment. In its absence I can see every emotion that passes behind Finn's eyes. Standing here in the presence of him when he is the most authentic version of himself makes me feel so lucky. Not everyone gets to see him this way.

He kisses me hard, drawing his hands down my arms then up my back into my hair. I wince when his fingers get caught in the tangled knots. Tears prick my eyes from the pain of him accidentally pulling my hair.

He gently removes his hands, placing a soft kiss to both my eyelids. "I'm sorry."

"Maybe we should shower. I need to condition my hair and brush it." I rub my arms. "It's also freezing in here."

He places a kiss to my cheek, and somehow it feels more intimate than making out. "You want to shower first?"

I shrug it off. "No, it's okay. Getting these tangles out will take a while. There won't be any hot water left for you."

"Can't argue with that." He steps away from me, unzipping his suitcase and grabbing only a pair of boxer briefs and black shorts. "I'll be right out," he says, closing the bathroom door behind him.

I daydream of joining him in the shower, but there's no way I'll be the first one to make a move like that.

~

Atlanta is *busy*.

Our hotel is near a suburban neighborhood, it's the closest place to get away from the chaos of the city.

Finn and I walk together on the sidewalk.

After our separate showers, we cuddled up and slept together, but when we woke up it was like nothing had changed. We bantered back and forth like always, no kissing, no proximity.

I almost think I dreamt the whole thing.

"Open house from eight a.m. to noon," Finn says slowly, like he's reading something far away.

I squint my eyes, finding the sign in someone's yard.

"It's a quarter after ten," I say, mischievously. "Can we go…pretty please?"

He nods his head with a ghost of a smile playing on his lips.

"I don't see the point of this," he complains, coming up to the house.

I tap his shoulder to let me down. "It will be *fun*." I drag out the word, reminding him of his birthday wish to have fun this summer.

You know how everyone has a specific smell? Well, the people who lived in this home smell freaking amazing. Like pumpkin spice, despite it being July.

Finn and I step into the well-lit living room, a tall lady dressed in business clothes eagerly approaches us.

"I'm Shanna, the real estate agent, and you two are?" She is full of energy, holding out a hand for us to shake.

"I'm Finn, and this is my fiancé, Adeline." He wraps a firm arm around me while shaking her hand. I awkwardly nod along with Finn.

She gives us a sincere smile. "Aren't you two adorable?" She pushes up her black framed glasses that keep slipping down her nose. "Welcome." She gestures with her hand to the house. "This is a four bedroom, I'm not sure exactly what you lovebirds are searching for, but this home is perfect for starting a family."

"Well." Finn looks at me with loving eyes.

I want to believe them.

He places a hand on my stomach. "Four bedrooms would be perfect for us and the twins," he says to me.

Shanna's eyes zero in on my stomach, widening as she realizes what Finn has just implied.

That I'm pregnant.

With twins.

To top it off, I ate the world's biggest breakfast at the hotel buffet and am wearing a fitted tank top. The tips of my ears are fire hot. I want to fade away and become completely invisible.

I force a smile.

"Well, sweetheart." He squeezes me even closer, acting all lovely dovey. "Let's look around. Tim and Timmy—the twins," he clarifies to the real estate agent, "might love it here." He finishes by giving Emily a nod, pulls me to his side, and walks into the kitchen.

Once we are out of ear shot, I push him off me, facing him head on. "You are the most annoying—" I try to find the right word to call him. Friend? Boyfriend? Summer fling who is also my best friend in the entire world and will probably break my heart when he goes back to college? Instead of assigning a name to what he is to me right now, I let that part of my sentence hang in the air. "You're a very annoying man." I point a finger so close to his face, I'm almost touching the tip of his nose.

My heart somersaults at the way his eyes flit over my features. He smiles easily, amused at my annoyance. He sweeps me up, carrying me like a baby.

It sends butterflies parading around my stomach, making it extremely difficult to stay annoyed.

"Are you done?" he whispers, placing a sweet kiss on my lips.

Butterflies wreak havoc to my organs. "No," I say. "Tim and Timmy?"

He laughs. "They were the first two names that popped into my head."

"What about Tom and Jerry?"

"Yes, lets name our twin sons after a cartoon mouse and cat," he says like the idea is ridiculous, which makes my eyes widen.

"Because giving them both the same name is any better," I say.

"They are not the same name."

"They're both nicknames for Timothy," I say like it's obvious because it is.

He smiles now. "I know, I just like arguing with you."

I roll my eyes and kiss him back. Since he started it, it must be okay.

He deepens the kiss, and my hands find their way into his hair, squeezing the roots as I starve for more of him.

Finn quickly pulls away, looking at something behind me.

Or rather, someone.

I blossom a bright shade of red, realizing another family is in the kitchen.

When did they get here?

Finn sets me on my feet. "Didn't you want to see the upstairs, sweetheart?" he asks, putting on the façade in front of the realtor when we pass her.

"I actually remembered I have groceries in the car, *honey*," I say the nickname a little too harshly.

"The Jack and Jill bedrooms would be perfect for Tim and Timmy, they're right off the master bedroom." Shanna swoops in, gesturing to follow her up the stairs.

"Oh, well actually—" I start.

"Jack and Jill?" Finn turns to me. "Sweety, that's exactly what we've been looking for!" he says, acting the part of an excited fiancé and soon-to-be dad.

We follow Shanna upstairs. I say so only Finn can hear me, "You must have a death wish."

His shoulders rise and fall like he's silently laughing, I want to kick him behind the knees, but I hold off.

For now.

～

"Hiking with you is a test of patience." Finn stands above me, hands on his hips while I violently try to catch my breath.

Hiking is not for me...let's just say that.

I try to blame my poor stamina on Florida's lack of incline but I'm pretty sure a turtle could hike this trail faster than I can.

Finn casually walks this trail like it's nothing. It's infuriating.

My feet ache, and my skin is coated in a layer of sweat,

not in a pretty, glistening way either. But nothing can beat this view.

The entire town of Authensville in a single glimpse, pocketed right before us.

It's breathtaking.

After the humiliating open house, the one where everyone started congratulating me on my pregnancy, we checked out of the hotel and decided to head north. We came upon this small town, the population of which is less than a shopping mall in South Florida.

The sun lays low, hugging the horizon. It rests in a golden hue, making Finn's eyes a polished shade of honey.

He has an after work out glow, his hair a darker shade of brown painted with sweat, and he somehow still smells good, I realize as he comes up behind me, loosely holding my hips. He whispers close to my ear, "I would climb a thousand mountains just to witness this again."

I try to keep my huffing and puffing at bay, especially with his proximity. "I know, this view...I've never seen anything like it."

"I wasn't talking about the view." He rests his chin on top of my head, letting his arms wrap all the way around my stomach. "I was talking about your smile."

The warmth of his words caresses me. "You can't even see my face. How do you know I'm smiling?"

"Because I can feel it," he whispers.

There are a few other people at the top of the mountain, taking photos and admiring the colors in the sky as the sun sets further.

"Excuse me, will you take a picture of us?" Finn asks. I turn around and see him handing his phone to a woman who is probably in her early thirties.

I turn around completely, wrapping my arm around

Finn and smiling at the phone, but in one swift movement, he grabs my face and presses his lips into mine in a wave of passion.

I am caught completely off guard and blink several times after he has pulled away to retrieve his phone.

Finn wanting a picture of him kissing me does strange things to my pulse. It lights me up and makes me want to take a million photos of his lips touching mine.

I breathe in the woodsy smell of a campfire nearby. The breeze carries Finn's expensive smell, entangling my hair. I've never felt so alive.

Finn hums the beat of *Perfect* by Ed Sheeran, and I make out the lyrics in my head.

Maybe he doesn't realize what the lyrics say, or maybe I read too much into things. I watch him, his amber eyes, and the gentle smile on his face as he watches the sun fall. The wind blows his brown hair, the words *I love you* scratch the back of my throat, begging to be said out loud.

But I can't, because then Finn would know how deep I'm in, and would definitely call this quits because he wouldn't want to hurt me at the end of the summer. Because one way or another, this will end.

He goes to school hours away from me, and I can guarantee there are beautiful girls at FSU lining up to get a taste of him. The thought of him with anyone else rips me apart with jealousy.

I close my eyes and wish that in some alternate reality, Finn and I would never have to go back home. Maybe in this other world, he would fall in love with me too, and I could shout from the rooftops, *I love Finn Walker!*

My eyes glass over, and before I can hide it, Finn wraps my arms around his neck, and rests his on my waist. He sways us back and forth, still humming.

The picture-perfect moment etches itself into my memory so I will never forget *this*. Finn's graceful voice, the wind that embraces me, Authensville's grand mountains… it's something straight out of a romance novel.

Finn twirls me, and my laugh cascades all around us. It isn't a graceful move like the ones in the movies. No, this one is chaotic and clumsy. I stumble over my own two feet. But I feel so beautiful the way Finn watches me.

His face is stoic, but with the slightest upturn in the corners of his lips; the kind of smile you wouldn't notice unless you were searching for it. It's captivating.

I let myself forget the future exists and get lost in the moment promised. Because right here, right now, Finn and I are no different than the couples surrounding us.

No one knows how hopelessly in love with him I am, and no one suspects he would feel any less for me. He looks at me like I'm the dream he never wants to wake from.

Or maybe that's me, projecting.

A gust of wind picks up, and a shiver runs through my body.

"Let's get you warmed up, love." He wraps an arm around me, leading the way to the trail.

"Charlie's Steakhouse seems promising." Finn walks behind me, his arms blanket me, doing the best they can to keep me warm.

I can hardly focus on anything but where he touches me.

Who would've thought it could be so *cold* on a July night? Not me. The weather app on my phone told me it was sixty-two degrees, the equivalent to Florida's winter.

"S-sure. It looks warm." I chatter the words out.

We've been walking along a strip of small businesses and shops. This is the first restaurant we've come across.

"Come on, love," he says, walking us toward the door.

The restaurant isn't what you would see back home, that's for sure. The place is like a log cabin inside, and we are immediately greeted by a deer head plastered to the wall.

A beautiful girl, who seems to be maybe a year or two younger than me, greets us with a welcoming voice. "Is it snowing out there or something? You're turning blue."

Finn squeezes me a little, and I melt into a puddle in his arms. He hasn't released his hold on me since two miles back. "We're from Florida, so we aren't used to the night-time chill. This one's always cold, though." He smiles down at me.

"We have a gas fireplace I can sit you near. We never have it on in July, but we can make an exception for the Floridians." She grabs a couple menus and Finn and I follow behind her. "Do you guys walk around in bikinis all day, or is that a myth?"

I let out a genuine laugh. "Is that what people think?" I ask. "No, we usually wear thick jeans and heavy boots. You never know when you're going to have to kick away an angsty alligator."

She turns around and narrows her eyes at me like she's not sure if I'm being sarcastic or not.

"Kidding," I finally say.

She laughs a contagious laugh. It wears off on Finn and me.

She guides us to a cozy booth, away from the other customers, and switches on the fireplace. The quiet is exactly what I needed.

I read her name tag. "Thanks, Chloe."

"Don't mention it. Oh, and I recommend the ribs, they're what we're known for."

"But...shouldn't you be known for steak?" I ask, confused. We are in a *steak*house, after all.

"We were a steakhouse about fifty years ago, when Charlie's father, who's also named Charlie, cooked the steak. When Charlie Jr. took over his dad's business, the only thing he knew how to make at restaurant level were ribs."

I cock my head in confusion. "Why not change the name?"

"Charlie doesn't want to deal with rebranding the place, besides, it's the town's hotspot. Rebranding could set long-time customers off. Believe me, you don't want to mess with these people when it comes to their beloved steakhouse."

"Do you guys have steak?" Finn asks.

Chloe laughs. "Nope."

"Then I will have ribs," Finn says, handing her back the menu.

"I'll do the same," I say.

"Good looking *and* simple, you guys are the easiest customers I've had all day!"

I reflect her smile, instantly feeling a sensation of warmth. It's rare you meet someone as kind spirited as her, I feel like I already know her, and we just met five minutes ago.

"I'll go put your order in with Charlie, he always gets excited when he gets new customers in here." She walks away gracefully, taking her sunshine with her.

Finn's hand lightly rests on my knee and all my attention goes to the small spot. I let my eyes fall shut; going to bed late last night is finally catching up to me.

"Two orders of ribs coming up!" I open my eyes. A man

who seems to be in his early forties holds two plates and walks toward us.

"These smell great," Finn says to the owner, I presume.

I gasp when I meet his eyes. I can't place it, but he looks…familiar. Do I know him from somewhere?

"Thanks." I smile as he sets my plate in front of me. "That was really fast."

"Welcome to Authensville, Chloe tells me you're from Florida."

"Yeah, we're on a road trip and ended up here," Finn says.

I'm starving, my stomach twists in a not so nice way.

Finn introduces us to Charlie, and I politely shake his hand. It doesn't go unnoticed the way his eyes hover over my face for a beat longer than they should, like he's trying to place me too.

Charlie clears his throat. "Adeline, what a unique name."

"Dad, let them eat their food." Chloe comes up behind him.

Dad?

"I'm just getting to know the new kids on the block," he says innocently.

"Well, the new kids on the block are hungry, and you wouldn't want them to try your ribs for the first time *cold*, would you?" she teases.

He slowly backs away toward the kitchen. "Enjoy your meal," he says.

"I don't think I can finish all of these ribs on my own." I admit. "Finn, we should've ordered one meal," I complain. I hate wasting food.

"Speak for yourself," he says, digging in. "I'll finish yours if you can't."

We finished our food about two hours ago but have been in no rush to leave. We've been talking to Chloe this entire time, and I already feel like we're best friends.

I learned she doesn't know who her mom is, her only parent being Charlie. We bonded over that, even though our situation isn't the same, it's similar. My mom was physically present, but emotionally and mentally, she was checked out of my life.

Finn's hand started on my knee but has teasingly moved up over the course of two hours. Each time his fingers gradually walk their way up my thigh, something builds between my legs.

Now, his hand is mid-thigh. His index finger gently rubs the cloth leggings covering my skin. I try to focus on what's happening around me, but it's nearly impossible.

My mind pictures things I've never imagined before. I'm afraid the people around me can read my mind, and I turn bright red.

"Time to pack it up, kids," Charlie says, dangling a set of keys.

"Where are you guys staying?" Chloe asks, sliding out of the booth. She stretches her long legs, and dramatically limps like she's been sitting for ages.

"You're almost as dramatic as Adeline," Finn jokes.

I elbow him. I am *not* dramatic.

"Finn's car," I say, taking one last sip of water.

"A car?" she repeats like it's the worst thing she's heard all year. "You can stay with us. Our apartment is right upstairs."

"Oh, we couldn't. Besides, his car is more comfortable than you'd imagine," I lie.

I squeeze my thighs together when Finn's hand moves inward.

"You're not spending the night in that car. I don't care how comfy it is, our spare bedroom is comfier," she insists.

I'm starting to picture Finn and I in his car, and we're definitely cozy.

"Are you sure...?" Finn asks, hesitantly.

"Yes, you're staying!" She jumps up and down, clapping.

I smile at Chloe, my new friend, and feel the waves of a new beginning crashing into me.

15

I don't know how to sleep. Before, I would climb into bed with Finn without a thought. We were just two innocent kids having sleepovers.

But tonight, my thoughts run wild and are anything but innocent.

I plop down on my side, facing away from Finn and staring at the plain wall. Less than twenty-four hours ago we were Adeline and Finn: inseparable best friends for as long as anyone could remember.

Now I don't even know how to sleep.

I freeze as the bed dips, Finn's breath is suddenly on my shoulder as he whispers, "Cute pjs, Miller."

I choke on the thick air. "Thank you," My voice comes out raspier than I intend.

"You okay?"

"Yes," I reply, a little too fast.

"Look at me."

I squeeze my eyes shut. I can't look at him, I'm awkward and nervous and horrible at this. Whatever this is.

I stay unmoving until Finn climbs over my body, settling in with his face an inch from mine.

"My left ass cheek is hanging off the bed, just so you know." His brows raise as he says this.

I scoot backward so he has more room. He manages to make me laugh like nothing has changed, and maybe in a way, we've stayed the same. He's still my best friend and the sweet boy from my past, all the parts of him I fell in love with are still there.

I've let myself get tangled in my own thoughts when reality is right in front of me. Maybe whatever is happening between us doesn't need a label… Maybe we can still just be us.

"What's got you all quiet?"

"Just daydreaming." I shrug.

He raises a brow. "Yeah?"

A genuine smile touches my lips. "Yeah."

"Do you want to know what I'm dreaming about right now?" he asks.

Yes, I want to know every thought that passes between your eyes. But I don't say that. I just nod.

"I'm dreaming about the taste of your lips." His grin spreads so wide, I want to poke his dimple.

I'm convinced this *is* a dream since it seems to be the only explanation to what is happening. But I see my reflection in his eyes, I count the barely noticeable freckles along Finn's nose, and there's a loose eyelash only a few blinks away from falling down his cheek.

Vivid details proving this is really happening.

"You're exceptional, Adeline Miller. Do you know that?" He runs his fingers through the roots of my hair, my eyes unintentionally flutter closed.

He moves his body closer, intertwining our legs and

holding me in his arms. His nose is hardly touching mine. He smells like mint toothpaste and my shampoo.

I smile at the thought of him using my products.

"Will you tell me a story?" I ask.

His eyes fall to my lips, hovering there for a moment before meeting mine again. "A make-believe story?" His rough voice is exceptionally appealing.

This piques my curiosity, so I smile and nod my head with anticipation.

"Once upon a time..." He speaks low, his raspy voice touching me places no one has before. "There was a lonesome worm."

I laugh, causing Finn to smile. "Are you going to let me tell you an awesome bedtime story or not?"

"Yes! yes! Carry on."

"Well, this worm didn't care for other worms. They were wiggly and boring, just as he was. So, he lived his life in solitude. Until one day he stumbled into a girl worm. She was unlike anyone he ever met. She was green with black stripes and made him feel emotions he never knew a simple worm like himself was capable of feeling."

I'm so captivated, I forget he's talking about worms and listen to hear the rest of his story.

"The two became inseparable. They did everything together...until one day the lady worm turned into a chrysalis. He didn't know what to do, she was stuck frozen for days. He had never seen a worm do this. He wasn't sure she would live." He pauses.

I stare at him expectedly. "Well? What happens?"

"For those long days, where the worm didn't know what was wrong with his best friend, he thought about their time together. He realized she made his life more than just survivable, she made it better than any other worm's life in history, and that's when he realized he was in love with her."

I gasp, so into the story I smack his chest to continue.

"So, when he saw her moving, he was ready to tell her everything. He was going to marry her, he wanted to spend every moment together until the day they died. When she woke up, she was no longer a worm. She was a colorful butterfly, and once she discovered she had wings, she flew free, and the worm watched her leave. The end."

My mouth falls open and actual tears sting my eyes. "That was a terrible story!"

"It was a great story, now go to sleep."

"Why didn't they end up together?" I ask, wondering why he'd let a sad ending happen in his own story.

"Because she was a butterfly," he states matter-of-factly.

"She could've flown back to visit him, or he could've stopped her from leaving," I argue.

He shakes his head. "He was a worm, Adeline. He knew he didn't belong in her world, and he let her go so she could do all the cool butterfly things."

"Maybe she wanted to be chased."

He tilts my chin up. "It's a happy ending, the butterfly gets to touch the sky."

"But the worm doesn't," I complain.

"No. No he doesn't." His voice comes out so quiet. "Sleep well, love." He pulls the switch to the lamp, turning everything to black.

"So, tell me about you and Finn," Chloe says with a mouthful of a giant pretzel. The food court is small in the so-called mall, with only a few restaurants which are all small businesses. Not a single chain restaurant in sight, I love it.

Chloe insisted on taking me shopping.

What a loaded question. "Not much to tell." I shrug, dipping my churro into mermaid magic sauce. If there's something to say about Authensville, it's that they *love* their names.

"There's always something to tell. How long have to guys been together?" she asks, prying as if hopeful for some juicy details.

"We aren't together."

She grins at me with squinted eyes like she is anticipating the punch line.

"We aren't," I tell her, point blank.

She frowns. "Why are you lying?"

I laugh, meeting her gaze and telling her I'm not lying.

"Fine, but just so you know, you guys are not fooling the entire world with all the touching and flirting. Just saying."

I hardly know this girl, but something tells me I can trust her. So, I explain everything from how we met to how hopelessly in love I am.

She hasn't said anything up until now, like she's really taking everything in.

"Wait," she finally says. "So, you mean to tell me you two aren't...well, you know?"

I cock my head in confusion.

"You guys aren't hooking up?" she asks, a little too loud.

An elderly couple gives us a judgmental look before returning to their pizza.

"No." I shrug. "Don't get me wrong, I want to. I don't know what is going to come out of this vacation." I lower my voice to a whisper. "I've also never..." My face burns.

She seems clueless, forcing me to say it.

I sigh. "I'm a virgin."

"Now you're lying." She shakes her head. "You ooze sexuality."

I laugh, "What?"

"I'm not making this shit up, Adeline. Look, two o'clock. All those guys are practically drooling over you. You carry yourself like you own the room."

She says this with so much conviction, but still, I don't believe a single word. Me owning any room? Yeah right.

"Fine, don't believe me and spend the *rest* of your life suppressing your true power."

I take a long sip of water. "You read a lot of self-help books, don't you?"

She brightens, like I've just brought up her favorite topic. "Yes! Why, do you want me to lend you one?"

I try to steer us back to the main point, reminding her of Finn.

"I think you should stop worrying, Adeline. You should see the way he looks at you." She shakes her head, as if picturing it now. "You're too wrapped up in your own thoughts to see it, but I'm willing to bet the restaurant he feels the same about you. I catch him watching you from across the room like you're a shooting star, or something. Like you're this exceptionally rare person he can't take his eyes off."

Hearing someone else talk about us does something strange to my heart. I try to picture Finn watching me how she says, but I can't.

Chloe's eyes light up in mischief. "I have an idea, follow me." She gives me no room to protest before she yanks me out of my seat, making me drop the last bite of my churro.

She drags me across the tiny mall. All the way to a lingerie shop.

"What is this?" I ask.

"I'm getting you laid, my friend. It's time you start embracing your potential." She nods like she's sure of her herself.

I glance hesitantly at the store, and then to Chloe. I don't know how comfortable I feel wearing...*that.*

A mannequin stands in the window, dressed in an array of thin leather and chains, covering everywhere *but* the intimate parts.

"Chloe, I cannot pull that off, and even if I could, I wouldn't want to. That's not me. Nope, not happening," I say, turning around to the opposite direction of the store.

"Let's just look, I'm sure they have *something.*"

With lots of persuasion and back and forth, I finally cave. We spend five minutes looking around the store, until a sales lady comes over with a tape measure and starts measuring my bust. No introduction, *nothing.*

I glance over at Chloe, who seems to enjoy watching me turn different shades of red. She discreetly pulls out her phone and takes a picture, immortalizing the moment.

"Thirty-two B, come this way," she says, wrapping the measuring tape around her neck as if it were a scarf.

I quickly turn to Chloe and shrug, trying to keep up with the sales lady as she travels in and out of aisles of lingerie. "I hate you by the way," I whisper.

The sales lady turns around holding a velvet hanger, and a beautiful set of red lace attached. "Dressing room is to the left." She hands it to me, and then she's gone.

"She's got some taste," Chloe says, examining the thin, lacy fabric. "Well...go on then. You heard the woman, dressing room is that way."

I roll my eyes. "Fine."

I fumble with the lingerie until it is in place. I stare back at the woman in the mirror, her head lifting high and shoulders back. She looks *sexy*.

"What's taking so long in there?" Chloe groans, right outside the stall.

I unlock the door and crack it as little as possible so Chloe can fit through. But she pulls it all the way open and steps inside.

I rush to close it. "Hey! Someone could've seen me."

"Holy shit. You look *hot*," she says, ignoring me.

I blush at the compliment, and instead of shrugging it off like any other day, I actually believe her.

The red compliments my skin tone and embraces my hair color. The lace wraps around my curves in a way that doesn't hide them like I usually do with my clothes. It embraces them in a way that makes me feel like a *goddess*.

"Now do you believe me?" she asks, rhetorically.

I almost do, so I buy the lingerie with giddy energy, imagining standing in front of Finn wearing it. It's a thought that terrifies me in the best way.

Chloe and I spend the rest of the day together. I've never really had a female friend in my life. It's nice.

After we get back to the apartment, we find Charlie and Finn arguing about a game on the TV, so I take this opportunity to throw my lingerie into the wash on delicate.

Chloe and I lay on her bed and spend the rest of the night talking about…well, *everything*. I feel like I've known her for years when it's only been a few days. Every few minutes we hear Finn and Charlie standing up from the couch with the squeak of the hard wood floor, followed by some sort of cheer or protest.

Chloe thought it would be a fun drinking game,

however I thought we would be blacked out after five minutes, so instead we just burst out into laughter each time we hear them.

"Can I tell you something?" Chloe asks.

"Spill."

"It's selfish, but...I hope you never go back home," she says, head hanging in shame.

I smile. A big, happy smile that only happens occasionally. I hug her and whisper, "I kind of never want to leave."

"It's just always been my dad and me. I don't have any siblings or many friends, and sometimes I just feel so... alone. Like no one *gets* me. Do you know what I mean?"

I do. I know exactly what she means.

"You guys ever been tubing before?" Charlie calls from his boat. Finn and I are sharing the tube in the water tied to the back of the boat. We lay on our stomachs. The cool water engulfs my toes.

"This will be my first time," I say, white knuckling the handle. We haven't even started yet.

"My parents used to take me," Finn says. He places his hand over mine and squeezes.

"I think Finnegan is going to fly off first." Chloe comes up behind Charlie, saying between bites of her sandwich, "Don't worry...we'll go easy on you." She gives her dad a wink.

"You ready?" Charlie walks over to the driver's seat. It looks much different than the boats in the Keys, I guess because this one is meant for a calm lake rather than the roaring sea.

Finn and I nod, and then the boat is dragging us along

the waves from the motor. Charlie drives straight for a while, to get to an opening away from any docks, so he can go in circles. Each bump we fly over sprays water in my face. My eyes are squeezed shut but I'm laughing hysterically.

"You having a good time over there, Miller?" Finn yells despite him being right next to me since the boat and splashing is so loud.

I swallow a splash of water when I scream, "Yeah!"

Finn's chuckle is drowned out by my yelp because now Charlie turns the boat in a tight circle. I hold on as tight as I can. My muscles strain and my body slides to the left and I'm going to fall—

Charlie cuts the other way. The motion slides me back to my place in the center of the tube right when Finn's hand leaves its place on top of mine. I turn my head and watch him fly off and sink below the surface.

Charlie slows down, both him and his daughter are laughing. So am I.

Finn points a finger to Charlie. "There was no way I could've held on with that maneuver." Chloe howls, and Finn continues, "Come on man, you're making me look bad in front of a pretty girl." He pulls himself back on the tube, rocking us so much we almost tip and fall into the water.

We each take turns, and when Chloe and I go together, we are screaming and laughing so much, the boys on the boat smile wide at the show. We both hold on so tight I'm almost positive my fingers will fall off, but neither of us let go.

Finn pulls out his phone to take a video. I hear him say to Charlie, "Don't go easy on them."

And then I can't tell if we are going in circles or infinity signs or if Charlie just invented a new shape, but Chloe and

I fly off the tube at the same time. I smack the water, my nostrils burn from not plugging them, and I almost lose my bottoms.

When I break the surface Chloe and I laugh so hard I have to hold onto the tube to keep from drowning.

Later into the day we're all wrapped up in towels, rocking on the boat. The sky is purple as the sun sets. I glance around at our group of four, sitting in comfortable silence with faint smiles on our face, and I feel for the first time like I'm truly a part of something. It's bittersweet to be so at home here. While I've had the sense of family through Finn and his parents, I always felt like the outsider, no matter how much they included me. I was never *one* of them. But for some strange reason, being here with Charlie and Chloe, I feel like I'm a part of something. Like I finally belong.

But as much as my heart is here in Authensville, my mother is back home in the Keys, and whether I like it or not, I'm eventually going to have to go home.

I can already feel my heart breaking when we leave. Not only do I love it here, but once we're back home, whatever happens between Finn and I…it'll be like it never did. The agreement of our fling will be over and left at a roadside stop, not coming home with us.

16

"It's nice, you know," Finn says gently stroking my hair.

I press my index finger into the shadow of his dimple, and my stomach flip flops. "What's that?" I ask.

I am wrapped like a burrito into the plush comforter, meanwhile Finn lays on the bed with nothing shielding him from the cold.

Charlie, much like Finn, keeps the air too cold. And on top of that, Finn cracked open the window in our bedroom —for the time being—and it's a whopping fifty-eight degrees outside.

"Seeing you so happy." The mattress dips when he whispers in my ear.

"Can you tell?" I respond absentmindedly, too distracted by the eight-pack staring back at me.

"You really like it here."

"I *love* it here," I admit, feeling a crack begin to form in my heart. Knowing one day this place, and these people will be a distant memory. A week here flew by in the blink of an eye.

"We have at least three more weeks, love. Depending on if your mom stays longer. Besides, we can come back to visit." He kisses my temple, then slowly peels the covers off my body. My skin pebbles against the cold but not for long because Finn shimmies his way on top of me and pulls the fabric over us. His breath is warm against my face, I can't see him beneath the comforter, but I know his lips are close. So very close.

The smooth pad of his thumb brushes over my bottom lip then along my jaw. My eyes flutter closed when his finger trickles down my pulse. *Lower.* I want to plead. His lips brush mine softly. He kisses me slow, his touch is tentative along my sternum, down my ribs, but he doesn't touch the areas that ache for him.

I need more. He swallows my frustrated groan, walks his fingers up my chest, squeezes my breast over the fabric of my shirt.

Yes.

His lips leave mine but only to move down my neck. Something hot builds in my core, and then he places a kiss to the area right below my breast. My heart picks up faster, like my body is subtly cluing me in on the fact that I'm falling in love every moment we spend like this.

I've always loved him. We're best friends, how could I not? But now I'm sinking into a never ending pit I don't think I'll ever be free from. *I'm words on a page falling so deeply in love.*

His rough, calloused hand lifts the hem of my shirt, scraping against my stomach as he moves up, grabs my breast, then stops.

He sighs, pulls my shirt down. He places a gentle kiss to

my forehead. He leaves his place from on top of me.

I stare at the ceiling blankly, trying to catch my breath. Finn turns off the lamp and gathers me in his arms. There's an obvious bulge pressing against my back, but for some reason he doesn't do anything about it. He doesn't let his own desires control him; he's the same gentleman he's always been.

My skin is hot from the ghost of his touch. I love him so much that I want all of him. He's the only person I trust to be so vulnerable and intimate with, and I'm ready, I just wish he'd make that next move. I would if I knew what to do or what to say, but instead I just starve in his arms.

Mom dreams are the worst.

I gasp for air, waking up in a layer of sweat from the horrifying nightmare.

My mother, lifeless in Finn's arms, cold to the touch, purple lips. Her chest unmoving—Dead.

"It's okay, love," Finn says, eyes still closed and half asleep as he sits up and holds me. I don't think he even realizes he's doing this.

I melt, already feeling the stress roll off my shoulders.

"I love you," he mumbles, then collapses and snores again like nothing happened.

But something did happen.

He told me he loved me.

He was sleep talking. He could've been dreaming about someone else...like his mom. This doesn't mean anything, you fool.

I close my eyes, trying to urge myself into sleep, but my mind doesn't shut off.

~

"You ready?" Chloe's sunshine comes into the guest room.

"Yeah, let me just put on some lip gloss," I say, dragging the cherry flavored makeup over my lips. I start to walk through the door, but Chloe stops me in my tracks.

"Wait!" She places a palm in the air, signaling me to stay put. She comes back only a second later with blush and a makeup brush in her hands.

I raise an eyebrow, but she just starts applying some to the apples of my cheeks. She packs even more on the brush and goes in for a second layer, but I stop her. "Hey, hey now. Let's not go ham on the blush."

"Fine." She playfully rolls her eyes. "Here, keep it. It doesn't show on my skin, and it goes great with your complexion."

Smiling, I put the blush in my makeup bag. She wasn't wrong, the coral shade on my cheeks makes me look more alive. It's pretty.

I follow Chloe out into the living room, and the magnetic pull tugs my heart toward Finn. He folds me into his arms without a second thought. It's starting to feel so natural. I'm worried I won't be able to go back to a time where I couldn't walk right up to him and touch him however my heart wants.

"Took you ladies long enough," Charlie says, taking the final sip of coffee. "I was worried Finn was going to wear a hole in the rug with all the pacing he was doing."

"What..." Chloe dramatically gasps, "are you scared, Finnegan?" She closes the lid of her to go cup. I hadn't even noticed her brewing the coffee, I was too focused on the way my heart changes when I'm with Finn. It's slower, calmer.

My body knows I'm safe.

Finn snickers at her. "Why would I be scared, *Chad*?"

I pinch Finn's tricep, but he doesn't even flinch.

"Oh, my apologies. You can go first," she chimes.

I frown. "I kind of wanted to go first."

"Hell no," Finn protests, peering down at me while his thumb rubs my lower back. "Chloe can go first, and make sure the line is reliable," he says, completely serious.

Chloe and I exchange a look and break out into laughter.

"A daredevil and a scaredy cat, what an interesting love match," Charlie jokes, giving Chloe a hug.

I try not to look at Finn's reaction to Charlie's choice of words while I put on my sneakers.

"Listen man, you're not the one going ziplining off a mountain," Finn says, ignoring the part about our *love* match.

"Touché." Charlie nods.

~

"Fuck me," Finn mutters.

"She's tried." Chloe pats Finn on the shoulder as he peeks over the ledge of the cliff, we are about to zipline over.

I give Chloe a wide-eyed look, but if Finn heard, he's way too absorbed in his fear of heights to say anything.

"Who's going first?" a peppy ziplining instructor asks us.

"Me!" I step up, and feel big hands pull me back into our three-person crowd.

"She is," Finn says, pushing Chloe toward the instructor.

I roll my eyes and pull on my harness, uncomfortable with the way it digs into my skin.

"Hey, hey, hey!" Finn says, stilling my hand. "Excuse me, Miss. Can you double check my girlfriend's harness? She's messing with it."

Ohmygod. I swallow down the storm of butterflies and act nonchalant. Maybe he said it as a joke, like when he pretended I was his fiancé carrying Tim and Timmy. "It's fine, Finn," I whisper, but the instructor checks anyway.

"Yup, she's all set!"

"Check again."

I slap his side, but his harness acts as a barrier.

"Please," he adds quietly.

She does as she is asked, or ordered, and Finn doesn't seem any less tense next to me.

Chloe is getting strapped in, while the instructor goes over the safety rules. I watch her nod her head and she gives me a peace sign before flying off the wooden platform.

She gives Finn a startled look, and when he leaps forward with panic, she lets out a high-pitched scream-laugh. A scraugh?

Her long blonde hair gets lost in the wind, and she becomes smaller and smaller, zipping through the forest onto the next platform.

"Did you want to go next, honey?" The guide has an outstretched hand toward me.

"Yeah!" I take a step forward, but Finn pulls me two steps back.

"Are you crazy? I have to make sure it can withhold *my* weight." Finn steps to the ledge, letting the lady get him ready. He stiffens more and more the longer she messes with his harness, double checking per his request. "Tell my family I love them," he says with a salute.

169

I shake my head in disbelief. And he says *I'm* dramatic. "What about me? Don't you love me?" I tease.

"The most," he says, and then he's off, zipping through the sky.

I try to laugh at his high-pitched scream but I keep replaying two words in my head. *The most.* I think those might be the vaguest words known to mankind.

"Something tells me he's not much of the adventuring kind." The lady gets my harness ready with a smile painting her face. I don't mind, I can talk about Finn all day, every day.

"If it were up to Finn, he'd be in bed with me right now." Wow that came out *so* wrong. "Cuddling," I add, but it sounds like a pathetic lie, and the guide's eyes light up in amusement.

"I'll see you on the other side," she says.

The air leaves my lungs as I fly through the mountains. My cheeks fill with air, I no doubt look like a cartoon character. My laughs echo through the forest, for only me to hear. I try to absorb the moment promised—the trees come and disappear all too fast, the rush of adrenaline filling the dull parts of my soul—but before I know it, a tiny platform comes into view.

When my feet touch the wood, Finn pulls me into a very public display of affection. He kisses me like we've been apart for ages. I deepen our kiss and let his tongue sweep over mine. It leaves me breathless.

I forget about our audience, until I hear Chloe's whistling.

Finn ignores her, continuing to knock me off my feet, but I'm not about PDA. I pull away, licking my lips, but still trying to savor every last bit of him while I can.

17

FIVE YEARS AGO

I hate throwing up. I grip the toilet seat while I profusely vomit last night's dinner.

It feels like minutes go by, but it's probably only seconds when I finally stop. I kneel on the cold bathroom floor. My throat burns, my hands shake, and tears stream down my face. It's four in the morning, and my stomach has been cramping all night.

I stand up and tiny dots interrupt my vision, I grab ahold of the sink and stare into the mirror. My under eyes sink in, casting a purple shadow beneath my brown irises. I brush my teeth and drag myself back in bed.

Luckily, it's Memorial Day weekend so I don't have to worry about going to school tomorrow.

That's something at least.

My abdomen cramps, and my stomach feels sour. My muscles burn with every movement. Finally, I settle and stare at my bedroom walls.

Finn's going to be so upset. I'm supposed to go with him on his family's boat tomorrow to spend the day at the sandbar. He says when I don't come, it's boring. But with the way my stomach feels, and my body hurts, I don't think I will be recovered within the next six hours.

My eyes eventually fall heavy, as the first light of dawn peers through my blinds.

～

"I really don't care if you think she's fine, I'm checking on her," a muffled voice wakes me up. It starts to get closer. "She was supposed to be at my house six hours ago, I'm worried, and maybe you should be too."

My door creeks open, my eyes travel from the hot pink walls onto a fifteen-year-old boy.

My fifteen-year-old best friend, Finn.

"She's fine, damnit. Get the fuck out of my daughter's room!" Jason yells.

"Look at her!" Finn points a hand in my direction. He glances at my clock. "It's ten past four and she's still in bed. The room smells like vomit."

Does it? I cringe.

My dad comes into view behind Finn. Their energies completely contrast one another. When Finn walks into a room, the air feels happier. Warmer. He's the sun.

When my dad walks into a room, everyone's pulse increases. His mere presence is the definition of unease. Until he speaks, his voice is what makes him a storm.

I sit up, but everything in me aches. I'm weak.

"Dad? Finn? What's going on?" my voice comes out hoarse.

Finn rushes to my side and inspects me. I hide behind my hands, remembering my appearance from when I threw up in the night.

The slight movement causes my stomach to rise, and I rush to my desk, grabbing the tiny garbage can.

I dry heave for what feels like hours until stomach acid comes out, leaving me completely empty. I sink onto the floor, using what little energy I have left to wipe my mouth with the back of my hand.

"What the hell happened to you?" My dad towers over me, annoyance is the only thing I hear in his voice.

Finn kneels beside me, glaring at my dad. His firm hands lightly touch my forehead, and then my cheek.

"Holy shit," he whispers to me. "You're burning up." He gently lifts me up by my arms and brings me to my bed. When I lie back, each tiny movement sends me silently crying out in pain.

Please let this end soon.

"Leave," my dad spits out, still standing in the doorway. His muscles make him wide and bulky.

I liked him better before he started the steroids and living at the gym. Well actually, I never liked him to begin with. If it were up to me, he'd be six feet underground so my mom could finally breathe.

"I'm not going anywhere until I know she is okay." He doesn't even look at my dad, all his attention still on me. "I'll go get you some medicine to break the fever." He strokes my hair and stands up.

"She don't need no medicine. She'll burn it off." My dad puffs out his chest, his scary voice sends chills down my spine.

Finn ignores him and walks downstairs.

I hear muffled yelling but am too tired to do anything about it. Eventually I drift off into a dreamless sleep.

Sharp pain sears through my abdomen, and I curl up in

agony. I urge my eyes open and glance around my quiet bedroom.

My clock tells me it's two in the morning, I must've slept the entire day. I turn over, trying to get comfortable to go back to sleep, when something catches my attention.

A folded piece of paper lays on my pillow.

I pull the corners apart. *Check your phone.* I smile at Finn's childlike handwriting.

I grab my phone from the charger that was placed right by my bed and turn it on. One long text message floods in.

Hey Ad, your dad kicked me out. Shocker, I know. I went home and grabbed some stuff, it's on your night table. I came in through your window, don't worry, I didn't watch you sleep or anything. It would only be cool if I was a hot vampire, I know, I know.

I gave you Tylenol at three (You were half asleep, it was pretty funny actually, you were talking about making donuts... Are you hungry?) you'll need to take it again at seven if you still have a fever. Oh, also I put your phone on "do not disturb" so my texts don't wake you up.

I will myself to sit up, grab the bag Finn left on my bedside table, and pull out my favorite candy, Hershey kisses.

I stick my hand back in the bag and pull out a bottle of Tylenol and a thermometer with a sticky note on it. *Take every four hours if your fever doesn't break.* I pull out a water bottle next, it's my favorite one from his house. A smile takes over my face as I turn it upside down, the glitter and tiny seashells float around like a snow globe. *The Florida Keys* is printed in my favorite color, hot pink.

I take a swig. The blue Gatorade coats my taste buds. It's my favorite flavor.

The bag feels empty, I peek inside just in case. Is that a

walkie talkie? I pull it out, and of course, a sticky note is attached. I press the button and say the secret phrase "ooga booga," per the sticky note's request.

I let out a weak laugh.

"Finally!" Finn's voice comes through almost immediately on the tiny machine. The volume is already turned down low.

"You bought me a walkie talkie?" I laugh.

"I already had it, and it was the quickest way for you to reach me. I have mine hooked on my shirt," his voice is raspy like I woke him up.

I smile.

"How are you feeling?" he asks.

"A little better now that I have my favorite water bottle," I say, releasing the button.

"I missed you today."

"You definitely didn't." I laugh, "How was the water? Cold still?"

The machine is quiet for a moment.

"It was warm," he says quietly.

I yawn, my body still feels weak. "I'm going to try to get some sleep."

"Sweet dreams," Finn's voice comes through one last time.

"Ad, wake up," a soothing voice whispers in my ear.

I feel a rough, calloused hand on my cheek and jerk awake. Amber eyes pour into mine with such concern and longing. The care that settles into his features makes him look...hot? Something fuzzy warms my chest, I try to shake away the strange feeling.

How have I never noticed how hot you were before, Finn?

I must've said that out loud because concerned eyes shift to amusement. Oh my gosh.

"You have a really high fever, Adeline. I don't think you're in your right mind right now."

The embarrassment goes away with a sharp pain turning my stomach. I must turn green or something because Finn grabs the trash can next to my desk and holds it under my mouth. The other hand holds my hair as I profusely vomit. It smells so bad, and my throat burns each time my stomach ejects more vomit. This would be humiliating if I didn't feel so weak. My body hurts and feels so strained. When my stomach gives up all its contents, I collapse.

I hear my father's heavy boots as he moves around the hallway. I freeze, Finn shouldn't be here.

He lowers his voice to a whisper, "I'm going to take you to my house. I'll be back in five minutes." He hurries away out my window.

My dad pulls open my door and with an angry face. "What the fuck are you doing, kid?"

"I—"

"I don't wanna hear it. Get dressed and walk to school. I'm goin' to work."

I try to protest but he interrupts me yet again. "I said I don't want to hear it." He walks further into my room a little, his voice threatening. "And if I come home and still find you in this god damn bed, you won't even be able to dream of what will happen next." He leaves without so much as a goodbye.

I hear the front door open and close, and watch his truck leave the driveway from my window. Tears well in my eyes, and each sob that escapes causes ripples of pain through my body.

I cover my mouth when I hear the front door open again. Is he back?

My heart races faster with each footstep, each louder than the last. My door creeks open, and Finn's smile fades when he sees my reaction.

"Adeline?" He rushes to me. "What's wrong?"

"My dad is making me go to school."

Finn immediately shakes his head. "You're not going to school," he says while lifting me, easily carrying me into the hallway.

"Finn!" I screech, but I'm too weak to fight him.

"I told you. You're coming to my house. I can take better care of you there."

"No. My dad will kill me if he finds out," I cry out. "And you have to go to school too."

"He doesn't have to know, and I can miss this one day, it's no big deal." He takes each step down the stairs carefully and puts me in the passenger seat of his mom's car.

He walks around to the driver's seat, buckles in, and backs out of my driveway. "Do *not* tell my mother about this. She won't let me get my license if she finds out I drove her car without it."

I nod.

We get to Finn's house. The car ride is silent. Every few beats Finn glances at me, as if I am not going to be here the next time he looks. *It's only a stomach bug.* I want to tell him this, but for some strange reason, maybe the fever, I *want* him to look at me like that.

Finn parks his mom's car and we both walk to the front door. He insisted on carrying me, and I insisted on walking.

The walk from the car to the front door is ten feet, max.

We compromised, and now Finn holds my hand, ready to steady me if I go weak. I try incredibly hard to ignore the waves of heat going through my body from the way his hand feels in mine.

Finn's house is silent when we go inside, but the Walker's infamous scent gives me a new boost of energy.

"I'll take you upstairs, you can lay in my bed."

"I've been in bed for the past two days, I'm starving."

I sit on the kitchen counter as Finn throws two pieces of bread in the toaster.

"I'm sorry about my dad," I say, while twisting a strand of hair around my finger.

Finn turns to me, with a serious demeanor. "Adeline." He walks toward me and peers straight into my eyes. "Please don't apologize for his actions. Ever again."

I swallow. "You're right. I'm sorry."

He points a finger, using it to touch my nose. "And stop apologizing all the damn time."

The toaster dings and Finn plates my toast, handing it to me. "You must be dehydrated, let me go grab you an electrolyte drink."

In his absence, I'm smiling because of how much Finn cares about me. He skipped school, risked driving without a license, and climbed his way through my window despite his debilitating fear of heights. All for me.

I realize Finn is my favorite person in this entire world.

18

NOW

"That'll be six dollars and fifty-five cents, dear," the older lady says, about to prepare my iced vanilla coffee with almond milk and caramel drizzle.

I hand her my card, and she swipes it with a smile. But her smile quickly falls as she swipes it for a second time. While leaning in she whispers, "It declined, sweetie."

I cock my head. I had a little over three hundred dollars saved up in my checking... How could I already have spent it all? "Um, could you try one more time, please?" I beg, the line behind me getting significantly longer.

I'm playing that fun game, the one where I go back in time and don't blow all my money on lingerie and ziplining. Technically I still have money in my savings, and a trust my grandparents set up for me in their will. But that money is for emergencies, and to eventually move out, once my mom can survive without me.

"Sure." She sympathetically smiles. She swipes it, handing it back to me with remorse.

A hand meets my lower back. "I've got it, love," Finn says, handing the cashier his card.

Relief washes over me. "Thank you."

We take a seat at a small table. The cozy atmosphere is inviting, with wood lining the walls, similar to Charlie's Steakhouse. Music plays at the perfect volume.

"Fancy seeing you here." I lean over the round table, going to kiss his cheek but he turns his head at the last second, my lips slamming into his.

The tips of my ears catch fire.

"Likewise. I thought you were going hiking with Chloe?" he says.

"She slept too late, so I figured I'd grab a coffee. I'm so embarrassed my card got declined," I admit. "I need to figure something out."

"Adeline," the lady who took my order calls, placing a latte on the counter. I stand up to grab it, but Finn stands, moving quicker than me.

Such a gentleman. *Nothing like my father,* I think for a second before I push the unwanted memories away.

I sit back down, and he takes a small sip of my drink before handing it to me.

"This cannot be classified as coffee. It's practically a milk shake," Finn says, scrunching his nose in an attempt to seem repulsed. But it fails and he looks adorable instead.

"I need to get a job," I say between sips.

"You have a job at Pete's."

"I mean here, in Authensville."

"Here?" He shakes his head. "But what's the point?"

"I like it here, and I can't afford to stay without a job."

"No place is going to hire you for such a short amount of time."

We've already been here for two weeks, I realize. When

we are together, time doesn't exist. I shake my head. The reality slowly engulfs me.

"Hey." Finn reaches across the table, placing a gentle hand on my shoulder. "We have at least two weeks. Why don't you see if this place will hire you for that amount of time?"

Two weeks. I have two weeks left as Finn's...fling. It's not enough time, albeit I don't even think a lifetime with Finn would be long enough. I want him for eternity, and now he's telling me I only get two more weeks?

"Okay. Good idea," I whisper, feeling a jolt of pain at the thought of summer coming to an end way too fast. I don't want to go back to the way things were. Not with Finn, and not with my life.

I'm having fun. I'm happy. I forgot what that felt like, but now that I've gotten a glimpse, I'm not willing to give it up.

Maybe after rehab, my mom won't need me as much and I can go to college with Finn. I nod my head in approval, the hope of a future with the man I love inspires me to be optimistic.

I pull back my shoulders, standing tall. I walk up to the counter, which by some miracle holds no line. This lady is a magician for filling all these orders by herself. The place is packed with happy customers, she might not need my help after all.

"Hi...Betty." I read her name tag. "It doesn't seem like you need it, but I was wondering if you wanted help back there. I'm in Authensville for at least two more weeks." I muster up my friendliest smile. "And you already know I need the money."

"Were you sent from heaven?" She claps her hands together. "We've been hiring for almost three months, but no one's applied! I would hire you on the spot, but I have to speak to the owner. He's away in Colorado, but I'll give him a call. What's your name and phone number?" she asks, grabbing a pen with a pink pom-pom on the end.

I give her my information and she reminds me to look out for a call. I make a mental note to answer any call from an unknown number, which I normally wouldn't. Telemarketers and all that.

"I can go run by the apartment and grab some more firewood," Charlie says, stroking his chin as if he had a beard.

"This should be plenty," Finn says, finishing off the teepee he's created with the wood. I toss him a lighter, and after a moment the flames catch. Finn blows gently on the fire, igniting it to life.

The sun has just dipped below the horizon, leaving a painting in the sky with purples, pinks, and oranges so vibrant no photograph could ever capture it accurately. The lake reflects the evergreen trees that grow along the shoreline. The campfire fills the air with nostalgia, leaving us with childlike smiles.

"Dad, you should learn a thing of two from Finnegan," Chloe teases.

"I've known how to build a fire since that boy was in diapers. I've been to a bonfire or two in my day."

"Sure, Dad." She laughs. Her eyes aren't as fully alert as they usually are, and based upon her lazy body language, it's safe to assume she's feeling the buzz of her drink.

I opted for a nonalcoholic drink, so instead of beer I sip on a can of soda. Finn too. When I finish, I attempt to throw the can into the fire, and Chloe cheers, despite me missing by a solid foot.

"I love you guys," Chloe says later in the night, wrapping an arm around me and one around Finn as she stands between us.

"We love you." I giggle, and Finn shoots me a side glance. "Don't we, Finn?"

He gives me a slight nod of confirmation, and I pinch Chloe to make sure she saw.

"Aw! You do love me after all, Finnegan." She messes up his hair before skipping along the shoreline, stumbling with a drunken smile plastered to her face.

"She really does enjoy having you two here," Charlie says, completely sober. Despite having a few sips of beer, I can tell he's not much of a drinker. For some reason, my heart opens more for him because of this. "And so do I," he says, pulling me into a side hug, and opening his free arm out to Finn.

Finn gladly accepts, and we hold on tight together for a moment before a song rips through the speaker Chloe brought.

We all turn our heads at once as Chloe displays a mischievous grin and turns the music even louder. The music echoes along the lake like a skipping stone. She walks back toward us and reaches her cold hand to mine, dragging me to the shoreline. She dances and I immediately copy her, swaying to the music on our makeshift dance floor.

I glance over at Finn and feel all the weight of loving someone. I only wish I could tell him.

The wind whistles through the trees, picking up my hair and entangling it as it blows around my head. We both shout the lyrics to the song, laughing and stumbling over one another as the crisp water engulfs my sneakers and her bare feet.

The song ends, followed by another from Chloe's playlist. I turn to make sure Finn and Charlie are okay. They stand around the fire, enjoying Chloe and I making fools of ourselves. Tiny balls of light pop in the distance— lightning bugs.

A splash steals my attention away, water ripples in a circle, and Chloe is nowhere to be found. Her wet hair breaks the surface. She wipes the water from her eyes and lets out a chilled laugh.

"Are you crazy?" I ask, already shivering from the water on my feet. I gasp as she splashes me. "Oh, it's *on.*" I dive into the lake's depths after her.

I swim until I can't hold my breath anymore. I'm already far into the lake, my feet nowhere near the bottom. A giddiness explodes in my chest as I shiver from the cold water. I see Finn watching me from the fire.

"Come in! The water's warm!" I lie.

"Not a chance."

I take it as a dare, so I pull myself under the water, letting out a scream before I go. I stay there, willing myself to keep from going up too soon for air, and then I feel firm hands under my armpits, lifting me up.

"Are you hurt?" Finn asks, water dripping into his eyes from his dark brown hair.

I break into a grin. Finn's concerned eyes shift to annoyance.

"She okay?" Charlie's voice calls from the shore.

I laugh. "I'm fine."

Finn's eyes don't leave mine as he says, "I think we should go to bed, love." His annoyance lets up on that last note.

I excuse us from the small group. Once Finn and I are in the living room, he stops walking and turns to me. "You have no idea the hold you have on me, Ad. I thought—" his voice cracks, but he quickly nods away the emotion. "I thought something terrible happened to you in the lake. Please, never do that to me again." He steps close enough to cup my jaw, then rests his forehead against mine.

I nod. I didn't realize I had scared him that much.

All my fears and inhibitions die when I gaze into those eyes. "Finn," I say gently. "How come you did that? On your birthday," I ask, remembering tasting his lips for the first time. Feeling so shocked and confused.

"What, exactly?"

"You kissed me that night, but then acted like you didn't the next day," I whisper the last part. I felt so... broken. Like the kiss had been a punishment for embarrassing him, or something.

He sighs. "I know, love. I didn't know how to approach it. So, I just—"

"Didn't," I finish.

"I wanted to touch you, to hold you, that whole day." He shakes his head. "You were so beautiful singing in my car, and your mannerisms were driving me crazy. I needed an excuse to kiss you and took it the first chance I got. I'm sorry."

"Don't be... I wanted you, too." My voice drops to a whisper, "I still do."

I think back to that day, it feels like ages ago.

I fought every emotion, every attraction I felt toward him, because I thought it would ruin everything. I didn't think friendship and romance could ever be interchangeable, but the truth is, they are one in the same.

At least for Finn and me.

Maybe it doesn't have to end here in Authensville. Maybe this is the first page to an exhilarating story.

I hold on to that.

Something shifts in this moment, like I can finally breathe.

"The moment promised is unimaginable," he whispers to me, whisking me away with his voice that drips with sex. He pulls me close until I'm pressed against him, draws his hand up my back and runs his fingers through the roots of my hair. He never once breaks eye contact. "You've been my favorite person since that day I saw you crying in the park."

My chest warms.

"Let me show you." his voice strains like the words are an effort to get out. As if he's holding himself back.

I nod, "Oka—"

Finn's lips don't allow me to finish my sentence. I wrap my thighs around his waist as he lifts me off the ground. He presses me against any and every possible surface on the way to the guest room, never *once* breaking contact between our lips.

My back meets the door to the room. Finn takes his time exploring every inch of my clothed body with his hands. I'm panting and shivering, we're both drenched from our swim.

I break away from our sloppy kisses, "F-Finn. *Please.*" I'm not sure exactly what I'm begging for, but the idea of his body heat against mine sounds alluring.

"Consequences, Adeline. Ever heard of them?" He bites down onto my neck, I whimper from the sting, which quickly turns to a moan as he sucks the sensitive skin.

"For?" I ask, completely sinless.

The click of Finn twisting open the doorknob answers me.

Panic spikes through me as I fall back, into the room. Finn catches me only a millisecond before my back hits the floor. I laugh from the adrenaline; it makes me feel alive.

He gently places me on the ground, with a quick kick to the door so it latches shut. He shimmies his leg between mine.

He closes the gap between our lips once again, except now his movements are careful. His hands get lost in my hair and I savor the groan he makes when I kiss him back, passion in every sweep of my tongue.

I push against his chest, encouraging him to roll off me, then slide on top of him. His hands burn me as he teasingly moves them down my back, squeezing my bottom as he whispers, "Fuck."

He sits up, taking me with him so I straddle his waist. His lips touch mine as he speaks carefully, "I want to learn every sound you can make." He slowly cocks his head, running a finger over my neck to move the wet hair away. "I want to be able to close my eyes and know exactly how you look beneath your clothes."

My breath turns shallow, my breasts rising and falling drastically.

"Is this okay with you, love?" His eyes are fixed on my lips, but as he says the nickname they look right at mine.

My voice is lost like I'm in a dream, so I nod my head instead.

One moment we're on the ground and the next he's tossing me onto the bed. It causes a loud thump as the headboard slams into the wall.

"Well, that's going to be a problem," he says, dragging the heavy bed away from the wall as my eyes roam his clothed body.

He's suddenly on top of me, his body weight easing all

the places that ache for him. My breath mimics his, heavy and fast. He wastes no time pulling his soaked shirt over his head, and then pulling my shirt carefully over mine.

Finn inhales a sharp breath, and suddenly I remember what I put on this afternoon. The red lace is out in the open, for only Finn to adore. And he does. His now swollen lips move along my torso, sucking, leaving me tingling. "When did you get this?" he whispers as if he's in pain.

"Well, Chloe—" I start but am cut off when he unfastens my soaked jeans and peels them open.

"Enough said." He gets the words out, but they are strained as he finds the companion lace. He works the wet denim down my legs, then tosses them across the room.

"You look—" He shakes his head. "Why am I always at a loss for words when it comes to you?" He settles himself back between my legs. "Irresistible." He breathes into the skin beneath my ear lobe. His kisses move down, my pulse speeds up.

His lips move sloppier the lower he gets. From my neck to my chest, by the time he gets to my torso he's breathing heavily. Sucking and kissing and biting.

I gasp when he leaves a kiss on top of my panties, the lace not doing anything to interrupt the warmth of his breath. "Is this okay?"

I nod my head, trying to catch up to what's happening right now.

My best friend kissing me—that much isn't new.

Him seeing me almost naked—not that new either.

His lips down there—*very* new.

I suck in a quick breath. The very audible sound makes Finn grin up at me. He holds eye contact as he slowly pulls the fabric aside, and places a soft, barely noticeable, kiss to my bare skin.

I let out a moan, nearly losing it from the soft contact. "Finn, I—"

But before I can finish my thought, his tongue flickers across my skin, lighting my entire body with heat. It's unlike anything I've ever experienced. The sheer pleasure has my head spinning, my lungs gasping, my toes curling. He kisses and licks me until I cover my mouth to keep from shouting out.

He carefully slips a finger into me, pumping it slow at first. His lips go back to the bundle of nerves. When I cry out, he increases the speed of his finger. My sporadic moans turn quick. I'm about to tip over the edge when he adds a second finger.

I sit up. The sight of his head between my legs is what sends me over the edge. I grip his hair and fall back against the pillows, pulsing around his fingers with a too loud moan. Once the shockwaves finally still, he grins up at me. "You taste better than I could've imagined." And he slowly takes his fingers away.

I gasp as he brings them to his lips. His eyes don't stray from mine when he darts his tongue out, licking the remains of me from his fingertips.

My attempt at processing what just happened is interrupted with his lips against mine. My head is in such a fog, I hadn't even realized he had come up here. I let out an aggravated moan, greedy and wanting more of him.

"Careful love, you know how much I like to hear you complain," he says, shimmying out of his pants, my eyes descend to his erection straining his boxer briefs.

He grabs a tiny wrapper from the pocket of his jeans, shimmying his boxers down his legs and sliding the condom on.

I try not to ponder why he had it on hand, but he stills

my worries immediately. "I wasn't expecting anything, but when you said you wanted to 'let this thing run its course,' I bought a pack with as much hope as winning the lottery."

I laugh.

He cups my jaw and kisses me again, making me feel like I'm the one who won the lottery. He carefully takes off the lingerie, so I am completely bare to him. He admires every inch of my body as his eyes rake over me. "Angelic," he breathes.

He lowers himself so he is on top of me, looking into my eyes as he adjusts himself. We both gasp when he reaches my entrance.

"Wait!" I widen my eyes. "I've never—"

He stills. "We don't have to do this."

"I want to," I whisper, pleading because the idea of not doing this terrifies me more.

"I'll go slow," he promises, slowly pushing into me. We both gasp as he fills me.

"Finn." His name barely leaves my lips because—*ouch.*

He stops, his eyes widening and looking down.

"Am I hurting you? I'll take it out—"

"No," I moan the word, the pain eases and pleasure replaces it.

He relaxes a little, pressing his forehead against mine. "Ad, are you sure?" His eyebrows bunch together in so much emotion. I watch his pupils dilate until his eyes are completely black.

I nod, I've never been so sure of something in my life.

He trails his fingers slowly down the length of my sides, squeezes my hips, and then feathers his way back up my body. His hands get lost in waves of auburn, hungrily grabbing onto the strands, his kisses devouring me whole.

I'm caught in a wave of passion like a rip current taking me someplace far, far away.

He possesses my lips with his as he slowly unwinds every nerve ending inside of me. Our pleasure filled sounds get drowned out in our emotional kiss. He's set a slow pace, teasing me, and leaving me wanting more. He takes his time, as if we've got forever left.

I hope we do.

He kisses my neck tenderly. So full of love. I gasp as he quickens his pace, I meet every one of his thrusts so we never truly part. His forehead presses into mine, his eyes are bright and focused so intently on mine. I grip his back, my fingernails scraping his skin, but he doesn't look pained. Instead, his eyes darken with his groan. "Come with me, my love," he rasps.

I widen my eyes, nodding quickly. His lips crash so hardly into mine and we come down together, letting the shockwaves crash into us as we come down.

It isn't long before he's inside me again. We try out best to make up for lost time in the span of a night, making love until we are physically unable to do it again.

My hair sticks to my forehead, which is shimmering in a coat of sweat. Finn and I are entangled in each other's limbs, so intertwined that I can't make out where I end and he begins. The cool air bites my bare skin, somehow the comforter ended up on the floor, and the pillows scatter across the bed.

"Wow," he breathes. "That was so…" He smiles against my lips. "Perfect—special." He shakes his head. "There are no words."

"As special as the other times?" I ask, not really wanting to know the answer but my insecurities forcing me to find out anyway. I flip onto my stomach, resting my upper body on Finn's chest. The thought of him being with another woman...or *women*...besides me makes me feels a possessiveness I've never known before.

He looks at me puzzled, so I elaborate, "The other times you've done what we just did." My cheeks heat up.

"Adeline," he says, "I've never done that before, just like you."

My eyes widen and suddenly my heart skips a beat because...that makes this even more special. Finn hasn't been intimate with anyone else.

He's only mine. And I'm only his.

19

"hloe's 'famous avocado toast' coming right up."
She beams, coming into the living room
balancing two plates. She gracefully sets them on
the coffee table and sits down next to me on the couch.

We eat in comfortable silence. "I had sex!" I eventually
blurt out. Finn made me pinky promise not to tell Chloe,
which I kept for a week...until now.

Her eyes widen, and she lifts a brow. "Was it the cute
guy from the café?"

A week ago, a boy, no older than fifteen, gave me his
number at a café, Chloe's been teasing me ever since.
"Chloe," I groan.

"With Finnegan?" She cocks her head.

I look at her like *duh*.

She shifts her attention to me. "Spill."

I fill her in, leaving most details out, but she pulls a few
out of me.

"He *wanted* to go down on you?" she questions for the

millionth time, only this time Finn had just walked through the door with Charlie. Both dripping in sweat.

Finn's eyes shoot bullets at us, and I feel every inch of embarrassment as I slowly glance at Charlie, who is just now pulling off his chunky wireless headphones. "What's with all the staring."

A wave of relief crashes into me, until Finn's eyes dart between Chloe and me.

"Really, Adeline? You *pinky* promised." He slumps down between us on the couch, grabbing the piece of crust off my plate and plopping it into his mouth. Charlie wipes a rag over his head and neck, taking the chair in the corner of the living room.

"Am I missing something?" Charlie asks.

"No," Finn, Chloe, and I say all at once…a little too fast.

"Okay then," Charlie says, unfazed by the weirdness that's very evident in the air.

Chloe changes the subject with ease, "So, are you guys planning on traveling anywhere else before you go back home to the Keys?"

I shake my head. I want to spend every moment until we need to go home here in Authensville. Before I can say that Charlie says, "The Keys? Which island do you guys live on?"

"Key Largo," Finn says.

Charlie's eyes widen a little. "Wow. Small world." He laughs. "I'm from there."

"I didn't know that." Chloe says, "I mean, I knew you were from Florida but not the Keys." She shakes her head. "You learn something new every day."

"You didn't like it down there?" I assume since he lives here in Authensville now.

He shrugs. "I loved it, actually, but I moved away after my high school sweetheart broke my heart."

I wonder what she was like. She couldn't have been the brightest letting someone like Charlie go. He's funny, respectful, kind. A good dad to Chloe. From what I've seen, there isn't a single bad bone in his body.

And the way Chloe looks up to him, the way they get along. It's something I've always dreamed of.

Being here with Charlie has healed a deep wound I hadn't even realized I had.

"Her loss," Chloe says, as if she's heard the story about Charlie's high school sweetheart before.

"Yeah," he says, with a hint of something behind his gentle smile—pain.

Early glimpses of dawn make their way through the blinds, casting faint lines of light along the wall to the guest room.

I've found myself unable to sit still here in Authensville, I want to be awake and present for every minute of it since our time here is finite. Even in my sleep, I'm tossing and turning, just wanting to wake up and enjoy the day. Usually, I would grab a book or scroll on my phone, but today I feel extra charged, like if I don't get out of this bed, I'll burn a hole through it with all this pent-up energy.

I slowly creep around the room, careful not to wake up Finn as I pull on leggings and Finn's Florida Key's hoodie he gave to me when he grew out of it. The floors are old, giving away any movement with loud creaks. Even when there's no movement, when the apartment settles you can hear it. I've almost convinced myself this place was haunted, but who would haunt such happy souls? Charlie and Chloe are as pure as pure gets.

The apartment is dark, with only purple hues coming in through the windows. I enjoy the silence, as I make my way down the stairs, through the closed steakhouse, and out the door.

The cool air touches my skin, the smell of trees and nature fill my soul. I can only see two small businesses past the morning fog, although there are at least ten along the downtown strip. No one's out here except for me, like I exist in my own little world.

I make my way down to the lake right past the strip, slowly dragging my feet along the cracked sidewalk. As the lake comes into view, I freeze, about to run the other way.

There's a man at the edge of the lake, his bare feet in the clay. I can't make much out about his appearance given how strong the fog is this early into the day. Right when I'm about to walk back the other way, he turns to grab a rock, spots me, and tosses me a wave.

"Morning, Adeline!" he calls.

"Charlie?"

He nods, signaling for me to join. I place my hands in the pockets of my hoodie, casually walking down to the shoreline.

Charlie doesn't say anything to me as I approach him, he just hands me a flat stone, tipping his chin toward the water for me to toss it. I do, and in one quick motion, the stone sinks below the surface.

"Skip it," he says, tossing another stone like a frisbee, I watch in amazement as it grazes the waters surface, skipping along once, twice, and even a third time before sinking.

I blink. "How did you do that?"

He smiles at me. "No one ever taught you how to skip a rock before?"

I shake my head.

"What about your old man, he never taught you?" he asks casually, letting his feet get soaked as he walks a little into the water to grab a perfectly flat stone.

"My dad never taught me anything," I say, almost low enough that he couldn't hear. But he did, and he gives me his full attention as he tries to understand my statement.

I sigh. "The only thing he's taught me was to be frightened of him."

His face remains the same, but the corner of his mouth ticks downwards. He hands me the stone, pointing at the water. "You have to flick it at the right angle, try to aim so it skids across the surface, low enough so it grazes it, but not so it sinks right away."

I nod, doing just that, but it sinks right away, ripples circling where it disappeared.

He grabs another stone, slowly flicking his wrist a few times to show me his range of motion, before tossing it and amazing me by skipping it four times.

I try again a few times, afraid we'll run out of stones. I'm about to quit, but it skips twice. I screech, jump up and down, ready to grab another stone.

"See, it's not so hard," Charlie says, arms crossed as he watches me toss the stone again. This time, it skips three times.

"Thank you." I smile wide, proud of myself. "Now I'll always know how to skip a stone."

He smiles at me, not saying anything, but he nods as if with pride too.

I sit down on the red clay, not bothering to care that it'll dirty up my leggings. The sun peeks through the mountains, casting rays of light along the lake, sparkling like a painting.

Charlie sits down beside me, mud all over his feet.

"Didn't bother to wear shoes?" I tease.

"I gave up a long time ago after I ruined so many pairs."

I nod, can't argue with that logic. "You come here a lot?" I ask.

"Every morning."

I look around, and the fog lets up a little, as the sun shines brighter. The sky is purple except for where the sun sits so bright, surrounded by orange. The clouds are painted pink. It's breathtaking.

"Chloe's really happy to have met you; she's been more chipper since you've arrived."

I smile at that, there's no greater compliment than to hear you've made someone happy.

"I'm sorry..." he starts, peering out at the lake, "about your dad."

Oh. How do I even respond?

Before I need to reply, he adds, "I know what it's like, you know. My old man relished in the power he had over me as a boy. I was so afraid of the guy. I hated him." He sighs, as if reliving a powerful memory. "There's not much you can do as a little kid, except strive to be better. A better person, a better parent. Make light out of the darkness within, make sure no one you touch in this life feels the way you've felt." He looks at me now. "Chloe has her own battles, growing up without her mom, but she'll never feel the suffering of being raised in abuse, and that's enough to bring me a world of peace. I'm sorry your father wasn't the kind of man who could give you that peace too."

Everything he just shared sits heavy on my heart, I feel tears stinging my eyes because the way he explained it is so beautiful. "And now Chloe's pain will ensure the people she touches in this life will never know the same pain she felt without her mom," I add, smiling at the thought. Our pain molds us to be better, to make sure the people we love never feel what we've felt.

It's heartbreakingly beautiful to be able to love despite the darkness we've lived, if anything, it makes us love harder. Better.

"You're right," he nods.

I nod too, happy with this new perspective. Thankful the children I come to know in this world will never feel such suffering if I have anything to do with it. I smile for my future kids, if I decide that's what I want. They will be so loved. They'll never know what it is to feel otherwise.

"Thank you, Charlie." I push off the mud.

"For what?"

"For bringing meaning to my dreadful past. For giving me peace, and hope for my future. For giving me more kindness, understanding, and wisdom in these past few minutes than my dad has given me in my lifetime," I say, my voice breaking as I try to hold in my emotions.

"Oh. You're welcome, kid. It's nothing." Charlie clears his throat as if he's also clearing away emotions he doesn't want to show.

I turn and walk back to the apartment, a newfound ability to skip rocks and peace in my heart. I shower and climb back into bed with Finn, easily falling asleep after my morning with Charlie.

Kisses along my jaw urge my eyes open. Finn's dimpled smile makes my lips upturn effortlessly. His eyes are puffy and glassy as if he has just woken up too.

He's beautiful.

"Good morning, love," he whispers in my ear.

I smile so hard, my cheeks hurt. How is this life? *No.* How is this *my* life?

I must've done something spectacular recently to have received this good of karma. I count my fingers. All ten, so I'm not dreaming after all.

"Morning." My voice comes out raspy.

I screech, lazily whaling around as Finn's fingers dig into my sides, tickling me into oblivion. I'm fully wrapped up in his embraces, his torso over mine as I squirm from the torturous act of tickling.

"Please," I say between clenching and gasps of breath, "stop."

My annoyance comes and goes all too fast, because his lips find the sensitive part of my neck. His hands no longer dig into my sides, now they grip my wrists as his kisses send memories flash through my head.

Fingers gripping the sheets, warm breath against skin, eyes fluttering.

We haven't had sex since that night. Unfortunately, Aunt Flow came to visit a week early. Chloe said to just do it anyway, but the thought makes me uncomfortable, especially since we've only had one night of experience together.

"I'm going to make us some coffee," Finn says roughly against my neck. "I'll be right back, my love." He places a kiss to my hair.

"Okay," I say softly.

The bed bounces, and the air feels as if it has dropped ten degrees without him. He closes the door to the guest room behind him and the mattress vibrates. I feel around for my phone and find it beneath my pillow, ringing with a random number.

It could be the owner to the café.

I take a deep breath and muster up my best customer service voice.

"Hello, is this—" I start.

"Adeline!" A deep *familiar* voice causes every organ in my body to halt to an abrupt stop. One word in that thunderous voice fills me with such dread, taking me far into my past. I can't breathe, I can't even blink. "I didn't raise a slut who runs away from home with some punk boy!" he shouts. I grip the phone with all my might, it shakes in my trembling hands.

"Get your fuckin' ass home *now* so you can explain to me why you put my wife in rehab."

A knife pierces my heart. The person on the other line slowly turns it with each word, sending every nerve writhing in pain.

"How dare you embarrass me? Everyone in town is askin' where my daughter is. I gotta make up some bullshit story, 'cause I don't have a fucking clue!" I pull the phone back a little, his voice so loud it sounds like it's on speaker. "I can't believe my fucking blood runs through your veins! Get your little ass back home before I come find you. I promise you it won't be pretty!"

The unhealed wound I've been brushing aside finally tears through my entire body. My heart beats a million miles a minute, my broken soul shakes so violently.

The voice is gone, replaced by a new one. "Adeline? Ad, look at me, love," he coos, the hot tears are wiped away by soft fingertips, but they keep falling.

I blink, for the first time, and find amber eyes staring back at me. I search for my phone, that lies on my lap. I still see the phone number, so I quickly tap the red circle, ending the call.

"Adeline, who was that?" Finn's calm demeanor has shifted, all I see is concern creasing his brow.

"He's b-back."

"Who?" His voice makes my skin raise in goosebumps. There's something hidden beneath the single syllable, as if he already knows. I see the moment his concern changes to rage, his nostrils flaring, his jaw clenched.

"Jason."

20

FOUR YEARS AGO

I don't know whether to be offended or amused as my drunken father spits obscenities to me at a bar.

I don't know how we got here. My mother is hidden away in the bar bathroom as my father tells me point blank that my mom is crazy, and how much he longs to have a different woman for each day of the week.

Occasionally the bouncer looks our way, but never intervenes. I'm only fifteen, sitting at the bar with a lunatic asking me to order him beer with a shot of liquor in it.

I have no idea how I was allowed in here, and why no one has called social services immediately at the sight of our clusterfuck family.

I've seen my dad drunk plenty of times, but as my mother stumbles her way through the Saturday night crowd back to her seat at the bar, her eyes are nearly shut, and she trips over her own two feet. She hardly drinks, but recently I've seen her drunk more times than I can count on my hand.

I perk up as the bartender hands her a fruity drink. "Can I have some?" I ask, smiling at the idea.

"The fuck is wrong with you, kid?" Jason smacks the back of my head. But with every sip, his sense of surrounding must disappear because my mom slowly pushes the drink my way and watches the bouncer while I take sips.

I don't feel that different, only slightly dizzy. And more at ease with my fucked-up life. Maybe that's how people become addicted to this stuff.

The night continues with my mom and dad taking turns going to the bathroom, telling me their horrible perspective of the other while we're alone. It's so incredibly fucked, I almost laugh.

The night continues with the same chaos, until I'm safe and sound in my bed, whisked away in a slumber.

Until something deep down urges me to keep my eyes shut, to stay asleep while the world around me erupts with noise. I battle with the louder voices telling me to open my eyes.

I resist as long as I can but finally my eyes shoot open and I'm suddenly trying to catch up to what's happening in my room.

Jason holds my mom by the throat up against my wall. "A-ask her," she chokes out, clawing against his face in one swift motion, causing him to drop her.

"You fucking bitch!" he spits, his voice shakes the walls and rattles my bones.

I gasp at the blood dripping from his face as he moves toward me. "Look what that monster did to your fucking father!" he screams at me, as if I'm the one who caused him to bleed.

I try to find my voice, but it's hidden away in my throat, like a terrified prey hiding from its predator.

"He was choking me!" my mom defends.

Rage bubbles up inside of me. I shouldn't be in the middle of this. I'm fifteen years old, I shouldn't be a part of their mess. Why are they even in my room?

"After we dropped you home, your father insisted we go to a club." My mom is frantic, shaking, and angry. "While he was throwing up in the bathroom, his little friend Erin introduced herself." The liquid courage helps her stand up to him, looking him in the eyes as he violently shakes like a rabid beast.

"You don't know what the fuck you're talking about, Marsha! She's fucking crazy and obsessed with me. I can't help that she told you some fucking story." He boils at my mom's audacity to accuse him of cheating.

But I know the truth, I know where he goes when he doesn't come home. I know the way that woman feels entitled to Jason, how she tried to break me for standing in her way all those years ago. I can only imagine the things she said to my mother, the woman Jason is married to. The person that makes Erin the other woman.

"Get your shit, we're leaving." Jason directs his angered voice at me, but I stay unmoving.

"Adeline, you are not going anywhere with him, do you hear me?" my mom says in rebuttal.

"*Shut the fuck up!*" he shouts.

I shake and sweat and think this might be how I die, but I would rather die than leave with him tonight.

"Take a fucking picture of my face, Adeline. Your mother's going to jail, and I need some fucking evidence." He points to the blood drips red down his cheeks and onto my floor.

I don't move.

"Can you believe her?" He tries to gain my sympathy, trying to obtain a disciple to stand with him, but I will never side with the devil.

I am so enraged by his audacity to involve me, to strangle my mom, that after all these years, everything I wished I'd said in the past barges through my lips like soldiers ready to fight.

"How *dare* you? I am *fifteen years old*. I shouldn't be subjected to this! No person should have to watch their dad hurt their mom! No mom should have to be hurt by someone like you. And you want me to be on *your* side?"

His eyes burn like hell fire, he moves so quickly toward me, I clench up and shout in a high-pitched voice, "Don't fucking touch me!" Angry tears burn their way down my cheeks.

"I'm your father, do you hear me?" he yells, it feels as if a dragon has spewed fire in my face. "Fuck you!" he curses me out, frantically shoving his middle finger in my face.

"No, *fuck* you!" I scream at the top of my lungs with everything in me, salty tears filling my mouth.

"I'm fucking done, with both of you." He points to my mom who stands frozen in fear, and to me. "I want you both out of my fucking life!" He stomps away, breaking the floorboards beneath him, or so it sounds.

My mother and I stare at one another in a state of shock, and complete fright. We flinch each time something shatters downstairs. It sounds as if he's punching holes into the walls. It's as if a tornado endlessly rages throughout our home, until finally the front door slams shut.

We're left in the quiet aftermath of a storm.

Jason is gone.

21

NOW

Adeline, slow down," Finn says.

"Get her to stop!" Chloe's voice barely registers in my head, I guess she's in the room now.

"I'm *trying*," Finn bites back.

I hear them talking but have no idea what they're saying. I can't focus on them.

I pull open drawers, gather clothes, and toss them into my suitcase, or maybe Finn's. It doesn't much matter anyways, they will inevitably end up in the same location. I push past a body, making my way to the bathroom. I'm stilled by a firm grip to my forearm.

"Adeline." Finn pulls me into his chest, the last place I should be right now, but the place I want to be the most. I try to fight the affection, but I sink into his breaths. Like an ice cube inevitably melting into warm water.

"I'm here, love. I'm right here." His hand rests on my lower back, the other brushes through my hair. "Will you join me?"

Here in Charlie's guest room. Right, the familiar smell

of cinnamon and clove and deodorant brings my heartrate down. I slowly breathe him in, my trembling hands easing into stillness.

"Chloe, go grab a glass of water," he says with ease, yet a hint of authority.

Some time goes by, and I continue to inhale and exhale. Waves of reality wash over me. I try to process what just happened, what this means. The only thing anchoring me to the present is Finn's hand wrapped around mine.

I slowly sip the water. A small hand takes away the glass when I am finished. Chloe's yellow nail polish finally registers, I turn to her, and then back to Finn.

Chloe is here.

And so is Finn.

Right, I heard her voice.

"Guys." My voice cracks over the word. I slowly back up to the bed and sink into it. "My dad... He's back. He's with my mom." I shake my head. "How is he there?"

Finn eases down next to me, bringing my head onto his lap. Chloe's blurry figure moves until she's sitting next to Finn. Her fingers stroke my hair.

More tears fall, I feel like anymore and I will drown.

"I don't know, love," Finn says as I weep in the fetal position. "But I'm here, and I won't let you go."

I hold onto the promise with all my might, gaining more clarity. Anger ignites fire in my core, and the tears stop.

"I don't know how he even knew she was in rehab." I wrack my brain, trying to find where I slipped. "I need to get my mom away from him. I hope she didn't relapse." I sit up, already planning.

"Okay," Finn speaks in a controlled voice. "Let's pack, but more...organized." He looks at the mess I've made.

I make my way to Charlie's bedroom. Apparently, that's where the washing machine is.

I grab the handful of clothes Finn washed last night from the dryer, but something catches my attention.

I drop the clothes and step over them, grabbing a picture from Charlie's shelf of framed photos and look closer at it. A young man, who looks like Charlie without the smile lines and crow's feet, and a woman with long, beautiful hair smiles at me.

"I was a looker, wasn't I?" Charlie's voice startles me.

I almost drop the black and white photo, but I grip it before it slips out of my sweaty hands.

"Sorry!" I blurt out. "I wasn't snooping. It's this woman, she's so pretty," I say, my cheeks heating.

He lets out a gentle laugh. "That's okay."

I stare at the photo again, their toes in the sand and the beautiful ocean only a few feet behind them. I can't make out the color, since it's a black and white photo, but I can tell the water was clear that day. "Is this in the keys?" I ask, remembering his brief explanation of his time there.

"Yes."

"Oh." Is all I can say. This is the woman who broke his heart, and I should despise her for it…but I can't help but feel something else toward her. I can't place it, but I almost feel like I knew her once.

Maybe my emotions are getting the best of me.

"She looks—"

"Beautiful," he finishes for me.

"I was going to say young. You looked young too."

"We were about your age," he says.

I start to set it back down, trying to change the subject since I'm sure this is the last thing Charlie wants to talk about.

"We were in love." He smiles easily. "I thought she was my soulmate. I've never made a connection like that since." He shakes his head, taking the photo from my hands. "On a random Wednesday afternoon, she left. No explanation, only a sticky note saying goodbye.'"

"That's it?"

"Yup."

I can't even begin to imagine how I would feel if I were in that situation, finding a sticky note in the place of Finn. "Have you ever thought about looking her up now?" I ask, maybe he needs closure.

"I searched for her for months, but she was gone. It's the reason I moved here, actually. Without her, living down there was pointless. I'm more of a mountain guy anyway." He shrugs. "I think it's best if I don't look her up now."

I get it. "Do you regret it? Leaving, I mean." Wondering if I've made a mistake leaving my problems at home, pushing away all the feelings Jason left me with... Running away.

Always running.

"I met Chloe's mother shortly after I moved here. Of course, as you can tell...that didn't work out either." He smiles, probably thinking of his daughter. "I wouldn't have changed a thing." He places the photo back in my hands. "Take it," he tells me.

"Oh...I couldn't."

"It's not doing much good here besides collecting dust. It's probably time I get rid of it, don't you think? Throw it away or tuck it into a drawer for all I care. Plus, I hear you're headed for the hills. Consider it a souvenir. A photo of me in my prime." He smiles, but his eyes glass over like mine do.

"Thank you for *everything*." I choke out the words. The

last one holding so much more meaning than he could possibly know.

He wraps his arms around me, entrapping me in a safe hug. "You are family now. Please don't be a stranger."

"I won't," I whisper.

"Do what you feel is right," Finn whispers against my hair. The color no doubt a bright shade of red reflected off the sun that's about to set.

Golden hour has been my favorite time to sit on Charlie's roof these past three weeks. It overlooks the peaceful streets of Authensville, the place I've called home for not long enough.

I consider his words. What do I feel is right? None of this is right. Jason at my house sitting on my furniture. I don't even want to begin to imagine what he's said to my mom... What he's *done*. "Right or not, I have to go home. My mom isn't safe as long as Jason is around."

No matter how messy our two-person family is, it's perfect I realize. It's been perfect all along. Sure, it isn't the most conventional, but is any family really? The love we have for one another lays the foundation, now all we have to do is put up walls.

How will we do that with Jason covering her eyes?

I won't text her or call her. I don't know if Jason will hear, what he will do to her the second she hangs up the phone. The situation is too fragile to mess with blindly. I need to access my mother's state of mind before moving forward. I pocket my phone and take a deep breath. I inhale Authensville's woodsy air. I pull in the memories I've made, the people I've come to love. When I exhale, I close my eyes, my mind painting pictures for me. Finn's husky laughter from my unfunny jokes, the warmth of his arms holding me while we sleep, the way he makes me feel like the most special thing in any room.

The uncertainty of what happens now becomes so real. Will everything Finn and I built come crashing down? Did I have enough time to make him want me after of this trip?

Jason has a miraculous talent for sucking dry my happiness.

I hate him.

I hate him.

I fucking *hate* him.

I still had a week left with Finn.

A week to make love with him and pretend he loved me too.

A week with my new best friend, Chloe. With Charlie who mends together all the wounds Jason left me with.

Jason has ruined everything for me. Again.

"We do this together, Adeline. I won't make you do anything alone, ever. You hear me?"

"I know." I lace my fingers into his, squeezing as I rest my head on his shoulder.

I smile at the city surrounding us. The last bit of sun that's about to dip below the mountain I hiked with Finn when we first got here. Little did I know I was going to fall in love with this town, meet my soul sister, and a guy who can heal any internal wound with just a smile. A part of me will always belong here. The hollow piece in my heart already aches as the sun finishes its descent, leaving the sky purple, then blue, and eventually black.

"Are you ready?" Finn finally breaks the silence with the one sentence I've dreaded since we got on this roof...since we got to this town.

"No," I admit.

"Neither am I." His gaze meets mine. "Let's be unready together, yeah?" His big hand engulfs mine. The simple gesture touches my heart in ways no one else can.

"Yeah." I find myself smiling, hardly surprised by Finn's ability to make me smile despite the current circumstance of my life. He hasn't changed one bit from that little boy holding a baby gecko.

"Did you pack your chargers? Maybe we should go buy you one just in case," Chloe says franticly, pulling out drawers and checking under the guest bed.

"I triple checked everything, Chloe." Finn's voice comes from behind me. His presence felt in every cell of my body.

Chloe hardly acknowledges him. She circles to the other nightstand and pulls it away from the wall, checking behind it. She moves around the bedroom, causing chaos in her wake. "We have a lot of cardboard boxes piled up, why don't we have a campfire?" Chloe finally faces us. There's a single stress line between her perfectly shaped eyebrows.

"We should really hit the road, Chloe." Finn's voice is gentle.

"It'll be really fast. Promise." She musters a persuasive smile, but her voice cracked over the last word.

"Chloe," I say, outstretching my arms.

Her eyes quickly turn to glass, a storm of sadness brewing within them. She pulls her shoulders back and shifts her features, but she doesn't fool anyone.

She wants us to stay, and based on a conversation we had weeks ago, she thinks it's selfish to feel that way. Which is ridiculous.

She takes three small strides and welcomes my embrace. Her body shakes and I feel the waterworks begin within my own body.

"I'm really going to miss you, Addy." Chloe's voice is higher pitched than usual.

"Likewise." I sniffle. "I can't believe how fast this ended."

"Promise you'll call?" The way her voice dips, I can tell she is afraid I won't. That this is it, I'll abandon our relationship just as her mother did.

"This isn't goodbye. It's 'I'll see you soon'," I say through stifled sobs.

She nods quickly, wrapping her pinky finger around mine, before using the backs of her index fingers to dry her eyes.

"Finnegan, it's been real." She goes in for a bro hug, trying to seem indifferent but I know better. They formed a bond over the past couple weeks. They act like bickering siblings that share an unspoken love for one another.

We finish putting our luggage in Finn's car and say our final goodbyes to Charlie and Chloe.

"I'm sorry we're leaving so soon, my love. I know how much this place means to you," Finn says and puts the car in drive. I look out the rear window. My heart shrinks the smaller Chloe and Charlie get, until we turn right, and they disappear altogether.

I want to cry, but I fight the tears that attempt to escape. "It's okay."

Leaving heaven to make the dreadful descent down to hell is a lot more pathetic than it sounds. I push away the thoughts of what's awaiting me down there. I'll deal with it once I have to, but right now, only this moment exists.

"What's your meaning of life, today?" I cut through the quiet.

Finn doesn't skip a beat. "To hold your hand through the bad times."

His promise buries itself straight into my heart. His hand feathers up my thigh, so close to the spot that begins to beg for him.

"Finn," I breathe. *I love you* claws at my throat, begging to be said out loud.

"Yeah?" He takes his eyes off the road to look at me.

I shake my head. Now isn't the time for proclamations of love. "Nothing," I whisper, looking out the window.

We make the journey back home toward a man I hoped would die without me ever having to see again. With each mile we drive, the more a fiery ball of confidence grows within me until I'm burning with it.

I think back to my younger self, the petrified little girl. Innocent. Helpless.

She had no one to fight the battles she'd been involuntarily thrown into. I close my eyes and picture her thin frame, big eyes, trembling hands… I make a promise to her.

You don't have to be afraid anymore. I'll fight for us now.

22

I'm coming," Finn says firmly, nothing but a serious edge to his voice.

I look at my dull colored house through the car window, and back into Finn's lively amber eyes. Cortisol heightens my instincts.

Do I fight or flight?

Finn's eyes say so many things—*Please don't do this alone.*

But everything about his body language speaks even louder. Back pressed against the door, seatbelt still intact—*I believe in you.*

"Five minutes," I say, my sweaty palms fumble with the seat belt. "If I'm not back in five minutes you can intervene." Each second that passes while I'm behind those walls will be hell for him, but I know he will wait. He knows I have this.

I know I have this.

War drums sound in my chest, my beating heart finalizes the decision I already knew I'd make—fight.

Trembling hands open the car door. They belong to me, and in theory I am the one who moved them, but right now my body moves before I tell it to, taking control. I beeline to my front door. Spine completely straight, shoulders pulled back, head held high.

Jason will never know how much the scared little girl is fighting the urge to run and hide. My exterior appears composed and confident, even if I feel anything but that inside.

I push my key into the door and twist until it clicks.

Unlocked. My neck begs to twist, to look back at Finn, to run. Ignoring it, something inside me tells me I have to do this.

Not just for my mom, but for that little girl who couldn't stand up for herself all those years ago.

Maybe it's the adrenaline junkie that craves danger or maybe I need closure.

I open the door and the lingering presence of my father barrels into me like a bulldozer. I don't see him, but I feel him. An uneasy chill trickles down my spine, and then I hear it.

Heavy boots clunking against the hard wood floor. Right above me. They move further away, toward the stairs, and that's when I see them.

Black.

Leather.

Boots.

Please Daddy, don't! I want to shout.

"*Get the* fuck *out of my sight!" His voice is directed at my mom, it's shaking the walls, or maybe it's me that shakes.*

I hug the corner, hoping he won't see me, but equally hoping he does *see me. Maybe if he sees I'm watching he won't do whatever he's about to do to her.*

My mother uses her gentle voice, the one she uses on me when I'm hurt or upset. "Jason, baby, please just calm d—"

A gasp leaves my mouth, but I quickly smack it shut.

My mother. *My* father.

His hands, wrapped around her throat.

No.

His muscles are so big. *He looks so* strong.

He is going to kill her.

I turn. I run. I run so fast I forget about the step right behind me.

The loud thud of my body falling turns my father's angry grunts quiet.

I can't move. My body lays across the bottom of the stairs unmoving, paralyzed.

His boots thud against the floor, getting louder.

Louder.

So loud that I finally can move again, so I run.

I bolt up the stairs, careful to watch my steps, he is right behind me.

My mother shouts something from below us, but I can't think to make it out right now. A terrified shriek escapes me when I reach the top floor, my quiet footsteps get drowned out by his heavy ones.

Light rain versus ground shaking thunder.

Innocence versus violence.

But I beat him. I make it to my room before him. I quickly slam it shut, twist the lock. I slide open the window.

The tree branch is so far away… Maybe if I were bigger I could reach—

The door gets kicked open. My father's black leather boots have demolished the wood.

I jump.

I run.

I try to scream, nothing comes out.
The neighbor is watering her garden.
I look back at my window.
My father sees the neighbor.
He walks away.
I made it.

The memory slams into me. Flight, such a natural instinct for prey. It's all they've ever known, it's what's always kept them safe.

I mount my feet in place.

Inaction is what hurt my mother. When I finally came back home that day, many years ago, I saw the purple around her throat, the stitches across her brow bone, the emptiness that took place of light behind her eyes.

Granted, I was only a little girl. Back then I did the only thing that gave me a fighting chance, I ran.

"Damn, kid, the fuck happened to you?" Jason steps down the stairs, as nonchalant as ever.

My mind tries to catch up to *this* reality, the one where we aren't baring our claws and fighting to the death.

He's dressed in denim jeans, and a camouflage T-shirt two sizes too small, showing off his huge beer belly. His hairline has moved back at least an inch since I last saw him, and his eyes are sunken in.

He makes it to the bottom level, where my feet are implanted, and then he really looks at me.

"Wow, you're all grown up." He doesn't say it in a gushy, sentimental way. The way you'd expect a normal dad to after not seeing his daughter, *his only daughter*, after four years.

I'm dumbfounded. It feels like a ghost has visited me from the past, only now the lights are on and I realize I'm about an inch taller than him.

I do a quick body scan of myself, and realize my shoulders pull back on their own, my chin sits above his without a conscious effort. I am confident, and it's not even for pretend.

I blink a few times, realizing we are just staring at each other, and I haven't said a single thing. Not that he deserves my words, but I speak for myself…closure, or something.

"Well, I'm an adult." My voice holds no sentiments, I'm completely ice cold. "Where's my mom?"

"What, I don't even get a fucking *hug* or something?"

I push past him and begin my search.

I try to shred the dreadful memory out of my head, it clouds my vision: Her limp body, slow breathing, hanging onto her life by a thread.

"You haven't seen me in what, four or five years, and this is my greeting? I didn't raise you to be a cunt."

My feet almost stop right in the middle of the stairs, but I push past my anger and take a deep breath. I imagine the lyrics to my favorite song to tune him out.

I walk briskly through the hallway, past my bedroom, straight to my mother's room.

Loud clunking trails me, and more nonsense leaves his mouth. "You know I could've died, right?"

What is he going on about?

"Hey! Don't you fucking ignore me. I'm your dad!" he shouts.

My nervous system remembers his voice, it knows exactly how to make my hands sweat and my body tremble, but I swallow the fear down. I just need to get to my mom.

I push open my mother's door. There are hints of Jason in every corner—his clothes sprawled out on the night-stand; the right side of the bed isn't tucked in neatly like it has been the past four years. I walk further in. With no sign of my mother, I check her bathroom.

While I don't find her, I do find a second toothbrush lying on the counter, which is dirtied by smears of toothpaste and tiny black shavings in her once clean sink. I spin around to continue my search but run straight into Jason's chest. I recoil. His arms are spread on either side of him, blocking the exit.

"Move." My voice almost shakes, but I force it to stay steady. I will not show him weakness. Never again.

But he doesn't budge. "My own blood isn't going to disrespect me like this, you hear me? I come home after all these years and get your mom out of that horrendous place and you don't even thank me?"

"I will never be grateful to you as long as I breathe on this earth. Move."

His eyes shift from anger to confusion to pure rage.

I stand tall and unwavering.

"What the fuck did you just say to me?" He puffs out his chest like an animal.

"You have one second." I cross my arms, mock checking my watch, and then say, "One." My knee makes abrupt contact to his crotch.

The tough guy façade tumbles the second he barrels over in pain. He breathlessly mutters, "Fuck."

I step over him, out of my mother's room, and back into the hallway. I ignore him groaning in pain, and any other day I'd take full delight in what just happened, and later I probably will. But the image of my mother passed out with a bottle of liquor and no pulse haunts the bliss away.

I freeze in place at her voice.

"Honey, I'm home," my mother sings in delight, the front door slamming shut.

I make my way downstairs, seeing my mother dressed to

the nines. Her hair is styled, she wears a designer dress that is casual but screams *I'm rich*. The cherry on top is the designer bag that probably costs more than any college tuition. I clear my throat and finally catch her attention.

She gently places her bag on the nearest surface before squealing and wrapping me up in a tight embrace, something I am completely and utterly *un*familiar with.

"Oh, honey! You're finally home, look who's here," she coos, as if she just came back from vacation and brought me back an exquisite souvenir. It's only been three weeks… How is she out of rehab?

She turns me around. My eyes lock with Jason's and bile rises in my throat. I look him square in the eyes. He glares at me like I'm the gum on the bottom of his shoe.

I turn around, not wanting to waste any more time on him. My anxiety skyrockets by having my back toward him. I assess my mother from head to toe. I hear Jason mumbling something about me being ungrateful. Something about shipping me off to boarding school. He doesn't realize I'm nineteen, way past boarding school age.

But if my mother is spiraling, she doesn't display it. Her nails are freshly painted, she doesn't smell like alcohol or vomit, and she's even wearing lipstick. The only give is the purple rings of exhaustion beneath her eyes.

Why would she let Jason back into our lives with a smile on her face? It just doesn't add up. I glance at her attire; she's wearing a turtleneck. I've never seen her wear a turtleneck in my life.

"I need to talk to you, Mom."

"Anything you say to me you can say in front of your dad, sweetie." She uses her old voice, the one she used as battle armer. To walk upon eggshells so they wouldn't shatter.

If I didn't just hear Finn's car door slam shut, I would've corrected her. Explained that the man who stands behind me is no more than a sperm donor. Instead, the front door opens and closes.

I step out of my mother's embrace and into Finn's. I whisper a quick, "I'm okay," but his worry doesn't disappear.

"You have some fucking nerve on you, kid." Jason walks completely down the stairs and passes my mom. He heads straight toward us. I step in front of Finn before he can lay a hand on him.

Finn doesn't say anything to my father, no handshake, no casual small talk. I respect Finn's disrespect.

"You take my daughter all the way across the fucking country—" Jason begins his rant. His face turns red, and he foams at the corner of his mouth like an animal.

"Out of state," Finn interrupts.

Jason looks like he's going to kill him.

"I took her out of the state Florida and into the state of Georgia, not across the country." Finn pulls me aside, standing directly in front of me. "Continue."

Jason's jaw ticks, he acts on impulse. I blink and Finn is in Jason's grip. My pulse misses too many beats, my body trembles, and adrenaline takes over.

"Get off him!" I shout, pure rage in every syllable.

My mother screams, her rich *stay at home wife* façade shattering to pieces. "Jason." She eases toward them. "Let's all just calm down."

"Calm down? Get back in the fucking kitchen and stay in line!"

You can't fight violence with violence. Nobody wins. Each side loses soldiers, wives lose their husbands, children lose fathers...innocent people die in the crossfire. It's a vicious cycle. I recall my ninth-grade history teacher's voice.

You can't fight violence with violence.

I swallow down the lava that burns my throat, that heats my muscles. It prepares me to fight with my body, but I won't. Instead, I pull out my phone and beg God to not let Jason break the man I love.

23

I make sure my phone is on silent, so when I press record, Jason won't hear the sound. I watch in the tiny screen the scene that's unfolding only a few feet away. I hesitate, my body screaming to protect Finn. But just as I'm about to lower my phone, my best friend quickly glances at me, realizing what I am doing. He gives the slightest nod and I know he understands how big this moment is. If I stand a chance against this war, I need to think with my head, not my heart, so I steel my resolve and keep filming.

My mother and I lock eyes. I see the wave of realization wash over her, and I silently plead with her to let me continue. She diverts her eyes and walks away; into the kitchen, as she was told.

Anxiety ripples through me more than it ever has before. I watch through the screen, trying to stand still to get proper footage but my hands tremble so much it's hard to make out what's happening.

"I've dreamt of this moment since you were a kid."

Jason yanks Finn by the collar, spinning them around. Finn looks winded as Jason slams him into the wall.

"You mean when I was an innocent kid playing with Adeline?" Finn eggs him on for me.

For evidence

For justice.

So Jason will be locked behind bars. For our safety, for the world to be a better place... If I can just stop shaking.

My heart catches in my throat at the contact of Jason's knuckles against Finn's ribs. A loud sob leaves me, I hear my breath as I hyperventilate.

I know it hurt, but Finn doesn't let on.

Now Jason's knee goes straight into Finn's groin. Finn groans in pain, but he still doesn't put up a fight. At least not a physical one.

Jason punches Finn's beautiful face. "I want you to look in my fucking eyes as I kill you!"

My stomach clenches. This has to be enough. I end the video and send it to Finn. Not taking a single chance in losing the evidence.

My confident voice causes every hair on the back of my neck to stand up. "You have one second to get off him before I call the cops."

Jason's flaming eyes burn into me, making me want to shudder, but I don't.

For the little girl that needed me all those years ago, I won't.

I stare him down, phone in hand, waiting for him to back away.

"You wouldn't call the cops on your own dad," he says with arrogance.

I pull my gaze away only for a second while I fumble with the screen. I type the digits and by the time I look up to show him my phone, Finn is free of Jason's rage. The wall beside him endures it, a fist sized hole in the dry wall.

Jason grabs his hand in pain, probably broke it in his temper tantrum. I ignore him and rush to Finn.

"I'm okay, love. Go grab your mom. We're leaving." His voice so normal, it's eerie. His cheek bone already turns a deep shade of purple and swells, and it hasn't even been a minute.

I enter the kitchen where my mom is collapsed in her chair, tears streaming down her face. Her shoulders hunch as if the weight of everything finally bears down on her in this moment. I carefully grab her hand. "Mom, we need to go." She doesn't even lift a finger, like she's completely wrung out.

"Mom, *please*," I practically beg.

"I deserve to be here, honey. Just go."

"Nobody deserves to be abused, Marsha. Please come with us." Finn enters the kitchen, and I selfishly thank God for him being here.

My heart rate slows a little in his presence, my mother nods in shame and follows us to the front door.

Jason sits on the couch, dramatically holding his fist as if it has been cut off. "Where the fuck are you two goin'?" he asks, dumbfounded.

I keep looking straight, hoping my mother will follow suit.

He doesn't deserve any more of our breath.

Her face shifts to uncertainty, like she might stay. Obviously, he's been here long enough to implant himself into her head again.

"Mom. Please," I whisper so only she can hear.

"I can't."

"I'm not leaving you behind, so either you come, or I stay too."

Something shifts in her expression. She steps through the front door.

For me.

It doesn't go unnoticed, and I make myself promise to hang onto the memory for the future hurt I can already sense I am going to feel.

Why would you let him back in, Mom?

"Oh, Finn!" Finn's mother cries out, taking her son's cheeks into her hands as she inspects the bruise Jason left on his perfect face.

"I'm fine, Mom," he mumbles, stepping to the side so she can see he isn't alone.

"Hi, Mrs. Walker." I gesture my mom to step up. "It's a big ask... but do you mind if we spend the night?"

"Oh dear, of course! Come in, come in!" She herds us inside, glancing the surrounding area before shutting us in, and locking the door.

"Did I hear my son in there?" Burt says, oblivious from the hallway. He enters the kitchen and takes in the chaos that gathers in his quiet nest.

After we all say our greetings, and Finn catches his parents up to our trip and what happened when we got home, we all sit around the living room.

I've never gone into detail to Finn's parents about my home life, but as I got older and would spend holidays like Father's Day and Thanksgiving with them, I think they pieced together that I didn't come from a conventional home. They seemed horrified to find out Jason put his abusive hands on their innocent son, and on my mother for years.

His parents take up the couch. My mother isolates herself to the furthest end of the room, occupying the accent chair. I wasn't sure where exactly I fit, so I sat on the floor next to Finn. As I retold the horrible tale that happened only moments prior, he gathered me in his arms and pulled me against his chest. It doesn't mean anything. He was just trying to console me. I don't know where we stand now that we are home and facing reality.

I inhale a deep breath once I've caught everyone up, and Finn places a kiss to the back of my head.

All of us have a serious discussion about what needs to be done. Jill takes photos of her son's face. Burt makes calls to find the best lawyer. Finn and I spend the rest of the afternoon filing a police report at the local station.

I insisted my mom come, but she refused. I try to be sympathetic toward her, choosing to leave with us today was a big step in itself for her. Going to the police station with us would mean finally accepting she'd been abused. She needs time, so I respect her wishes to stay back.

Finn and I told a police officer what happened. He took pictures of Finn's face, but when I pulled up the video I took earlier in the day, my heart sank. It had all been for nothing. The footage was so blurry from my trembling, the audio only picked up my panicked breaths. The police report wasn't enough evidence to lock Jason up.

The next morning, all of us eat breakfast together, deciding to take a break from how serious everything truly is, even just for the duration of this meal.

"Coffee?" Jill offers everyone.

I'm the only one who declines. Once Finn takes a sip from his turquoise mug, a bright smile overtakes his face.

"This is the best stuff I've ever tasted." He pauses for a moment then says, "Well, maybe not the best." He winks at me when no one is watching.

My face heats.

Finn chuckles then scoots his seat as close to mine as possible. He rests his arm across the back of my chair, surprising me when he places a kiss to the top of my head.

Jill glances at Burt, gets up, and leaves.

"That was weird," Finn whispers into my hair, then takes a bite of his bagel.

She comes back only a moment later, giving her husband an eyeroll, and then a ten-dollar bill.

"Thank you very much," Burt says to his wife, and then looks at Finn and I, "And thank *you*." He inspects his money with a pleased smile.

"What the fuck is going on here?" Finn mock gasps when I jam my elbow into him. I think he got a little too used to cursing in front of Charlie, but these are the Walkers. A picture-perfect family that frowns upon cursing.

It's a mystery to me how we ended up as friends to begin with. Our families were from two different planets.

No.

Galaxies.

"Oh nothing, son. Just a friendly bet between your mother and I." He wraps an arm around her, placing a smug kiss to her cheek.

She gives him yet another playful eyeroll before explaining. "Burt here was convinced the past ten years that, well, you two would end up as…" She shakes her head searching for the right words. "More than friends."

I wait for Finn to correct his parents' judgement, my entire body tensing like I've been turned to stone by Medusa.

Burt continues, "And of course, your mother just *had* to disagree with me."

"Has it ever occurred to you that I may have my own thoughts and opinions. Not everything that leaves my mouth is just to spite you," Jill rants.

"Oh, come on, Jill. There's no way you never caught on to these two." My mom finally joins the conversation, breaking out of her shell.

Jill looks at my mom, completely dumbfounded. The red that paints my face moves all the way down my body, I realize as I glance at my splotchy arms.

"Finn has been following my daughter around like a lost puppy since I met him," my mom says, like it's been so utterly obvious, taking a sip of coffee.

I'm on the edge of my seat, just waiting for Finn to interrupt them and tell them how stupid the idea of us together is. How stupid I am for imagining it to be real.

"Wait a minute," Finn finally says. "You mean she followed *me* around."

"Nope," my mother says confidently. "I got it right the first time. It didn't take a genius to figure out how head over heels you've been for my daughter." She shrugs, sitting up straighter.

"Apparently it did," Jill says.

Finn's composed laughter disintegrates every bit of tension from my body.

"So let me get one thing straight," Finn says, over our laughter. "You guys *bet* on us?"

"Yup," Burt says.

∾

"Come with me," Finn says out of nowhere. The yellow light from the bathroom I stand in floods his dark bedroom, painting him gold as he rests on his bed.

I comb through my hair in an attempt to ease my mind, but the truth is there are just way too many emotions in this tiny body of mine. I stare back at myself in the mirror, purple hollows out my eyes like I haven't slept in days.

"Where?" I ask.

"You know where, Adeline," he says in this low, raspy voice.

I sigh, setting the comb onto the vanity of his bathroom. "I couldn't leave my mother before, and I certainly can't leave her now," I say, tears stinging my eyes because going to FSU with him could change everything.

I could finally be a nineteen-year-old girl in college instead of my mother's caregiver.

She might be sober for now, but even if she stayed sober, Jason is here, and there's nothing I can do about it with the little evidence we have.

Right when hope starts to light up my life, something always creeps in to steal it away.

I hear Finn shuffling from his bed, and when I look at him, he's walking toward me, then behind me. I stop breathing when his stomach grazes my back. Finn spins me around.

We are touching almost everywhere.

His head is tilted down, he glances at me through pleading eyelashes. "They are both adults, Adeline," he says. *"Please."*

I would follow you into a hurricane if it meant being with you a little while longer. I peer down. "Why?" I ask.

His eyes scatter across my face, like they are examining

every edge and contour. "Why?" he repeats with a sarcastic laugh. "Because I want you to."

I'm in a daze looking at him this close up. "Why?" I ask again.

"Because."

"*Why?*"

"Because I do, Adeline, that's why."

I force out a breath. "Well, do you want me there because I'm your best friend and you miss me? Or is there another reason?" I bite my lip, realizing the recent circumstances of my life has done something strange to my filter. Maybe I've got nothing left to lose.

He reels back an inch, not saying anything.

All my fears catch up to me in this moment. He's left us in Authensville, and the worst part is there was a final moment of us together that I hadn't realized was our end. If I had, I would've memorized every detail of it.

We agreed things would be back to normal once we returned home, and that's exactly what he's trying to do.

My chest caves, it feels like my heart is an avalanche. I know he's just honoring the fling, but there was a moment where I truly believed he would want me beyond that. I push at his chest to leave, but his hands encage my wrists, trapping me in place.

His eyes turn glassy. "Don't go." His voice cracks. "I'm sorry," he says, letting my wrists go and grabbing the arch of my back, pulling me closer. "I know you wanted a fling, but God, agreeing to that with you was the worst decision I've ever made."

I shatter.

He holds me tighter when he says, "I knew from the start how much it would break me to go back to being friends. I knew but I still agreed because even a few weeks with you is worth the lifetime of misery that follows. God, Adeline, I wasn't failing economics. I took the summer off because I was so miserable being away. Every day without you is like a fist in my chest squeezing my lungs. It was unbearable, but it let up the moment I saw you in the parking lot. I could finally draw a full breath." He pinches my chin, angling my face so our gazes meet, "I know this is the last thing you would want to hear from your summer fling…" He hesitates. "So I would understand if you needed some space." He releases me and takes two steps back.

A tear rolls down my face, then another. I whisper, "What are you telling me?"

He sighs, "I can't even look at another girl because my mind returns to auburn hair, and blushed skin scented with vanilla." He laughs without humor. "I have dreams where you're my girlfriend or my bride or my senile wife… Hell, my roommate even knows your name from hearing me talk in my sleep.

"I fell in love with you a very long time ago, Adeline." There's a long pause, my heart doesn't even beat. "I love you as a person, a friend, and as the other half of my soul." His voice breaks, "I've loved you long before I knew what the word meant, so when you said you wanted a fling, I talked myself into believing it wouldn't end this way for me…" his eyes glass over but they never leave mine, "To experience what it would be like to be loved by you too, even if it was for pretend."

There are a million words whirling throughout my mind like a tornado, so fast I can't grab a single one. I'm speechless, but Finn keeps going, "And now—" his voice breaks as if he's in pain, "I know exactly how you sound when we make love. You gaze up at me as if…as if you love me too, and—"

"I do." The words fall from my lips, Finn's eyebrows bunch together, he shakes his head as if he didn't hear me correctly, so I whisper, "I love you."

His expression is frozen in what seems like denial. I take two steps, eating away the distance between us. I reach for his hand and place it over my heart that beats so rapidly for him. "This is what you do to me."

His eyes are filled with emotion as he watches me, so I keep going, "You look at me and my stomach flips. You laugh and I forget everything that's wrong in the world. And when you touch me, it feels like I'm free falling." I step even closer, so we are pressed together. "You're the only person in the world who brought light into the worst years of my life. You know me better than anyone."

He moves his hand up my sternum and around the back of my neck, holding me tenderly. I say carefully, "I've fallen in love with you little by little each day we've known each other... I just hadn't realized until I saw you again this summer. It was like ten years' worth of love caught up to me all at once." I drag my palms up his chest and wrap them around the back of his neck, similarly to the way he holds me.

He leans down so our foreheads press together.

"I never wanted a fling with you, I just didn't know what else to do. I wanted to be with you, but I was so scared of your rejection that I—" I never finish that sentence, Finn lips crash into mine in a wave of dizzying passion. He's urging his tongue past my lips and devouring me.

I swallow Finn's moan, similar to a sigh of relief. His arms wrap around me so tightly I can hardly breathe, but I've never felt such excitement...such arousal...such *love*.

"I love you," he says desperately between kisses. Like

whatever is happening is moments from an end. Like he's trying to fit everything he's ever wanted into seconds.

The words heat up at the pit of my stomach, fueling my desire further.

He sweeps me off my feet, and the next thing I know I'm beneath him on his bed. "I got my wish, you know." he says.

"What wish?" I ask out of breath while he kisses my neck tenderly.

"Well," he starts, "I've learned every inch of your body. There's a tan line in place of that green bikini you always wear." His face hovers over mine, eyes shut. "A constellation of light brown freckles between your perky breasts, the left one is slightly larger than the right."

I self-consciously bring my hand to my chest even though I'm fully clothed. With his eyes shut he catches my wrist and gently brings it to my side.

"Your hip bone juts out, casting the slightest shadow along your soft skin." He smiles as if remembering something to himself.

"Wha—"

"I can close my eyes and see beneath your clothes, just like I wanted." Amber eyes open and glimmer with adoration looking down at me. "You wrinkle your nose when you lie," he continues, placing a ghost of a kiss to the tip of my nose. "When you're excited you squeeze your hands together, like you're trying to contain it." He gently laughs, resting his forehead against mine. "And when you told me you loved me, there was fire in your eyes."

A rainstorm of emotions pours down on me. My nose burns and a wet tear slides down the side of my face, falling right into Finn's hands.

"I've fallen in love with every part of you." He kisses me

strongly, firm hands touching me everywhere. "Just to be clear," he pauses, eyebrows bunched together, "the fling is over. I want to be your boyfriend and eventually your husband. I want to be the old man sitting beside you in a rocking chair sixty years from now still bantering with you over everything." He smiles. "I want to be your best friend and the love of your life."

There are no words. I am nodding—fast. He interrupts my emotion filled laugh with a kiss.

My clothes are gone, along with his, and he makes love to me like he's been starved of it for years. I lean into his hand that cups my face. Our love is euphoric. It washes over me…

Through me.

I'm so submerged and consumed by it that I can't tell where I end, and Finn begins. Together we're one.

24

I haven't seen Finn since last night. He woke up early to run errands with his parents. I felt a gentle kiss on my forehead sometime during my sleep, probably him saying goodbye.

It feels wrong being in the Walkers' house while they aren't here. My stomach twists and growls at me. The tile is cold beneath my feet as I walk into the kitchen, open the fridge, and pull the tray of eggs out.

I open almost every cabinet and drawer, unable to find a pan to cook the eggs. I could call Finn, but I don't want to bother him with something so insignificant. I put the eggs back and sigh; there's a bagel in the pantry, but it's the last one. My stomach growls some more, like there's a rabid beast living within me.

"Morning," my mom says, coming into the kitchen still in her pajamas, hair knotted against her head and purple rings around her eyes.

I close the pantry, and fill a glass with water to hold me over. Maybe I'll grab drive through, but as the thought of getting in my car to get food comes, I remember the orange juice in my fridge and the pancake mix in my pantry. My stomach rumbles so loud my mom looks at me with humor.

"I want pancakes," I state, leaning against the cool granite of the Walker's kitchen counters.

"Do they have pancake mix?" my mom asks, wrapping her arms around herself.

"We do, at our house. And orange juice. That is, unless Jason drank it." I push off the counter, walking closer to my mom. "Want to go outside? You look cold." I gesture to the goosebumps along her arms and the way she tries to rub them away with friction.

She doesn't respond, but she follows me out the sliding glass doors.

The sun is naked today, without a single cloud to conceal its heat.

"What's the plan?" I ask a little too harshly, the beast within my stomach controlling my words and the feeling of being too hot making me the worst version of myself.

I try to push past the aggravation occurring within my body, but this conversation can't wait another minute. We need a plan. We need Jason gone.

My mom won't look me in the eye, she shrugs her shoulders and kicks a pebble by her foot.

"We can't stay with the Walkers forever. Sooner or later, we are going to need to go back to our own house." I take a step closer to her and place a hand on her shoulder. "Without Jason living in it."

She focuses past me. "Adeline—" She shakes her head. "I think you should give him a chance—"

I interrupt, "No." I ignore the sweat beading off her forehead, I hadn't even asked her how rehab went, or had the chance to really speak to her about how she's feeling.

What she's going through. My head pounds so loudly, it's all I can focus on.

"I know it's a lot to take in." She lightly caresses my head like I'm a child who hasn't gotten her way. "Him being here and everything, but we can't make him leave. It's his house as much as it's ours."

"Mom, you aren't in your right mind." My voice doesn't belong to me. This one is frantic and shaky. "I don't know exactly what went down. He found you at your lowest. Made you feel weak, like you were nothing without him. Am I right?"

She fumbles backward, as if my words are punching her in the gut. "Adeline—"

"Don't you get it?" I barely take a moment to breathe before I start again.

She just blinks. She doesn't try to interrupt me.

"Jason abused you, Mom. For years. You jumped every time you heard a loud noise, you had bruises all over your body, your life didn't even belong to you."

All she does is look at the ground.

"He broke you down until you felt like you were nothing. You couldn't leave him, not even for *me*." My voice breaks. I point toward myself, feeling every ounce of pain she made me feel. It barrels into me all at once. I've always tried to push it down, always knew it wasn't as simple as leaving. But here I stand for the first time in my life, angry at my mother for not putting me first.

For allowing me to witness everything that I did.

For having a child with a man like Jason.

Hurt and betrayal bubble up inside me. I back away a little.

I will never allow my children to be fathered by someone that hurts me, someone capable of making me feel like I'm nothing. I'll die before letting my future children feel even an ounce of the pain I've survived.

I can only see her silhouette now, as my eyes fill with more and more angry tears. She's just a blurry blob of color when she mutters, "I'm sorry."

I back away a little more, tears pricking my eyes. Emotions I've kept buried deep down take over.

"Please, just listen to me." My mother uses her calm voice on me, the one she hoped would seep into my father's temper tantrums.

I can't stop.

Whatever meltdown my body is unleashing, I can't control it. I can't put out the fire that burns within me. It has too much control over me.

"Let me just explain—"

I shove her outstretched hand away from me. The world turns red and everything else fades away. "Just when I had hope we could ever be more than an addict mother and her neglected daughter, you take back the person who destroyed us."

I don't look at her, I just let everything out at once, hoping to feel relief from the words. "I don't know what's worse, the fact that you neglected me all my life or the relief I felt when you went to rehab and weren't my burden to keep anymore!"

"That's enough," Finn's firm voice breaks through my hysteria.

I blink away my temper as fast as it was brought on. I glance back and forth between Finn who must've just got home, and my mother.

I've never seen her so broken. Her faraway expression and wet cheeks make me hate myself. There's not a single part of me that's relieved from saying the words that caused the pain written all over her face.

I leave my body in that moment, watching myself from a bird's eye view. The way I let my anger and hurt speak for me...

I am no better than Jason.

Dissociated completely, I give Finn a blank expression before entering the house and leaving through the front door.

If I want Jason out of my house, I'll just have to do it myself.

I only get three feet from the Walker's yard before Finn is right beside me, matching my fast strides. "Where are you going, love?"

"Home."

"Okay... And what do you plan on doing when you get there?"

I stop walking and face him. Realizing how pathetic and thoughtless my plan was. What was I going to do anyway? Scream at the man until he packed his bags and goes on his merry way? That's not how things work in the real world. Maybe in one of my fiction reads, but I live in the world where my father leaves scars on my mother.

Finn must read every thought from my facial expression because he says, "We'll get rid of him. Together. Once we've figured out a safe way to do so." He brushes my cheek lightly with the tips of his fingers, the touch reminds my body of what he can make me feel.

"I don't know what I was thinking," I admit. Tears pool in my eyes and slide down my cheeks.

"You weren't, love. You weren't," Finn coos, pulling me into his arms.

I cry for what feels like eternity before either of us say

another word. Embarrassment and regret tear me apart. I'm so ashamed. I will fully understand if Finn seeing me like this drains his feelings for me.

"About what happened with your mom," Finn starts.

I squeeze my eyes shut. Remembering how the hurtful words tasted as I spoke them. Preparing myself to hear Finn's *I'm not interested in you anymore*.

"You were hurt. She'll understand," he says instead.

I don't deserve to be let off the hook that easily. I deserve ridicule and shame. And no matter how much I apologize to my mom, it won't make the words any less true. You can't take back words, and you can't deny them if they're true.

"I meant what I said," I whisper, as if I were spilling out all of my sins. Afraid God might hear them and shun me away.

"I know." He cups my jaw. "And that's okay." He softly smiles.

The world isn't just black and white after all. I'm allowed to think and feel the way I do toward my mother, given the circumstances I was delt, while loving her at the same time. Yes, she let Jason back in. Yes, she drank herself into poor health. But no one does those things without reason. Maybe once I hear her side, I'll be able to be rid of this weight that's been pulling me down since I was a little girl.

And then maybe, just maybe, I'll find forgiveness.

Maybe I can finally heal.

It's been three days since the blow out with my mom. Three day's we've been tiptoeing around one another in a house that isn't ours. Three days of wishing I could go back in time and stop myself from adding lighter fluid to the devastating forest fire that is our relationship.

I should've waited to have that conversation with her. I couldn't have chosen a worse time—with her just out of rehab, still incredibly vulnerable mentally and physically, and with Jason doing God only knows what to her. I'm the worst person.

The worst daughter.

I inhale, trying to pull confidence from a source that doesn't exist. I grip the sink, and stare at my reflection. I pull my messy hair out of the bun that lays on top of my head, the crazy red strands float around my face. This girl in the mirror looks fierce. Fiery. Like one wrong look at her and she'll devour you whole like a lioness.

Looks can be deceiving.

My shoulders sink and my eyes drop to my nails that are bitten to the nailbed.

Inhale.

Exhale.

Repeat.

I need answers. I need to understand what my mother is going through. How did Jason brainwash her again?

Once I can grasp how far he's dug into her, I can finally untangle the knot of lies she's been convinced are truths. Maybe once I can erase Jason altogether, it will be enough for her to gather the strength to heal. To heal herself so in time *we* can heal.

No matter how much the truth might pain me, I must know. I'm the only one who has a chance to fix this huge mess that is my life, that is my mother's life.

"Knock-knock." Finn's knuckles tap on the door frame of his bathroom.

I take in his attire. Loose army green joggers hang low on his hips. A black cotton T-shirt grips his biceps and shoulders. An expression of pure adoration and love glimmers in his eyes.

Ever since we told each other how we feel, we can't keep the touching and flirting away, despite the circumstances of my life. He's a trooper for sticking around. *There are good guys out there* he told me not too long ago.

You are a good guy, Finn Walker.

"Hey." I smile.

"Hey." He lifts me in one swift motion, resting my butt on the edge of the sink. "Did I tell you that you look beautiful today?" he whispers against my lips, closing the space before I get the chance to answer.

I gently push his chest, separating from his hungry kiss. "I'm going to talk to my mom."

He doesn't back away. His eyes shift from hungry to searching. He assesses me, trying to figure out my state of mind. I put on my best poker face, maybe I can appear confident without actually feeling it.

"You'll do great," he says with ease.

I guess my poker face is strong after all. "I'm scared."

He brings my hand away from his back, placing gentle kisses along each knuckle. "Do you want me to be there?" he offers, but I immediately shake my head.

"No." I have to do this by myself. I can be brave. I have to be.

"I'll be close by, the second you want me I'm yours," he promises, kissing my lips.

I savor the taste of him. Our chests move in the same heavy pattern. I hop off the sink and make my way past him.

Downstairs is empty. Burt and Jill are at work. The

search for my mom ends quickly as I look out the sliding glass doors. She lays on a lounge chair in the backyard, with a mug in hand.

When I step outside, the hot patio burns my bare feet. I make my way into her view, and she jumps a little, as if my presence was unexpected. Startling.

"I'll just finish my coffee inside—" She starts to sit up, but I place a gentle hand to her shoulder, gesturing for her to stay.

"I'm sorry, Mom. The things I said were horrible." I stiffen when she grabs my hand, holding it.

"I'm not upset with you," she says so maternally I almost lose balance. "I know what you said was how you felt, and all I saw was passion behind your words. You were angry and hurt, rightfully so. I'm the one who should be apologizing to you." She sets her coffee on the ground and sits up.

I grab a patio chair that's only a few feet away and sit across her.

"I haven't been the best mother to you, Adeline. But I don't want you to hate me." She chokes over the last words. Her fair skin blotches with red.

"I could never hate you." It comes out as a whisper.

"Your dad—" She shakes her head. "Jason. He started sending me letters four months ago."

Something inside me sinks.

I should've known, but I had no idea he'd been lurking in the shadows for that long.

"The first letter had a thousand dollars in it." She looks around, uneasy. "I kept the money and threw away the handwritten note as soon as I saw who the sender was."

A thousand dollars? Jason never had that kind of money to be giving out.

"A few days later, another envelope from him came in the mail. I decided I would skim the letter, maybe he was dying or something." She clears her throat. "He was sorry, Adeline. He apologized to me. For hurting me. I finally read the words I've spent years waiting for."

I can't look at her anymore. In this vulnerable state, she seems so fragile. I'm afraid the slightest breeze will crumble her into nothing.

"He said he changed, in that second letter. Then the third letter came, with even more money." Her voice shakes so much it's hard to make out what she is saying. "He told me he knew he messed up. He was a bad dad but an even worse husband."

Letters and money.

Is that the true driving force that made her decide to get clean? Not her daughter begging her to stay alive so she could be there to walk her down the aisle at her wedding. Not meeting her grandchildren. Just more promises from the man who abused her mind, body, and soul for years.

"I didn't believe him. Not with those first three letters. But then the fourth letter came, with promises of a future. He said he would make it up to us. That he would prove to me he changed."

I finally look back up at the mess she is right now. Oh Mom...

"So, I decided to finish the last of my liquor, finish the last bottle of pills, and try to get clean." She admits exactly what I feared. "But then I overdosed..." Her hands shake, her gaze isn't on me. It's somewhere else, somewhere far away. "I guess he was still my emergency contact since we are still legally married. The hospital called him and kept him updated, and then at the end of my second week in rehab, he showed up to visit."

I've been clueless as to what's been going on this whole time.

"He convinced me to leave with him, to start our future. So, I did."

"You didn't go to rehab for me? Or for yourself?"

"I didn't want him to see how pathetic I had become," she cries.

"Right," is all I can say, massaging my temples.

How can you be there for someone when every word that leaves their mouth guts you from the inside out?

"Do you hate me?" she whispers, finally meeting my eyes.

I don't even blink. "No." I bring my thumb up to my mouth to bite the nail, but I stop myself. "I'm just hurt."

Quiet sobs shake her, and she hides her shame away in her hands.

"Keep going. I need to know everything," I say numbly.

She sniffs and wipes her eyes, trying to gather her composure. "The fifth letter came when I was in rehab, it had a ten-thousand-dollar check attached. It felt like everything I have ever dreamt of was at my fingertips. The very thing that destroyed me promised to put me back together." She sighs. "I was broken, Adeline. He was my only saving grace...or so I thought."

I'm an empty shell. I've been cracked open, my yolk dried out, and then poorly glued back together again. I feel nothing.

"The first few days felt too good to be true. He was so kind and affectionate. He took me shopping and we went on dates. Actual dates, Adeline. He never once made the effort to take me out before, but he finally was." She stands up now, walking back and forth trying to appear okay. "I felt like my dreams were finally coming true. But then..."

You know that moment, when your heart stops beating in your chest, because you know you're about to hear something tragic?

"He took me to Key West for the weekend. The place we had reservations at gave up our table, the only place left to eat dinner was a bar. It was like the universe was laughing at me. There was alcohol everywhere. The smell, the way it affected the people around us. Jason ordered whiskey, Adeline. It was on his breath; the smell and the craving made me insane." Her brows pull together in regret. "That's when someone tapped me on the shoulder. An old friend from college, a guy friend. I wasn't in my right mind, I couldn't think. I introduced Jason as my friend, instead of my husband."

An angry breeze flips my hair in every direction. A gray cloud hides the sun, and a chill breaks out across my entire being.

"He made us leave after that, without a single bite to eat." She speaks so fast now, it's hard to keep up. Physically, she's here, but her mind is somewhere else. "He sped between the Saturday night traffic. In and out of cars, missing them by a hair." She trembles in fear, like she's back there again. "When we got to the hotel, I was terrified of the man. But I was trapped, I followed him through the lobby to our suite. We were the only people staying on the 10th floor. He reserved every room on our floor so we could be alone."

I hadn't realized until now, my body shakes with hers. Tears roll along my cheeks. I hurt right with her.

"He pushed me against the wall of our hotel room in what I had hoped was an attempt to be seductive." She tries to laugh at that, tries to ease the heaviness of it all, as if it wasn't a big deal. As if it was nothing.

"But then he wrapped his entire hand around my throat and *squeezed*." Her voice is so choppy, each syllable sends shock waves through me. I want to reach up and hug her, to hold her, but I'm trapped in place.

"He squeezed so hard, taking the air out of my lungs. I thought of you, puffin. How disappointed you'd be when you found out how I died. How naïve I was to fall back into the cycle." She stands now, pacing, like there's too much happening within her body to sit still.

I can almost feel it. The sensation of someone strangling you, the instinct of trying to fight for your life but not being strong enough. That's why she's been wearing turtlenecks everyday. To hide the bruises.

"*Mom.*" I cry. I break. I fucking die.

"Something clicked behind his eyes. He let me go, and I thought it was over. I felt hopeful, and then he kneed me with everything he had in him, right to my side." She pulls up her shirt and my eyes zero in on the deep purple bruising beneath her skin. My heart stops beating.

"The back of my head slammed into the wall faster than I could register what was happening to me. What was being done to me." She backs up, resting her body against a pillar, like the words are just too much to be able to hold herself up on her own.

"I didn't feel anything though, I guess my body had enough adrenaline and self-preservation to shield me the only way it could." Her back slides down the pillar and she sinks into the ground. I can tell that's where she would rather be right now.

I should do something, say something. But what?

"He said he wanted to put a baby in me—" Her voice comes out so high pitched it stings my ear drums and I flinch.

"He said I'd never be able to leave him if I was carrying his child. He ripped off my jeans and—" She disintegrates right before my eyes.

"Oh my god." I cover my mouth and run to the bushes. I vomit everything in my stomach, and rest there for a second. I finally gain the strength to stand up and then I hold my mother and promise to myself that I'll never let go again.

If there's one thing I know, it's that Jason can't get away with this. I won't let him.

I quietly walk into Finn's bedroom in a daze. I feel a wave of relief when I see him sitting at his desk. He types away on his laptop. "Hey, love. How did it go—" He turns his head, and his eyes go wide. "Shh, it's okay." He rushes to me.

I look at him, puzzled. Then I feel water drip onto my neck, I glance up. No leaks in the ceiling. I touch my cheek and realize I have been crying.

We sit on his bed, everything that just happened pours out of me. I give Finn the short version quietly, trying not to let my emotions take over. My mom wanted to sleep the rest of the day. She rests only a few doors down on an air mattress in the Walkers' home gym.

"I just don't get it," I say. "How can somebody do that to another person? How can anyone treat someone so cruelly and feel no remorse? How could Jason look into my mother's eyes and hurt her in such unthinkable ways? I just —" I stumble over my words, "I can't fathom it." I laugh without humor, "I have no words to describe how much I...what I *feel* toward him."

"Oh, I can think of some words." Finn finally breaks his

far away glare. His knuckles are white, gripping the blue comforter we sit on. "It's not about me, though."

For some reason, his words jolt me a little. "Tell me," I urge him. "I think it would help me to hear."

"There's not a single word in the English dictionary to describe just how much I loathe that man." He spits the words out.

"Why?" For some reason, I want to hear Finn get angry about Jason. It feels righteous to hear someone speak thoughts I've left buried deep inside myself for my *entire* life.

"Why? Where do I even start?" I can tell by the way he speaks so swiftly this is something he's thought about before. Something he's gotten angry about in the past. "He's the worst kind of person, Adeline. The only thing he gives to the people around him is pain and trauma. A true man doesn't have to make himself frightening and inflict pain onto his wife and *fucking* daughter. It's pathetic." He inhales slowly.

I watch, mesmerized at the way he calmly collects himself, despite the rage I can clearly see burning him up.

My dad probably would've thrown something by now.

"I saw what you went through, Adeline. He had a tight hold on your well-being for so long. He hurt you on such a cellular level, and I wanted to fight it. For you." He grabs my hand and squeezes it.

"I always felt like I had to be the knight in shining armor. To protect your heart from his abuse, but then as I got older, I realized how stupid that was. For me to think you needed me for protection. I watched in fucking awe as you fought back."

Fought back? I didn't, though. I was scared and I hid. I

would let him yell at me and then walk away like his words didn't break me in half.

"You did," he says, so confidently. He must see the confusion on my face. "Adeline, he tried to kill your spirit and you did the complete opposite. You kept smiling. You kept laughing, and most of all, you kept loving. You are *good*, my love. You spread your light everywhere you go, that's how you fought." He tips my chin up so I meet his eyes. "That's how you won."

I grab his face with urgency and press my lips into his. It's sloppy and uncoordinated, and it burns every inch of me with passion. I am so fucking in love with this man. He's everything Jason isn't, and I am so thankful I went down a different path than my mother. I could've so easily fallen into the wrong type of love, finding someone just like my dad and feeling comfortable in the familiarity.

As Finn pulls me onto his lap, warmth fills me from head to toe. I know this is what love should feel like. And I deserve the real thing.

I have since I was a little girl.

So does my mom, and I hope that one day she will find it.

"This doesn't feel right," I say from Finn's passenger seat.

"Adeline, if we let every bad thing that happens in the world keep us from having fun, we are never going to live the life we deserve." He puts on a pair of aviator sunglasses, then looks at me.

I see my disheveled hair and shallow eyes in the reflection. I bring my hand up to smooth my hair. "But my mom—"

"Wants you to have fun. Come on, love. Live in the moment promised with me." He smiles seductively.

I look at him warily, but I accept his outstretched hand, and get out of the car.

The salt fills the air, and I can already sense the way I am going to feel when I finally dive into the calm sea. Maybe its effects will wear off on me.

A gust of wind blows my hair and takes away the surrounding sound. All I hear is mother nature singing her lullaby.

After a few more talks with my mom, she quickly realized what she has with Jason is not love. It's abuse. He's blown up my mom's phone and mine with texts asking where we were along with several angry voicemails. I took the liberty of blocking his number, and my mom handed me her phone in case she was tempted to unblock him in a moment of weakness.

I thought it was the strongest thing ever.

We reached out to a lawyer. I took pictures of the bruises on my mother's ribs and the one on Finn's cheekbone which is now a faded yellow. I put all the evidence that Jason hurt the people I love in a folder on my laptop, along with the video I took when he beat up Finn.

The lawyer Burt found told me what I already knew. The video was pretty much useless. We might be able to use the pictures and claim we feel unsafe around him to file for a restraining order, but I want him locked away so he can never hurt so much as a fly again.

But we need better evidence.

My legs burn with overflowing energy, I run. I run so fast, Finn struggles to keep up with me.

My laugh echoes in the wind embracing me and I don't stop. Not when my lungs beg for more air, not when my muscles strain to keep up, and not when I hear Finn dropping towels in the sand.

The setting sun airbrushes the world around me with gold. The sand looks less grainy, the water is as flat as glass, the palm trees are as perfect as a painting.

When my feet are submerged in the gentle waves that meet the shore, I slow to a walk. Finn was right, I needed this.

"Wow." I jump at Finn's sudden closeness.

He stills me before I can turn around. He tilts my chin, that begs to see him, back toward the ocean. The surface of him presses against my back, my head goes with the heavy fall of his chest.

"You're the most beautiful girl in this whole fucking world, Adeline." His hands skim the hem of my shirt, lightly brushing the skin on my abdomen.

"I'm not," I whisper, letting my head lull back as my eyes fall heavy against his touch.

"Oh, yes you are." His breath hits the side of my neck, sending tingles exploding throughout my body.

The air leaves my lungs, and everything spins as he swiftly turns me around. Before I can even process the shift in position, his lips are on mine and everything surrounding us disappears.

He kisses me like it's the first time, always. He picks me up in front piggyback, and then takes off running.

I laugh into the nape of his neck, and a rush of giddiness overtakes me. I squeeze my arms tight around him to keep from falling.

A flock of seagulls rain on our parade—well that's one way to put it. I reel back, eyes wide and burst out into heavy laughter.

Finn doesn't laugh, but his eyes are as wide as mine as

he sets me down. He doesn't break eye contact as he brings a hand to the top of his head. He slowly examines the white on his fingers: seagull poop. "Those mother fuckers." He takes his time, growling out the words.

I grip onto my kneecaps and let the waves of laughter roll out of me.

"You done?" I hear Finn's voice, but I can't stop laughing. Not until warm, wet fingertips brush my cheek. "Finn!"

Now he's the one laughing.

I mutter a colorful string of curse words under my breath, then run to the ocean to wash the bird poop off my cheek.

Finn follows suit. I dive beneath the surface too many times to count, Finn by my side doing the same.

"You see that bridge over there?" I ask between plunges.

"Yeah, what about it?" He tilts his head, jumping up and down trying to get the salt water out of his ears.

"You think you can just wipe seagull shit on my face and not suffer the repercussions?" I raise my eyebrows in a playful challenge and watch Finn's eyes go wide in realization.

"Hell no." He slowly backs away toward the shore but I'm a faster swimmer.

I dive beneath the blue depths, toward the small island only fifteen feet out.

When I break the surface, I hear Finn's, "Fuck." Followed by a splash, and before I know it, I feel a presence behind me.

I walk up the incline of the sand, until I'm fully out of the water.

"Don't even think about it, Adeline," he says firmly, running a hand through his wet hair to get it off his forehead.

I ignore him with a painfully wide smile on my face, I grab onto the large rocks that make up the beginning of the jetty, climbing them with excitement.

"Come back!" Finn calls as if he was still standing in the sand, but he isn't. He's climbing the rocks, following me to the bridge that connects the small island to the beach.

There's a three-foot stretch between the rocks and the concrete ledge of the bridge. I grip the bridge and hoist myself up and let out a murderous laugh.

"Quit evil laughing up there," Finn says, exacerbated behind me.

I turn around, kneeling on one knee with an outstretched hand to help Finn onto the bridge. He rolls his eyes and easily pulls himself onto the tall platform without my help.

Rude.

"Okay, we're here. Can we leave now?" He lets out a breath.

I slowly ease backwards to the edge of the bridge, until my heels are over the ledge. It's a good twenty-foot drop.

"Adeline, don't—" He rushes to me with his arm out as if he could grab me.

I step back with a screech and the thrill of adrenaline invigorates me.

The loud splash of my body against the ocean knocks the air out of my lungs. I guess it takes the pure silence of being underwater with salt burning my nostrils to make me feel alive again.

But hey, I'll take it.

I kick my legs and breech the surface. Finn's still on the bridge, counting. "Eight…nine…ten." He jumps over the ledge.

I laugh when he comes up, gasping for air as if he's been free diving for three minutes straight.

I squeeze my eyes shut as he splashes my face. "Just for that, the last one back buys pizza."

"What?" Finn asks, but I'm gone without answering.

I push and kick through the water until I reach the sand of the beach. Finn doesn't catch up to me for another twenty seconds.

He's soaking wet with shoulders slumped and an even expression. "We're getting a full meat lovers," he says as he passes me on the way to his car.

I love this man, even when he's a grump.

Hell, that might be my favorite version of him.

"So, this is the place you two were always running off to?" My mom observes the exterior of Pete's. The place I've spent working endless hours for but never felt fulfilled.

"It's the best pizza place in town," Finn says, proudly grabbing my hand and pulling me close to him as we walk toward the door.

Finn holds the door for my mom and me. The jingle at the top always boosts my mood somehow. It reminds me of Pavlov's experiment, and I salivate every time I hear the welcoming jingle on Pete's door.

Or maybe it's the overpowering smell of pizza. Or possibly it's the happy atmosphere I grew to love Finn in.

I walk in after my mom, allowing Finn to grab my hand as we take our usual booth.

"Well, well, well. If it isn't my favorite customer and employee," Pete says, walking toward our table with a bright smile plastered to his face. The most prominent creases in his skin are the crow's feet and smile lines, as if he's spent the last seventy years smiling. "And you must be our Adeline's mom." He offers a hand to shake, and my mother takes it happily.

"Marsha." She smiles.

"Pleasure to meet you, Marsha. I'm Pete." He sets a menu down in front of my mom, leaving the table bare in front of Finn and me. We know that menu on the backs of our hands, but we stick to half meat lover's, half cheese.

But Pete already knows this.

"Well, well, well. I see the 'engagement' stuck," Pete says to Finn with a wink, noting Finn's arm loosely resting over my shoulders.

"Yessir, it seems to look that way," Finn says, squeezing me a little with pride.

We haven't talked about the future. What will happen when he goes back to school, what will happen to my mom and Jason… Everything still hangs in the air. I try to focus all my attention on the here and now. I can't help but feel doomed. How can this possibly end well? How will I survive if it doesn't?

"Yeah right! If I hadn't made a move at the campsite we wouldn't even be here right now." I point a finger into Finn's chest, and he playfully tosses it aside with laughter.

"I made a move way before that, love. You were just too wrapped up in yourself to realize it."

I scoff.

"Pete, back me up." Finn snaps his fingers, looking to Pete expectantly.

"Hey, hey now." Pete holds his hands up. "I'm just here to look pretty and make pizza."

"Adeline, didn't you say Finn kissed you after he 'proposed'?" My mom joins in on the conversation, remembering what I told her a month ago while we bonded before she left for rehab.

"Yes but—" I start.

"Aha! See, I did make the first move. Point made. We will have a large meet lovers, Pete." Finn eyes me as if he just won some unspoken game. "Go heavy with the mushrooms."

I hate mushrooms.

"I guess I'll need my notepad after all." Pete digs into his apron, pulling out a small note pad and grabs the pen from behind his ear. "I guess all that time away changed the fiery one's appetite?"

"Nope. Finn's just being annoying. Mom, what do you want?" I nudge Finn's side. He mock winces. There, now who's had the last laugh?

"I'll have the chicken parm, please," she says, handing Pete the menu with a polite smile.

"When should I expect to see you back at work, lava girl?" Pete asks easily.

It would be so easy to take this job again and fall into the endless loop of unhappiness I spent so much time in. But maybe comfortability isn't the best thing for me anymore. Being happy is an endless process, and now that I've had a taste, I'm not willing to give it up so easily. This is the part where I put myself first. "You won't." I smile.

Pete slowly nods his head, a smile curling his lips. "Good."

Finn raises an eyebrow at me. I smile and pull my shoulders back. I have no idea where to go from here. My life is a blank canvas and I plan on filling it with every color.

"I expect to be invited to the wedding," Pete says, walking toward the kitchen.

I turn bright red, but Finn is at ease. He gently tugs a strand of my hair. I scooch even closer to him, sagging against him and letting his arms wrap around me.

Pete is back, balancing three cups of water. "Here you ladies go—woah!"

A little girl on roller skates knocks into Pete, sending the last cup of water spilling all over my phone.

A middle-aged woman runs after the little girl, followed by a much older woman who comes straight our way.

"I'm so sorry about that, Addy!" Pete says, handing me his rag that rests on his shoulder.

I shrug him off. It's no big deal.

I slide off my phone case, and a folded picture falls out onto the table. I completely forgot about the black and white photo Charlie gave me. I took it out of the picture frame he gave to me and put it in my phone case. I unfold it, using the rag to gently pat it dry. I set it back on the table while I dry the rest of my phone and the case.

"Kids, I'd like you to meet someone very special. Adeline, Finn, this is Barbra." Pete pulls the older woman to him, placing his hand on the small of her back.

She smiles with the equal amount of joy that Pete always emits.

My mom grabs the photo off the table and gives me a look I can't place.

"Oh, my goodness! It's so great to finally meet the famous Adeline and Finn! Pete's told me so much about you two love birds." She reaches out with both hands to squeeze our cheeks as if we were her own grandchildren.

"Barb is my girlfriend," Pete says so proudly.

Barb introduces us to her daughter and granddaughter who just so happen to be the little girl on the roller skates and the woman chasing her down.

Eventually Pete and Barb's family say their goodbyes and occupy the largest table in the restaurant. I watch from afar at the picture-perfect family Pete plays a role in, and I couldn't be any happier for him. I even feel relieved, knowing he finally has what he's always been silently searching for—companionship.

"Are you crying, love?" Finn brings a thumb to my cheek to catch the fallen tear.

"I'm just so happy for him," I whisper. It's about time I get to cry tears of *joy*.

"I know, my love, me too." He kisses my hair and giggles at me as if I'm the most adorable thing in the room, sobbing over another person's happy ending.

"You okay?" Finn asks.

I look up and realize his question wasn't directed at me. It was directed at my mom, who just stares at the black and white photo.

"Who are these people?" She turns the photo around toward us.

"Oh, that's Charlie," I say.

"Yeah, we stayed with him when we were away in a little town called Authensville," Finn clarifies, and my mom's eyes slightly enlarge.

The town's name leaves a hollowness inside me.

My mom slightly nods as a waitress sets a large pizza between us, along with my mom's chicken parm.

"Who's the girl he's with?" Finn asks casually, grabbing a slice of pizza despite the steam that rolls off it.

"Oh, that's a sore subject," I say, waiting for the pizza to cool before grabbing a slice.

My mom chokes on thin air. She grabs her water and slowly sips it, resting the straw between her teeth to chew.

"Charlie's ex," I whisper, ignoring my mom's weird behavior.

"Oh. The one from the Keys?" Finn asks around a mouthful of food.

"Yeah. She left him heartbroken with no explanation. Kind of a bitchy thing to do." I flinch at how sour the words are on my tongue.

"Hey!" My mom starts. Smoothing over her features, she clears her throat and hands me back the picture.

I cock my head, waiting for her to continue whatever she was about to say.

"Um, she's pretty, that's all." She shrugs, smoothing back her hair. "Maybe you shouldn't call her names," she whispers.

I shrug as if I'm indifferent toward it, but I feel anything but. I almost feel…guilt for calling her names.

But I don't even know her.

There's a dull heaviness to the air as we finish our food. I can't place it, so I ignore it and attempt to act as if it doesn't exist. But it does.

It's in the way my mom's shoulders are stiff, and the way her eyes glass over as if she isn't even here with us.

Finn tries to make polite small talk but fails miserably when I'm the only one to engage in it with him. My mom hardly nods her head as we speak of mundane topics.

It becomes a very uncomfortable afternoon. The drive home is loud with silence. My mom sits in the back seat. Her presence is so heavy, but at the same time she's not even engaging with her surroundings.

I start to worry a little, when we hit a speed bump on

the way to Finn's house. He flew over it a little too fast and the momentum of the car caused us all to jolt in our seats.

I even let out a slight yelp, but my mom remained stoic.

What's going on?

Did she relapse and I didn't notice? Maybe she took something before we left, and it just started to kick in when we were sitting at Pete's.

I glance at her in the reflection of the rear-view mirror, a worry snakes its way into my stomach, wrapping around my intestines.

Fuck.

I knew leaving her today was a bad idea. I should've stayed with her until I knew for sure she was at a good place mentally. I was too busy catching butterflies for my best friend at the beach to realize she had taken opioids.

My blood runs dry.

I've been too preoccupied with Finn to even notice my dad was sending her letters. I didn't notice the change in her. I had no fucking clue of his invisible presence.

But as I look back, he was there all along.

Has Finn innocently been standing behind me, covering my eyes to the truth that's been right in front of me this whole time?

Does my happy ending compromise my mother's?

Everything shifts.

My heart still pounds in my chest, but now it hurts. My lungs still expand with air, but for what? Blood runs through my veins, but it doesn't matter to me.

Everything I've done—every thought, every action—has been out of love. But it's cut the power to all my other senses.

I glance at Finn. His easy expression, laid back and relaxed, loosely holding the steering wheel. What will he look like when I break the heart he so generously let me into? When I tell him it's over, that it has to be over? That we've blindly hurt my mother and inevitably, ourselves, in the process of falling in love?

How silly of me to get wrapped up in having fun, losing sight of everything I've been doing for my mom.

I look out the window, careful to not let Finn see the silent tears that begin to fall.

I knew I wouldn't get a happy ending, and it was only a matter of time until I was handed my tragedy on a silver platter.

The world around me loses its vibrant color, and as if mother nature could reflect my state of mind, a gray cloud rolls in and releases her silent tears.

I don't confront my mom about the drugs or have a chance to talk to Finn. I'm simply a hollow shell that's been gutted too many times to recover, so instead of facing reality I put on my wireless headphones, leaving the Walkers and my mother without so much as a goodbye.

I won't be gone long, so they probably won't even notice I left.

I just need to *breathe.*

I strut down the sidewalk, eyes glued to my phone as I walk aimlessly with my headphones. It's a tough decision, picking a happy song or a sad one.

I doubt any song could uplift my mood, no matter how upbeat it is. If anything, I'll feel like a phony, pretending to be okay, happy even, when I'm on the other end of the emotional spectrum.

I'm broken and soul crushed, so I find a song to match

how I feel. At least I won't feel so alone in this. I crank the volume all the way up, drowning every realness of my reality out.

And then I run.

I read once that running releases feel good hormones in your brain, and until I feel good, I won't stop running.

Or until I pass out.

I don't know how long it's been since I've started, but several songs have begun and ended. My lungs burn. Tiny dots prickle my vision, but I don't stop. I keep running, even when the outer edges of my vision turn black.

I pull out my phone to let my mom know I'll be gone for a little bit longer. The phone shakes so much in my hands as I try to keep my pace that I click on the camera app and my thumb accidently hits the red button.

Sweat drips into my eyes and impairs my vision, and I put my phone in my leggings, but the black edges in my sight take over.

25

I 've always wondered how it would feel to die. Not the part leading up to it, but the actual moment your soul plunges from your body.

As a little girl, I would try to feel the sensations within my—very alive—body. Maybe my stomach would wrap around my heart like I was falling. Or perhaps one second, I would have all five senses and the next I would have a new one. Like instead of sight, I would just *know*... I'd know what was around me, know who I was. Maybe I would just be a conscience without the weight of my own body keeping me in one place. Maybe I'd be everywhere all at once.

Or maybe everything would just fade to black.

It wasn't until this very moment I'd start to wonder the *how*.

How would I die? What would force my soul out of my own body, or better yet...who?

It's dark behind my eyelids, but I'm awake. All my senses slam into me, one by one.

"52nd street. Yup, that's it, I'll let you know when." A voice spits off Finn's house number.

Every single organ inside my body stops functioning, even my heart.

I just…exist.

I can't move, I can only sense my right side against cold tile.

I can't see, I can only smell something metallic burning my nostrils.

I can't scream, I'm stuck in paralysis. Frozen in place.

I open my eyes.

There's a white washing machine against pale blue walls. I'm in my laundry room.

I slowly place my left hand on the ground to boost myself into a sitting position, my muscles scream in agony with each inch of movement. My hair is matted to my head on one side, it's wet and sticky and before I can stop myself, I'm feeling the blood that clumps my hair together. I examine it on my fingers and my stomach twists and bile rises in my throat.

I swallow it back down and force the fight or flight response to keep me focused. I can't be discrete about my sudden consciousness if I am throwing up. Who knows what Jason will do to me once he knows I'm awake.

Okay, okay. *Think*, Adeline.

The injury can't be that bad if I'm awake. I'm in my own house, which gives me the upper hand. Granted, Jason is the one who bought this house.

Fuck. Fuck. *Fuck*.

Okay, okay. I'll put on my big girl pants and just walk out, what's he going to do? Tackle me to the floor and tie me down?

Well, he did kidnap me when I was passed out on a sidewalk and put me in a room with no windows.

I'm lightheaded when I stand so I feel the walls with unsteady hands until I'm holding the cold door handle in my sweaty palm.

With an all-too-loud click, the door is unlatched and the hinges squeak.

I inhale every drop of confidence I can muster and brace myself for what's outside this door. My muscles strain trying to push the door, creating a loud thud every time I push, but it won't open.

A tear rolls down my cheek and my torso constricts in a way that begs to be in the fetal position. I suddenly feel like a little girl again, like I'm two feet tall and stand no chance against the ginormous man who I'm forced to call Dad.

A salty tear slides into my mouth. A heart wrenching sob leaves my throat. "Open this door, Jason!" I scream with everything in me.

But I get no response.

My palms sting with each smack I take out on the door. The thud of whatever blocks it sends my nervous system into turmoil, but I don't stop. I scream with each blow to the door, my blood hotter than hell fire. I throw myself into the door, but it doesn't open.

"Shit." I succumb to the reality that I have no control here. My fate has been unfairly handed over to Jason.

I take four steps back until I feel the opposite wall hit my back, and I slowly slide down to the floor.

Only a second passes, and then something heavy is dragged away from the laundry room door. My heart picks up and slams into my ears.

The door slowly creaks open, in a mocking manner. As if it were that easy all along.

My eyes make the dreadful journey from the stomach-turning boots, dirtied jeans, a beer belly dressed in a wife beater tank top—how disgustingly ironic—and meet crazed eyes.

I stand up and take two shaky steps forward, toward the door and inevitably Jason. He doesn't move a muscle. He just stares at me with blood shot eyes.

I move around his wide frame, inhaling a shaky breath as I graze him, but a rough hand yanks me back by the forearm.

I wince at the soreness that spreads throughout my body.

"If you don't let me go—" My voice trembles.

"What will you do?" he shouts, my back toward him and his mouth only a few inches away from my ear. "But before you answer…" He scrambles through what sounds like his jean pockets. Suddenly I am staring at a phone—his phone—I squint my eyes at the text messages displayed.

Finn's address.

A detailed description of what Finn and my mom look like.

Jason ordering the unknown number to kill Finn on his demand.

All the air leaves the room until I'm left gasping for relief.

52nd street. Yup that's it, I'll let you know when.

No. It can't be. The world around me spins so quickly I'm losing balance. He's texting…a hitman? My dad hired a hitman—someone to kill Finn.

My brain tries to grasp that the person I love the most in this world is unknowingly a call away from death. One call and the person holding me to this earth, like gravity, will be wrongfully taken from me. From his mother and father.

I focus in on the presence who stands behind me, fearful I might not live to see tomorrow. Or even the nightfall.

Jason—my narcissistic and abusive father—just reached a whole new level of insanity. He doesn't just want to injure…he wants to kill.

"You're sick," I seethe, my vision turns red as I shake uncontrollably.

He just grips onto my arm harder. His fingernails break my skin.

I quickly turn around, feeling unsettled with my back toward him. The look in his eye is something I could never imagine in my worst nightmares…the image of someone who's thinking of killing you.

Never in a million years did I think my world would collide with dark things like hitmen.

How can he even afford…*that*?

Now is not the time to dig deep for answers, but I make a mental note to find out the second I'm free. If I ever get that chance.

The corners of his lips curl into a crazed smile.

"I won't hurt your little boyfriend," he coos, bringing fingertips through my auburn hair in an uncharacteristically soothing way.

A cringe ripples through my body and I pull away but not before he yanks me by my hair. My neck is bent in a way that makes me cry out in pain. Tears prick my eyes.

"As long as you return my loving wife back to me," he says.

Over my dead body.

"Oh, and not all fucking brain washed." He lets my hair

go, pushing my chest with strength so I fall back and hit my head against the wall.

I boil over, but he slams the door in my face right as I reach for him. I grab the door handle and push but I'm not fast enough, because it hits something and doesn't budge.

"I'll give you time to think it over," he laughs.

He.

Fucking.

Laughs.

My consciousness comes in waves. I'm in and out of my own impending fate, only able to catch glimpses of it.

Here and there I hear Jason's boots walking back and forth throughout my home. My nervous system knows what those boots mean and tries to protect me by releasing even more fight or flight hormones. But I do neither, I just sit and accept what was done to me.

The happy ending that's being ripped so painfully from me.

I close my eyes and let a hazy memory sweep me up and away from here.

A raspy whisper digs into my subconscious, but not enough to wake me. I welcome it as a part of my dream.

"I shouldn't tell you this, but it's killing me." Finn's voice is comforting, and I try to open my eyes, but I'm tired. We've been on the boat all day. I'm not allowed to sleep at a boy's house, but my mom told my dad I was with a girl friend from school. I'm probably the only girl in tenth grade that's having a sleepover with a boy.

"You are the best thing that has ever happened to me." I

hear a smile in his voice. "You're my favorite person in this entire world."

Something soft presses against my shoulder, followed by a kiss sound. My entire body breaks out into goosebumps. Or maybe this is all just one very vivid dream I'll forget about in the morning.

"Even if all I get to be in this life is your best friend, I'll hang onto that title with pride. I know I may never get to call you mine, but I'm yours. I always have been." Finn's voice has dropped to an almost inaudible volume, as if he knows he's not really talking to me. "Always will be."

My dreams take over, but I still hear his voice.

"I know you are hurting right now, with everything happening at home. It's painful to see you get knocked down, but I know you'll get back up." It's quiet for a moment before the voice starts again. "You always do. I'm amazed every time you brush yourself off and look life straight in the eye with bravery, you are the most amazing woman I've ever seen."

The memory must awaken some dormant part of myself. I inhale a shaky breath, and slowly rise to my feet. I remind myself I'm not that little girl anymore.

I can fight, and I will.

I open the dryer, knowing my mother's habit of leaving clothes in there and forgetting they exist. I grab a T-shirt, wipe the blood off me, pressing the cloth to my injury for a few minutes in hopes it clots.

I can kick and scream and beat at my chest, but that's only going to get me as far as another injury. My head hurts, my muscles scream, all I want to do is shut my eyes and forget this is happening…but I can't.

I refuse to lose without so much as a fight.

Happiness is an endless process and I plan to fight like

hell for it. This isn't the end of my story. I won't allow it to be.

"Jason," I call calmly.

My stomach sinks, I want to tumble over and die picturing the words I'm about to willingly speak.

26

I stare at the door, imagining the way it will slowly creep open. The dead eyes I am going to be forced to peer through, while I sink to his level.

But the door flies open in a quick breath, and I am knocked back by the surprise. I quickly gather myself before he can recognize the shift in my composure.

I didn't notice before, but his skin is modeled with so many broken blood vessels. He looks frail and older than he is. He doesn't feel as scary as he did a little while ago.

Funny how my brain picked this moment to reveal the hidden memory of Finn, as if I subconsciously knew I'd need it on a rainy day.

"Mom's been using drugs, Dad." I contort my face to seem worried, as if I've been thinking this over the entire time I've been locked in my laundry room. I know he knows this, since he's the one who picked her up early from rehab, but I make sure to remind him.

I notice fury building up within his body.

I can almost hear his thoughts. I'm sure they aren't

worried for her, but rather for himself. Like her doing drugs is a disrespect to *him* and *his* property.

I hate him. "It's like ever since you left, she's been so—" I shake my head, and let a tear roll down my face. It's a real tear, from real pain…but it's not attached to the words I'm about to speak. "She's nothing without you. I mean, she takes whatever she can get her hands on just to make it from one day to the next."

His demeanor changes and he slowly walks over to me, grabbing both my hands.

Disgust rolls off my entire body, but I keep my reaction at bay.

"Dad…" I cry, letting him sweep me up into his arms. He holds me rigidly while I weep into nothing in his arms. At least that's what I want him to believe. That I'm nothing without him.

"She needs you so badly." My voice is a broken whisper. "So do I." My hot tears fall onto his shoulder, he slowly releases me, assessing me for cracks of the truth.

But I leave none, I am completely sealed from head to toe with these lies.

"I love you, Dad. Please forgive us for leaving." I want to vomit the words back up, but I'll say them a million times if it means the people I love will be out of harm's way.

"You just needed a push in the right direction. I knew you were just rebelling like every other teenager." He believes his disturbing words, and I let him.

"Let's get your mother and be done with this bullshit," he says like this whole thing was no big deal.

As if he isn't the reason I'm bleeding as we speak.

"Maybe I should be the one to talk to her," I say, pulling an excuse out of thin air. "She's really fragile right now. I think if I asked her to come home, she would without the blink of an eye. But if you're there, she might think you're making me say those things." I gently laugh, "You know how much she hates being told what to do."

He looks at me for twenty long seconds before rolling his eyes. "Fuck. You're right." He holds a finger right up to my face, and in the most threatening voice he says, "I have my guys all over that place, don't go playing some fucking game. You hear me?"

I just nod.

"Oh, and no more seeing the brown-haired boy. That fucking delinquent pisses me off."

I nod again, trying to be as compliant as possible so I can get out of here.

He grinds his teeth, like he's expecting some type of rebuttal from me, so I give him one so he doesn't suspect anything. "But Dad, I like him—"

My eyes are wide with shock as I bring my hand up to my stinging cheek.

He just slapped me.

"I fucking swear to God, Adeline, if you don't do what I fucking tell you, I'll have those guys kill him." He shoots me a glare. "And I'll have them make sure you're watching."

I shudder. "Okay."

He stares me down one last time, before releasing his gaze and stepping aside so I can leave.

I walk at a normal pace toward the front door, trying to seem as normal as possible, despite the urge to sprint. Once I twist the handle, I toss him a wave and a gentle smile. "Be right back, Dad."

He watches me with pride in his murderous eyes, letting me go like I'm his trusted disciple.

I walk casually down the street, but once I make the turn so Jason can no longer see me, I run. I don't have a plan yet. I can't go to the Walkers house and go back to normal. But I have to do something to protect the people I love, even if it means breaking Finn's heart to protect him.

My legs burn and my body is weak, but I don't stop. I can't mess this up, I peek over my shoulder, and when I face forward again I instantly halt.

"Adeline!" Finn rushes to close the gap between our bodies, he cups my small face in his ginormous hands. I watch as his expression slowly breaks down and shatters. "Thank God. Are you okay?"

I push him away. "Fuck you!" I shout.

I don't know who's around and who's watching. I look over my shoulder, hoping Finn can somehow read between the lines. "Just leave me alone, okay?" I set my eyes on the stop sign because I can't look at his face any longer, if I do, I'll break and take it all back.

I'm saving your life, Finn.

"I can't believe I could've ever loved someone like *you*," I say with hatred, picturing I'm speaking to Jason, and not the man I am so hopelessly in love with. I walk past him, falling to pieces.

"No one is going to kill me," he says from behind me.

I spin around with wide eyes.

"The men Jason 'hired', weren't hitmen." He laughs, like having to say that sentence out loud is insane. "They were undercover FBI agents that advertise themselves on some sketchy forum to catch people like Jason." He slowly walks over to me.

Sirens sound in a distance, and before I know it, red and blue lights are speeding past me, headed straight toward my home.

Toward Jason.

"Finn—" I burst into a million and one pieces, but Finn rushes to me, picking me up before I split one last time.

"I'm *so* sorry, Adeline." He holds me as if he would never let me go. "I should've realized you were gone. I mean, I *did* realize, but it was too late." He pulls away to assess me, gently running a finger along the dried blood that dripped down my face. He looks like he's been punched in the gut, and then I see him cry for the first time. I let him pull my body against his.

"You were there with me." I smile past my tears, remembering what he said to me all those years ago while I was asleep. I peel myself off Finn so I can finally watch the justice I deserve. That my mother deserves. She should be here—

"Fuck you!" Someone shouts over the dozens of sirens. My mom.

I run back to my street, into view of my house, with Finn on my heels. I watch in complete shock at the scene unfolding before me.

"You are under arrest, mother fucker!" my mom shouts, while police officers lock hand cuffs around Jason's wrists.

I can see one of the officers is talking, most likely stating the reasons for his arrest and reading him his rights, but all I can focus on is my mother.

I can finally see it now.

Fiery hair blows around her like oxygenated flames, her strength hitting me harder than a semi-truck.

She isn't this broken person I always made her out to be.

My mother is the strongest, bravest woman I have ever met, and here I stand, watching that very essence of her come alive.

Often times you don't know a moment is big until after

the fact, but I can feel the weight of everything as it plays out.

Jason sitting in the back of a cop car.

The tons of weight dissipating off my shoulders.

Finn's touch on the small of my back, like he's subtly telling me he's here, feeling it too.

I let my mom have her moment. I spin around and kiss the man of my dreams like I never have before.

"Unfortunately, we can't guarantee he'll go to prison for a lengthy period of time," a short, friendly, man wearing a police uniform tells my mother and I off to the side while the rest of the officers start leaving.

Finn sits on my porch, out of ear shot to give us some privacy.

"What?" I demand, flabbergasted he even could suggest Jason being a free man after the day I hardly survived.

"I know it's frustrating, but even with the proof he tried to hire a hitman, he never actually worded anything that would insinuate he wanted to kill someone. It wouldn't be enough to hold up in a court of law."

I have dried blood all over me, isn't that enough in itself to have him locked away for the rest of his life? I still have the folder on my laptop with the photos of my mom's ribs and Finn's bruised face...even the blurry video. But it's not enough, and all of this was for nothing. My stomach sinks and I feel like I've died.

I can take a photo of myself now, and add it to the collection, hoping one day it will be enough.

"I'm sorry I can't give you ladies better peace of mind.

The justice system is flawed." He gives a sorrowful shrug, one that say's *don't shoot the messenger.*

"Thank you, Officer, for all your help." My mother still has the strength to smile at the man who just delivered us a world full of future battles.

He nods his head with a tight lip and walks away.

~

Paramedics assessed me and offered to take me to the hospital. After the day I've had, I just want to scrub it all off in the shower and curl up in bed with Finn, who left a few minutes ago to pick up dinner for us. Besides, once they cleaned up the dried blood, they found it was only a minor cut. It bled a lot because of how thin the skin on my head is.

It's finally quiet, all the nosey neighbors and first responders left. I haven't been able to go back inside. My mom sits on the grass with me, even as the sun sets, until I'm ready to go through those doors.

Finn's only been gone for fifteen minutes, but with everything going on we hadn't really had the chance to talk. I feel a pull to speak to him now that I finally can. "Can I use your phone?" I ask my mom since I must've dropped mine somewhere along my run when I passed out.

"Why, what's wrong?" she asks, handing me her phone.

I don't know if it's my mother asking me what's wrong or if losing my phone was the last straw, but the floodgates open. Everything that happened hits in one sweep of a massive tsunami. The world shrinks around me, strangling me. I'm gasping for air when I hear a familiar string of notes coming from my abdomen.

Specifically, the area where my leggings meet my stomach, where a rectangle vibrates against me. I slowly pull out my phone and set it in the grass, not even bothering to check who's calling me. I had my phone the entire time. It registers numbly that a call for help was perfectly within my capabilities.

Jason didn't even check me for my phone, I want to laugh with how ridiculous it all is. So, I do, I laugh hysterically. It's the sort of laugh that knocks the wind out of you and has you gripping at your knees, only this one doesn't end with a deep inhale, it turns into a full-blown break down. I collapse onto the grass and let my mother soothe me.

She holds me in her arms, I'm a flimsy feather incased in diamond armor.

"What can I do for you? Did you want to call Finn?" my mom asks, reaching for my phone that lays face down in the grass.

I just shrug, not in the right mind to make decisions right now.

She picks it up and looks at it.

I glance at my phone in her hands, there is a timer at the top of the screen, five hours and thirty-one minutes and counting. The screen displays the scene right in front of us.

"Oh my—" Life is breathed back into me, just as easily as it was lost.

"I'm confused, why are you taking a video?" my mom asks.

I stand up, with so much strength, I could withstand the entire world's weight *and more.*

"I'm not. I hit record by accident right as I passed out." I grab the phone from my mom's hands, she still kneels on the grass from when I needed her support. Little does she know I have the final puzzle piece that's going to ensure our safety for the *rest* of our lives.

I can see as it all clicks behind my mother's eyes, because she slowly stands up and walks toward me and my phone as if it's the most fragile thing in this entire world. Like, if she walks too fast the wind will knock it right out of my hands and shatter it to pieces.

"Upload it to the cloud so we can share it with the lawyer," she says quickly, like the evidence is seconds away from disappearing. "Please tell me he said enough to incriminate himself on the video."

I nod and quickly do as I'm told, connecting to the Wi-Fi so it goes through.

"Oh my god!" my mom shrieks, grasping my hand. She squeezes so hard that her knuckles are completely white, but I don't care.

This is how we are going to reach the finish line.

This is the part where we win.

I look up at the sky, I've never been a religious person, but I close my eyes and thank whatever God is up there.

27

W hy do bad things happen to good people?" I trail my fingertips along the dips of Finn's abs. Jason's murderous face flashes across my vision until Finn brings his thumb over my bottom lip, looking up to me as I sit beside him on my bed, leaning against the headboard.

He brings me out of the vivid memory from a week ago. A part of me is thankful for what happened, because if it didn't, I would've never gathered the evidence I needed. But another part of me wishes it never happened. It's tainted my last bit of time with Finn.

The flashbacks and the post-traumatic stress have put a damper on the mood. We haven't talked about the future, not once.

"I don't know, love." His face contorts from the relaxed expression it was a moment ago, to a pitiful one.

"Don't pity me," I wince.

He sits up straighter on the bed, pulling me onto his lap. I adjust myself so I straddle him.

"Bad things happen to good people because they are the ones who make good of a bad situation," he whispers, brushing my hair away from my face and tucking it neatly behind my ear.

I grin at him. "Since when did you become a walking fortune cookie?" I smile against his lips, that somehow ended up so closely to mine. They reflect my smile. His hands slowly inch up my thighs.

I want him to wrap me up in bliss and whisk me away from what happened.

I let him kiss and make love to me until I'm dizzy, until I forget about everything.

My bedroom is painfully quiet, except for the low hum of Finn's snore. The quiet is too *loud*, it's as if my ear drums are seconds from bursting inside my head.

I should be happy.

We have a court case soon, but my lawyer is doing everything she can so my mom and I don't have to attend. There's so much evidence in that five-hour video, there should be no need for me to relive the horrors of that day. No need for my mother to tell a room full of strangers about the most traumatic moments of her life.

Not only are we going to win, finally get the justice we deserve and rid the world of Jason's abuse while he's locked away for good, my mom is *okay*. I confronted her about my suspicions today, about her using again. She told me she remembered something that bothered her, that's why she was so quiet leaving Pete's. *She didn't relapse.*

I should feel relieved by that.

What memory could possibly have my mom so

distraught, that she wasn't comfortable enough sharing it with me? What other demons has she lived through?

If I had been a better daughter, she wouldn't have succumbed to pills and alcohol in the first place.

No, Adeline. Addiction is an illness, just like any other disease.

I know I did the right thing when I made the decision to stop helping her, to stop enabling her. It eventually got her where she needed to go—rehab.

But my worries torment me on a repeated loop until exhaustion puts me to sleep.

But I can't even escape them in my dreams…

Ping.

I open my eyes at the sound of a text notification and take in the scene of my bedroom. Memories of Finn's lips along my skin in an erotic haze come rushing back to me. I squint my eyes, my clothes are still thrown across my room, only Finn's aren't beside them.

Ping.

I feel around my bed until I find my phone. I turn it on and see I have a text from Finn.

He's sent me a file named *The Edge of the World*, so I open it.

Adeline,

I don't know why I'm writing this, or what it's even for, but I feel compelled to put my thoughts into words…if that makes sense.

Today at school you said something.

Well, you're always saying something, *but for some reason, this something really hit me.*

We were sitting at our usual table for lunch, talking about our plans for next year...Senior year. I spent five minutes complaining to you about SAT prep.

But you didn't say anything, you didn't even look at me. You just stared off at the cafeteria wall, nodding every few sentences, as if you were in a trance.

I'd assumed you just zoned out because you weren't interested in hearing me complain. If you were any ordinary girl, I would've been insulted.

I didn't care that you weren't listening to me, though. I was too busy wondering what the hell was going on behind those big brown eyes.

I talked and talked and talked *about SAT prep, not because I cared about it, but because I wanted to watch the way you stepped outside of the world, and into your daydream.*

The most authentic you, I guess you could say.

If I were as selfless as I wish to be, I'd say my motives were to give you a break from the thousands of thoughts you always seem to have.

And there's some truth to that, but it's only twenty five percent of the reason.

Seventy five percent was so I could just stare at you, and you wouldn't notice how interested I was, because you'd be so uninterested.

Gosh, does this even make sense?

I hope it does, Adeline.

Anyway, after the best five minutes of my life, you suddenly spoke.

"Too bad Earth isn't flat," you said. Your eyes hadn't left the spot they had spent the past five minutes.

And oh my god, Adeline, the way my stomach somersaulted at your voice. My heart sped in anticipation just to hear the way your brain worked.

I could spend every second of every day listening to you narrate your train of thought.

"Why?" I asked.

You smiled like you've been waiting decades for me to ask you to elaborate.

I didn't realize a smile could hurt your cheeks, but mine did, when I watched your eyes look at mine and smile right at me.

This girl, this spectacular girl, whom I've almost convinced myself was a figment of my imagination, was sharing a smile with me.

Was smiling at me.

In that moment, I decided I would do anything to get you to smile at me like that again...for the rest of time.

"Because," you said, "I bet the edge of the world would have the best view."

I laughed.

You laughed at me laughing, brightening and pinkening.

Gosh, you're beautiful, Ad.

I've always known it, but wow.

I thought about what you said, about the edge of the world having the best view. I pictured the world, squished down from a sphere to a pancake, pictured the treacherous journey to the very edge.

It made me sad, Adeline.

That in your hypothetical train-of-thought world, the most beautiful thing was just outside of it.

Untouchable, but punishable enough to be where you could see it.

Every worldly view would be mundane by comparison.

So, yes, you were able to experience the very outer edge of heaven, and for that moment when your eyes touch it, your soul tethers to it.

Once you walk away, back to where you came from, you'll always feel the tug, calling you back to the place your soul calls home.

I realized that's what you are to me.

The edge of the world.

A beautiful, unworldly place…heavenly and too perfect to exist in this plane.

Finn's words bring tears to my eyes.

I catch my reflection in my mirrored closet. My smile is undeniably cheesy and wide. I try to remove it from my face, but I can't. It's going to be plastered there for the rest of the day, no doubt.

I never knew Finn thought that *deeply* about me. The way I've caught myself secretly thinking of him all those months ago.

All along, I've asked him questions to understand how his beautiful mind saw the world. Little did I know, he was doing the same with me, in his own way.

I can't think of another person more perfect to love than Finn Walker.

Amber eyes and a dimpled smile come to mind.

My soulmate's face.

I jump out of bed and throw on a pair of cotton shorts and a matching tank top. A familiar smell seeps into my nose and my mouth waters…bacon.

I love bacon.

I run downstairs with an extra pep to my step, when I get to the kitchen, I find the source of the smell.

"Well, hello there, you must be my personal chef," I tease. When Finn turns around, I wag my eyebrows.

He takes two long strides, pulling me into him and presses his lips to mine.

He holds the small of my back, a pair of tongs in the other hand, careful not to get bacon grease in my hair.

"Sleep good?" he whispers against my lips.

"Extremely." I smile against his, even though I slept horrible. Anxiety plagued my night, but I try to keep my worries for the future at bay for now. I want to enjoy what's right in front of me like it's the last time.

"Good," he says with a deep smile that shows off his dimples.

It's cute. "Good."

"Well then, I better get back to work." He steps back but doesn't release his gaze. It sweeps over every inch of me.

My mother's presence fills the kitchen.

I turn to her, the heaviness to her expression causes my heart to race.

She hardly acknowledges Finn, like whatever is on her mind is too vast to capture anything else.

"What's wrong?" I hate the way my hands automatically shake. My nervous system picks up the smallest signs of distress and runs with it.

"There was never a good time." She shakes her head, and I realize she's holding a piece of paper.

I stand frozen. Everything about her freaked out demeanor sends me into panic.

She gives me a weak smile and slowly hands me the paper.

I stare at her, trying to gather information about the situation before looking at it. Her expression tells me nothing, so I let my eyes fall to what she handed to me.

It's not just a piece of paper, it's a picture. A familiar one.

Charlie's smile eases my anxiety, but the red headed girl

wrapped up in his arms makes my heart jolt in an unfamiliar way.

"I don't get it," I admit. This is the picture I showed my mom at Pete's.

I recall that day, and the way my mind reeled for an explanation for why she was so quiet after that. It was because the picture meant something to my mother.

Maybe because she had the colored version, when mine was black and white.

But why?

My mother gives me a look, like I'm supposed to know.

I don't know what she's trying to tell me, so I look to Finn for answers. He somehow ended up right next to me, peering at the image in my hand.

"Who is that girl?" He directs the question at my mom.

"Evia Monroe."

Monroe? "Isn't Monroe your maiden name?" I question.

"It is," my mom says, like she's admitting a truth that's supposed to upset me.

I look down at Evia Monroe, long auburn hair with almond eyes, fair skin, and a bright smile.

"My aunt," I breathe, I never realized I had an aunt before. "She's beautiful." I smile at my mother, but she just frowns.

"She looks like you," Finn says, nudging my shoulder.

"What happened to her?" I ask, gathering that something did in fact happen to her by my mother's sad expression.

She slowly takes the picture out of my hand and peers down at it, with tears welling in her eyes.

"She met a great man," she begins, bringing her fingers to the inner corner of her eyes to keep the tears from leaking down her face. "Charlie. They were inseparable," she whispers, like she's thinking out loud rather than speaking to me. "He treated her so…right."

I can't ignore the way my mom says the last sentence with so much gratitude, like her sister deserved every bit of goodness Charlie gave to her.

"They were young and in love, around your age. Seeing the way you two are together reminds me a lot of them." She looks between Finn and me. "When Evia missed her period, I bought her a pregnancy test from the drug store. We sat for three minutes, waiting for lines to appear, and when they did, she cried from pure happiness, and I joined her."

My stomach sinks.

I reach out for my mom's hand, trying to comfort her before she gets to the end of this story. I can see it in her eyes that telling it is close to reliving it.

"Charlie and Evia were going to make great parents, despite how young they were." She sniffles. "I told her that. But the thing about Evia, is she never wanted to be a burden to anyone." She shrugged. "They were so wrapped up in each other that they never had the chance to discuss children. She didn't want to put Charlie in the position where he felt obligated to step into a role he didn't want to be in." She clears her throat. "She decided to casually bring up the idea of having kids together. He made a joke about how he was too young to be a dad, and that was all it took."

I shake my head. Charlie loves being a dad, I can tell by the way he is with Chloe.

"I tried to talk her out of it, but she broke up with Charlie without explanation. She always put others above herself, and she was stubborn as a mule." My mother sighs. "She wanted to raise the baby on her own, without ever telling Charlie about their child. She didn't want to burden him with a responsibility he wasn't ready for."

For some reason I'm grateful Evia never told Charlie. I don't know where this is going, but I can sense if he knew this story, it would haunt him for the rest of his life.

The air weighs a thousand pounds, making my chest heavy as I inhale. I can sense tragedy, and she hasn't even finished the story.

"So, she bought a house in the Keys he didn't know about. He searched for her for months. He came to me several times and asked about her. I told him I didn't know where she was, hating the situation but respecting my sister's wishes." She massages her temples. "Evia cried over losing him as much as she smiled from the pregnancy.

"Eventually Charlie moved away, and I never knew where he ended up." She looks back down at the photo, running her thumb along the image of young Charlie. "I helped her set up the nursery, took her to all her doctor appointments, and cried with her when we heard the baby's heartbeat." She wipes at her eyes. "It wasn't ideal, but she made it work. She always did." She smiles, reminiscing over her sister's strength.

She stands straight, preparing to get the next sentence out. "I drove her to the hospital when her water broke. I was so frantic, making sure she had everything she needed. My hands shook in anticipation, my mind in a million other places."

Tears stream down her cheeks now.

"I forgot to check my blind spot—" She chokes on the words.

Finn stiffens beside me, and my heart stops as if I am living it too.

"The passenger side of my car hit the one in the lane I

was switching into. Everything after that was a blur. I woke up in a hospital room. A doctor told me my sister died."

My heart breaks for my mother, and Evia, and her unborn baby. Just hearing the tragedy causes pain throughout my entire body, and I'm only hearing it secondhand.

My mom clears her throat and takes a deep breath. "They handed me her daughter. I fell in love with her instantly." She smiles past the tears.

What?

"We bounced back and forth with baby names throughout her pregnancy, but she always came back to one name—Adeline," she whispers.

Everything spins.

I can't breathe.

I can't—

Breathe...

"Mom—" I pant, not knowing who I'm directing the name toward. The room spins faster.

My knees meet the ground. My head feels like it will collapse off my shoulders.

I *know* I'm having a panic attack.

Putting a simple label like panic attack on *this* feels insensitive.

Girl finds out her entire life has been a lie and all the abuse and torture she endured wasn't even meant to happen to her: just a silly little panic attack.

"Breathe in your nose and out your mouth," Finn coos, as if it's that simple.

As if breathing properly could fix my life.

Could bring back Evia.

Could rewrite my childhood.

Thanks Finn, for the helpful insight.

It feels like my lungs are filling with water.

I'm drowning.

This is the way it ends. I'm going to die. Right here, in my kitchen. My lungs try to keep up with my panic, as I pant so quickly everything just fades away. Darkness sweeps me up, engulfing me whole.

"Adeline!" A rough hand lightly smacks my cheek, signaling for me to open my eyes.

I take in amber eyes that hold a world of worry and pain. "Thank god," he whispers in relief.

"Puffin—" My mom gently nudges Finn aside, peering over my destroyed body. "I'm *so* sorry." Her voice breaks up, like it's impossible to get the words out when everything inside her dies.

I'm right there with her.

I lay still on the cold kitchen floor, while the world around me continues.

The smell of burnt bacon fills the air. The clock ticks quietly, reminding me time still moves relentlessly...even though I want it to stop.

I close my eyes, picturing what it would've been like if Evia had given Charlie a chance. Would she have died? He would've driven her to the hospital, everything would've been different.

I would never know how it felt to watch my dad abuse my mom. I wouldn't have had to learn ways to comfort myself while his voice rocked the walls. My whole life would've been different. Better.

What was she like? Would she have been a good mom? Would she have hugged me every chance she got and spoiled me with love? Would Charlie have taught me what it's like to truly be loved so I could learn long before Finn would teach me?

Would I have even met Finn?

And Chloe.

Our lives would've been so different if we had grown up as sisters. She wouldn't have felt so alone in the world. I would've been the best big sister.

I can't recall the rest of that day...or the week that followed.

All I remember is time moving painfully slow.

Instead, I just felt every stab, every punch, every gut-wrenching pain known to mankind. I felt it with every beat of my heart.

I wished it would just end, the pain, the pity from Finn and my mom.

And now I feel nothing.

Still, as I let Finn rub my feet and feed me ice-cream in my bed, I don't feel a single sentiment toward him. Toward anything.

I feel nothing.

I had so many questions, but the most prevalent was *why Jason?* I guess I always asked myself that, but at least before I could make the excuse that he was my dad, and that's why my mother never left him.

If my mom could choose any man to father me, why would she choose Jason?

It was horrible timing, she had said. *We had broken up nine months before you were born. When he showed up at my doorstep and saw me holding a baby with auburn hair like mine, he assumed you were our child, and I never corrected him. I was vulnerable and broken and I let him back in. It was the gravest mistake I've ever made, one that we've both had to live with. One I'll spend a lifetime trying to make up to you. I am so incredibly sorry.*

My phone rings, filling the silence of my bedroom.

Finn hands it to me and I stare at the screen feeling a tug at my heart.

The contact photo I have for Chloe is of us squeezing each other tightly at our bonfire while Finn captured the candid moment.

The photo alone sets off an emotion I can't place, I answer her call and put the phone to my ear.

"Girl you better have a good excuse," she says, her voice cheerful, not hurt.

My lips upturn into an effortless smile, but my heart hurts and my vision turns blurry with tears. "What?" I ask softly.

"I haven't heard from you in ages! What the hell happened to your psycho dad? Did you kick him in the balls yet or what?"

I haven't spoken to her since we left Authensville, it's just been too crazy, I haven't had a chance to breathe.

I catch her up on everything that happened, leaving out the most important part—*you're my sister...Jason isn't even my dad because Charlie is. Evia is my real mom.*

"If I didn't know you, I'd think you were making this shit up!" She laughs into the receiver, and for the first time in a week, I laugh too.

"I miss you." I hold my breath to keep her from hearing me cry.

"Aw, do you really? I was starting to think you'd forgotten me." I hear the smile in her voice.

Chloe doesn't pity me. She doesn't hone in on the horribleness of it all, she makes light of the situation and spreads her sunshine all the way to the Florida Keys without even trying.

I need her in my life.

I don't think, I just speak with my heart. "I was actually thinking of moving to Authensville."

The air suddenly weighs a thousand pounds. Finn's expression remains stoic, but I catch the flicker of heartbreak in his features.

Chloe squeals and screams into the phone, laughing giddily and declaring to whoever is near her, "Adeline is moving back, bitches!"

She updates me on her life, telling me about the cute guy Charlie hired at the restaurant.

When I end my call with Chloe, I can't look at Finn. I can only look down. He doesn't speak. He stands up, walking with slumped shoulders to my bathroom and closing himself in.

Please don't let this be the moment I've feared, please don't let this destroy us.

28

I'm filled with anxiety as I wait for the bathroom door to open again, dreading what's on the other side. I can feel the happily ever after I almost believed we'd achieved being ripped away.

A future without Finn Walker isn't a place I ever want to be.

But I can't live this life anymore. I can't be *this* Adeline Miller: child of abusive father. With this agonizing life I wasn't supposed to live.

I need to start the life I was destined to live, even if I am nineteen years late.

With Charlie and Chloe.

But what about Finn? He belongs in that life as much as I do, but I can't ask him to uproot everything for me. His life is here. I think mine is a thousand miles away.

The door slowly opens, Finn's expressionless as he walks to my bed and sits on the edge. He's far enough to where I could only touch him if I extended my entire arm. He's quiet for a moment, as if he's gathering his thoughts.

I speak first. "I'm sorry for catching you off-guard like that, but I didn't know I wanted to move until the moment I said it—"

"I wasn't caught off guard, love." He gives me a gentle smile. "I know you, Adeline."

I know you.

Those words do something strange to my soul, lifting it up while shooting it down at once.

This isn't fair. Anger thickens my blood. I'm not sure who to direct it toward.

My mom, since she was the one driving the car that changed my entire life. Even though it was a tragic accident.

Or Jason, for his relentless rage and the years of anguish my mom and I survived.

Or Charlie, for not fighting harder to find Evia. For joking about being too young to be a father.

Or myself, for not being able see the good through all the bad in my life. I might not have met Finn if I didn't run away that day, ten years ago, and cried on that swing set.

I wish I could split myself in two and give one half to Finn and my mom, the other to Charlie and Chloe.

"I don't want to leave you," I whisper, feeling every fear and doubt I've had become a reality.

We shouldn't have allowed ourselves to fall in love because this is how it ends. We won't end up together, Finn.

"You have to go, love. And I have to be happy for you." He smiles through tears that fall fast down his face.

"You don't have to be such a good guy all the time."

"It's what you deserve." He pauses for a moment. "Maybe we can do long distance. I mean we can talk on the phone everyday—"

I sit up and move closer to him, placing my hand on his cheek. "I want every bit of you, Finn. Not a relationship

300

through the speaker of my phone. I want to kiss you every time I tell you how much I love you. I want to sleep in the same bed and see you the moment I open my eyes."

"Okay. Yeah, you're right," he whispers and looks down. "So, this is…over then."

The pain in my chest is incomparable to anything I've ever felt. It's like my heart shattered and every sharp edge stabs inside my chest. I hold his face in my hands so his eyes meet mine once again. His tears drip into my palms, I want to hold all his pain like he's held mine for so many years.

He kisses me softly with raw, heartbreaking emotion. I want to kiss him forever, but I know once our lips break apart, this is it. The reality of what's happening doesn't stop me, instead it drives me.

It's the last time we'll get to be more than best friends living in two different states, so I absorb every millisecond of the moment promised, making sure I won't forget a thing.

The way his tongue glides past my parted lips makes me want his body to possess mine, our souls intertwined…tethered together until the end of time.

"I love you *forever*, Adeline," he whispers against my lips, our tears mixing. "The past, the present, and the future… Wherever you are," he strains to get the words out, "you have my heart."

"I'm so sorry."

"Don't be."

We kiss and make love with everything left of us, making sure to savor every second.

I'll remember this moment for the rest of my life. The end of our story.

∼

I couldn't see Finn after that.

It would break me to have to say goodbye, so instead we left off on a high note, saying *I'll see you later.*

It's better this way, I reassure myself as I zip my last suitcase.

I woke up the next morning to a new luggage set and a note from Finn I read for the millionth time. *Fill that beautiful mind of yours with memories of the entire world, you deserve to witness it all. I love you in every timeline.*

I fold it neatly and put it in my phone case, so I'll always have his words with me.

My mom lightly taps on my door, eyes puffy with a scrapbook in hand. "Done packing?" she asks with a smile that battles to become a frown.

"Yeah, I'm all set." It's going to be hard to leave my mom, but we agreed she needed to finish rehab and figure everything out down here before joining me in Authensville.

She's been working on packing up our home and finding a realtor to show the house.

Along with the legal issues of filing for a divorce to a man in prison. It turns out we don't have to worry about him getting out anytime soon since kidnapping me and arranging to have Finn killed weren't his only offenses. My mom didn't go into too much detail when she found out from the lawyer, but apparently, he was getting all his money from fraud.

We won the case, which would've been enough to ensure me a lifetime of peace a few weeks ago.

As much as things are finally falling into place, like Jason's life sentence and my mom being in a good enough place for me to finally go my own way, it's equally falling apart.

I can't help but feel like all of this had been a waste. Finn and I were planning on going to college together when we were kids, and now that I can finally leave my mom without worrying so much, I'm leaving the state.

Leaving him.

I fell in love for the first time, trusting the only person worthy of it. It was exhilarating while it lasted, but now I'll spend the rest of my life grieving what we had. What's now already over.

When I told my mom I was moving, she was *happy* for me. Instead of holding me back and asking me to stay, she said, *when do we leave?* She wants to come with me, and I couldn't be happier about it.

I know the former would've been the easiest approach, but she's going the hard way of uprooting her life and finishing rehab *for me.*

She's taking care of everything down here. I'm taking care of everything in Authensville. I'll make sure there is a good support group for her there and look for someplace for her to live.

Chloe and I talked about getting our own place together, and it was the first shiver of excitement I've felt in a while.

Her and Charlie don't know I'm their long lost sister and daughter, and I'm hoping the news doesn't drive a wedge into our easy relationships.

I take a seat on the hard wood floor, a double edged sword of happiness and heartbreak pierces through me, and I let it.

My whole life I pushed away the pain and memories of what I've lived through as a child, but I won't do that now, because the pain means I experienced a love that usually only exists on the pages of a novel. Our story happened, and it was beautiful. He taught me what real love is.

I won't force the pain to let up because the moment I do, it becomes a distant memory instead of a vivid one.

I want to always remember the way my heart dropped to my stomach when he kissed me for the first time in Pete's, the way his voice was strong when he told me he loved me, the way he tasted when we made love. I want to find Finn in every moment promised, so the sharp pain is a reminder and a blessing.

"Here." My mother sits beside me, squished together since my suitcases take up most of my bedroom. She hugs the scrapbook to her chest before placing it in my lap. "Your mom started this when she was pregnant with you," she whispers, tucking my hair behind my ear.

I grasp her hand quickly, giving it a squeeze. "*You* are my mom."

I can tell my statement puts to rest a fear she's been battling my whole life. Her eyes redden and shine immediately. "I'm so proud of you, puffin." She sniffles.

"Oh, Mom," I say, my emotions quickly surfacing. I pull her to my side in a tight embrace. If young Adeline could see this moment, she'd be taken aback. This isn't a place I ever thought my mom and I would get to, but it is something I've spent years dreaming of.

I open the scrap book; the first page is full of ultrasound pictures. I run my finger slowly over the pen ink at the bottom of the page. In loopy handwriting, it says, *I got to see you for the first time today, my baby girl. I already love you so much! I cannot wait to squeeze you.*

Everything I could've had rains down on me.

The perfect family. A dad who loved me, who didn't yell

and abuse his family. One who would've given me the moon and the stars and the whole world.

I have to go.

I tuck the scrapbook into my carry on, grab my suitcases and let my mom drive me to the airport.

~

I couldn't help but look over my shoulder throughout the line at security, walking to my gate, and even when I stepped onto the plane.

He wasn't there the first time I looked, and he isn't here now as I check the completely clear aisle of the plane.

Everyone has boarded.

I don't know why I'd hoped Finn would show. We agreed it'd be too hard to say goodbye.

A part of me selfishly wishes he'd leave with me, but a much larger part of me knows his life is right here.

A muffled voice zips through the aisle, passing the flight attendants that are getting in place to do their safety demonstration. "Excuse me. Sorry. Coming through."

Someone's late for their flight, and I judge them a little since it inconveniences hundreds of people if the plane waits on one person.

I check my carry on one last time, feeling like I forgot something...but I know the feeling isn't something, it's *someone*.

I jolt as a tall body suddenly appears in the aisle, hovering over me. I stare straight ahead, ignoring the person, hoping their seat isn't the one next to mine. Maybe if I don't make eye contact, they'll leave.

But my hope goes out the window the second a finger taps gently at my shoulder.

I glance up and my heart stops beating in my chest.

Eyes of amber and a dimpled smile.

"Finn—" I say, the wind knocked out of me.

"I love you. I love you. *I love you,*" he says swiftly, dropping to his knees right in the aisle. Before I can even catch up to what's happening, his lips crash into mine and kisses me fervently. He holds my face in his hands. The smell of him breathes life back into me. Cinnamon and clove.

Tears trickle out the corners of my closed eyes. I didn't realize how much I needed this kiss until this moment. My body floats and my pain dissipates.

He grips my jaw firmly, like he'll never let go.

I ignore the flight attendant telling Finn to sit down, that they are about to close the doors.

Finn whispers painfully, "I have to go."

No.

I fight back a sob and nod my head quickly. *I love you, Finn Walker, down to the very beat of my heart.* I try to get words out, but my throat closes. "I love—"

"I know," he says, looking so deeply into my eyes.

We exchange a silent I love you, and then he's gone, zipping through the aisle and taking my heart with him.

He can have it. It hurts too much when it's without him anyways.

I replay the last minute in my mind, smiling and crying as the plane moves toward the runway.

He bought a plane ticket to say goodbye.

That's the all-consuming love I'd always brushed off as fiction, but it exists, and I live in the aftermath.

I open the window shade, watching the world shrink down as we take off.

Normally I'd enjoy the feeling of being small, but right

now, I can only hope to God our story doesn't die right here on this plane.

But how could it not?

We belong in two different states.

I let everything go, closing my eyes and thinking of a new beginning.

The one where Adeline Miller has a true family, one of her own.

"Ohmygod! Adeline, I swear I almost forgot what you looked like." Chloe's high pitched excitement rings in my ears as we squeeze each other so tightly in the airport.

I peer over her shoulder, meeting Charlie's eyes.

My dad's eyes.

"Hey there, kiddo." He smiles with emotion, like seeing me really means something to him…he has no idea.

Chloe releases me, and I go straight for my dad, hugging him and breathing the miracle in.

I found you, Dad. And I wasn't even trying to.

He laughs, shocked by how long I hug him for, but he doesn't try to release me any more than I do.

How do you spend an hour-long car ride with two people who have no idea you're their long lost daughter and sister?

I've swallowed down the truth many times, even though it's begging to be said out loud. But this isn't the way to tell someone, *oh hey, by the way, you got your ex-girlfriend pregnant, and she didn't tell you. Oh, and it's me, I'm your daughter. And Evia is dead. Surprise!*

We are almost to Authensville, so I test my patience for a little longer.

They really need to build an airport closer, but I guess that's the price you pay for living in a small town in the mountains.

Everything that's not within the town is miles away.

Like it's our own little world.

I kind of love it, and it's my new home.

I unlock my phone, opening my texts with Finn. I fumbled with the keys, backspacing and retyping, not sure what to say. I settle on, *I landed, Chloe and Charlie just picked me up.* I want to tell him I love him, but we can't say that to each other anymore, it'll just hurt all the more.

Once we get to the apartment, Chloe talks, never once letting up to take a breath. She listed adventures on the bucket list she wrote for us, told me about some apartment listings, and is now telling me about the cute boy she works with.

She brought up Finn a few times, but I just shook my head, not wanting to talk about it yet. I figure once I tell her the truth about who my real parents are, it'll be easier to admit we're over.

Charlie sits on the couch, watching his daughter with amusement, an easy smile on his face. He's happy when she's happy.

I don't think I can go any longer without telling them. Something bursts, and I just interrupt her mid-sentence, "Chloe!" I take no time to think over my words before speaking them. "I'm your sister."

Her face doesn't fall, and she doesn't gasp in shock, she just looks confused.

"Oh, wow. Um, that is not how I wanted to say that." I

clear my throat, looking past Chloe and straight at Charlie. "I know who Evia is." I slowly step past my sister, then sit on the couch beside our dad.

Now his face does fall, his mouth hangs open slightly, like he's just heard me say the name of a ghost.

"I know who she is because…" Here it goes. Please don't hate me, Dad. "She's my birth mom."

His eyes ping pong between mine, confused and shocked and even more confused. His facial expression goes from denial to probability. Like he's questioning if this is true. His fingers touch a strand of my hair, his eyes fill with water. "You have her eyes," he says as emotion floods his vocal cords.

I laugh past a tear that falls down my cheek. I feel Chloe's presence as she sits on the floor between us.

"Wow. Evia Monroe's daughter." He shakes his head in disbelief. "How is she?"

In his shock, he hasn't registered what I said to Chloe.

"Dad," Chloe says, eyes wide with tears. "Oh my god, Adeline. Are you—"

"Charlie's daughter." I fill her silence. "Your sister." My hands tremble.

Silence. Heavy, loud, raging silence.

"Wait." Charlie stands to pace back and forth. "How?"

"I'm nineteen." I answer with the logistics. "I was born April twenty-ninth in Key Largo," I say, so he can do the math.

Chloe sits there, staring at me in disbelief. Her eyes graze over my features, the shape of my nose, the width between my eyes, finding all our similarities.

He stops pacing, looking me head on. "You're Evia Monroe's daughter?"

"Yes."

"You're *my* daughter?" he asks.

"Yes."

"I'm your dad." He echoes his thoughts, a smile breaks across his face.

I smile wider than I ever have before, reflecting his.

"Holy shit." His hands reach up to squeeze his hair. "Shit. Sorry, no cursing, you two." He points between Chloe and I. "Wow, Evia and I have a daughter together," he says, dumbfounded. "Where is she, I've got to see her. Why didn't she ever tell me?"

My heart sinks. I tell him what my mom told me, everything from why she hid to the way she died.

His head shakes in denial, like it can't be true. The woman he loved, who broke his heart, who carried his daughter…is dead. Has been dead for nineteen years. Nineteen years he spent thinking she was alive.

"Just because of a stupid joke I made, she's gone?" He laughs, but without humor. "'*I'm too young to be a dad*' is what drove her away? Is what killed her?" He looks as me with gut-wrenching sorrow. "I'm so fucking sorry." He cries, face reddening as his hands clench in and out of fists. "That…*guy*—" He's so angry now. "He got to know my daughter since she was a baby. He hurt my *baby*. My daughter?!" He means Jason.

"Charlie," I say, hot tears falling down my face. "I'm here now."

Something shifts behind his eyes. He pulls me to him, hugging me the way a father would hug his daughter after not seeing her for a long time.

Chloe joins in, squeezing us so tight, nothing can penetrate the love in this room. The bad parts are over now, and I'm ready to live out all the good life has to offer.

We all spend the day together, completely dumbfounded by the life-altering news. I've had a little longer to process it, but it's still a shock. I imagine I'll wake up in my hot pink bedroom, and this would have all been a dream.

But it's real life.

We've talked about how crazy it was that Finn and I ended up in this town, in Charlie's restaurant. That we got along and became friends right away.

How one-in-a-billion the chances of us meeting this way were.

We cried over the years we lost. Cried over what happened to me, to Charlie, to Chloe. The abuse I survived. The love Charlie lost and years of my life he unwillingly missed out on. Chloe's years of growing up feeling alone in this world, almost as if she knew someone was missing all along.

It's going to take time to process everything, to heal from the past, and to establish our routine as a family, but they want me in their lives as much as I want to be here. All that matters is we finally found each other.

But the moment promised is missing two people: Finn and my mom.

I imagine what Finn would say if he were here. How he'd talk to Charlie knowing he's really my dad.

I imagine how my mother and Charlie would be, with the history they share and grieving the person they both mourn.

I try not to think of what this moment is missing.

I take in this time with my dad and sister, remembering every second and every detail.

My new bed is cold without Finn to hold me while I fall asleep. I stare at the wall, trying to imagine him behind me. How he would scoop me into his arms and gently play with the ends of my hair.

It's been a month since I last saw him. Chloe and I moved into our two-bedroom log cabin a week ago. Charlie was hesitant to let her go, but she's almost eighteen, and we are only a five-minute drive away from the restaurant and his apartment.

My phone rings and when I see who's calling my stomach flips. We've only spoken a few times over the phone. I answer on the first ring, "Finn."

I hear the smile in his voice. "Adeline."

I flip onto my back, putting the phone on speaker and resting it on my chest.

"I needed to hear your voice. I miss you," he says. I hear sheets ruffling through the speaker, like he's getting comfortable in bed too.

My ringtone goes off, and when I look at the screen, I realize he's trying to Facetime me, so I answer with a bright smile.

I was right, he's lying in his dorm room bed. He went back to FSU shortly after I left. His face lights up when he sees me. "You are beautiful."

I feel my cheeks warm. "I miss you." I lift my thumb to my mouth to bite the nail but stop myself, "Every night I lay in bed wishing you were beside me."

"Me too, love. I'll see you for Thanksgiving." He promises, "I booked my plane ticket last night."

Thanksgiving isn't for months.

"I'm starting college soon." I've been waiting to tell him

about my newfound passion. I wanted to see his face when he found out.

His eyes widen and he sits up. "That's great, love! Do you know what you want to study?"

I remember what he told me a month ago. That bad things happen to good people because they are the ones who make good of a bad situation. I smile widely when I say, "Law. I'm going to be a lawyer that fights for children who have no one on their side." I'm going to be the person I needed all those years ago.

His eyes light up. "I'm so proud of you," he says in awe.

I chuckle. "I haven't even started yet."

He shakes his head. "I can already see the finish line, the children, and families you'll impact. You're going to be an amazing lawyer."

I can picture it too, and the thought brings tears of joy to my eyes. The new future I see for myself lights me on fire, in the best way. I think of my mother, and all the people out there who are experiencing what she did, right now as we speak. I think of the justice they deserve, that their kids deserve.

I'm going to fight like hell to give that to them.

"Are you happy?" he asks.

"Yes…and no." I sigh, "I have everything I've ever wanted." I squeeze my phone a little tighter. "Except you."

Emotion flickers across his face.

"I know it's impossible, but I wish you lived here with me." I brush away the tear that slips from my eye. "What I would give to wake up next to you every morning."

"I wish for that too, love."

All I do is nod, trying to hide the tears from him. I tell him it's getting late, and I'm tired. We say goodnight and end the call.

29

"Get your butt up, sister." Chloe's sunshine battles my gray cloud as she enters my bedroom a couple days later.

Boxes clutter my room. The curtains are pulled shut and I lay in bed despite the time. Noon.

"I'm recharging," I groan, pulling my hot pink comforter over my eyes to shield them from the light as she pulls open my curtains.

I squeeze my eyes shut as she pulls the blanket off me, the cool air covering my skin in goosebumps.

"We are going hiking, sister." She crosses her arms in a confident manner. She's been calling me her sister every chance she gets, like the word has been missing from her vocabulary for far too long.

"No way." I turn over, but she pulls my hands so I'm sitting up, straining to get me the rest of the way out of bed.

"Adeline, you have not seen sunlight in a week," she says, sitting on the corner of my bed.

Moving into the cabin was a heavy reality check that

I'm living a thousand miles from my home. And I don't mean Key Largo, I mean Finn.

Chloe reels me back into the present. "Please come with me, you wouldn't want me to get mauled by a bear, would you?"

I roll my eyes, I'd much rather wallow in my dark bedroom, but I'd do anything for my sister. No matter how simple. "Fine."

She claps her hands with excitement, opening one of my boxes and sifting through my clothes until she finds the outfit I wore when we met. When Finn and I hiked a mountain together for the first time.

It makes me smile that she picked it, and that pain digs into my heart, making me smile a little harder.

Chloe bounces with energy as we hike. I ignore her, panting and dying. She's way more in shape than I am.

"I love you, sister from another mister," she says easily, smiling giddily. She uses this expression a lot.

I laugh. "We're from the same mister, Chloe," I tell her for the thousandth time, but she just laughs it off like she always does.

Her phone pings, she stops to check it, glances around, and then widens her eyes. "Be right back!" she says in one breath, running off the trail into the forest, leaving me completely alone.

"Chloe?" I shout, about to go after her.

I yelp as someone grabs my shoulders. *I'm going to die.*

I am turned around to face the perpetrator, I squeeze my eyes tightly, refusing to look my fate in the eyes.

"Adeline." His breath trickles against my face, my eyes shoot open and meet amber eyes.

I gasp, mouth hanging open as he pulls me hard against him, this time, not letting go. I'm in complete shock, I don't even think I'm breathing. I cry into the nape of his neck as he lifts me off my feet. "Is this real?" I ask myself.

He sets me down, kissing me like we've been apart forever. It feels like we have. He deepens our kiss, never wanting it to end. His hands touch everywhere he can reach. Cinnamon and clove invigorate my senses until thoughts form in my mind.

"What are you doing here?" I ask against his swollen lips, never letting my hands leave his body. They constantly move to touch a different part of him, like they've missed what he felt like. I squeeze his bicep, then his shoulder, then his hair.

"What, you're not happy to see me?" he teases with a goofy grin. "I came here to tell you something."

His face is serious. All the blood in my body drains, leaving me pale and terrified. I step back, thinking back to the plane, to that split second where I thought he was coming with me.

But then the disappointment I felt when he left.

Please don't leave and break my heart again.

"You're such a spectacular woman, Adeline. I've always known it." He stands tall, confident, his eyes never straying away from mine. "When I saw you sitting on that swing set, crying into your hands, I felt so angry."

I brace myself for impact, not knowing where he's going with this.

"There was something about that initial moment when my eyes met yours that changed my entire fucking life. I

316

can't put it into words properly, other than saying I simply fell in love with you, right then and there."

My heart sings, begging to hear more.

"I knew you were special. I knew you were too good for this world. I see you as an angel, Adeline. A girl a simple man like myself wasn't enough for." He looks down, his confidence wavering. "But I fell in love with you before I even knew what love meant. All I knew was I wanted to be around you all the time. You became my breath, my thoughts, *my life* since the moment we met."

He steps closer to me unconsciously, like we're magnets. "Ten years later, when you told me you felt a sliver of what I felt, I couldn't fight my selfishness," he says. "At the time, I believed I wasn't good enough for you. I knew you deserved the whole fucking universe and everything outside of it, and to be honest with you, Adeline, I wasn't sure I was the person capable of giving you that." He stands tall again, pulling his broad shoulder back. "So, when you told me you wanted to move away, I let you go, feeling like my selfish time with the most amazing woman in the entire world was up. I wasn't going to invade your life anymore. I didn't want to dim the happiness you deserve." His hands hold onto my arms, rubbing me and lighting me on fire.

I can't look anywhere but his face, not caring what exists outside of us.

"I realized shortly after you left that my life without you was close to meaningless. I realized I should be with my fucking soulmate, and I can work every day to make you happy. To give you everything you deserve." He laughs. "I realized a world without Adeline and Finn together was a shitty place, so I transferred schools, packed up all my belongings to be with the person my soul calls home." He smiles with tears shining in his eyes. "Fuck, sorry that was cheesy."

I laugh against his lips. "You're the place my soul calls home too, Finn." I close my eyes. I realize how significant this moment is.

This is the finish line. This is my happily ever after.

It's here, and I can finally touch it.

"So, Adeline Marie Miller," he whispers against my lips, before slowly moving down.

My eyes widen as his knee meets the dusty trail we stand on.

He grins up at me, like he did all those months ago at Pete's. "Put me out of my misery and marry me already," he says like he's been waiting ten years for this. I glance down at the dainty ring in his hand, the stone glittering in the sun.

Everything from my broken past disappears, becoming a hazy, faraway memory. It happened, but I survived, and now I get to live.

"Yes, yes, yes!" I scream more than say. I feel every ounce of the moment promised, as I jump up and down, fogging the air with dust before Finn lifts me higher than the sun.

He whispers slowly against my lips, "I think we've reached the edge of the world, my love."

Whispering to my fiancé, I say, "I think so too." I smile, like I always do in his presence. Like I will for the rest of my life.

"And they lived happily ever after," he says into the next kiss.

EPILOGUE

There are childlike smiles plastered on everyone's face as I plug a cord into the wall, lighting up the entire log cabin I share with Finn and Chloe with colors. I slowly step back, staring at the now decorated Christmas tree, and its colorful lights that paint my family's faces.

Someone that smells like cinnamon and clove slips an arm around my waist, placing a kiss to my neck, right where my pulse beats rapidly for him. "Don't you think it's a little much?" Finn whispers.

Chloe must hear him because she playfully smacks him across the chest. "It's perfect, Finnegan." She rolls her eyes.

The only tree we could find that would be small enough to fit our cozy living room was a nearly dead tree, with only a few spots left of green, the rest an orange color.

I like orange, I told Finn when I picked it out, *it's like the sunset.*

I bought too many ornaments at a local business by Charlie's steakhouse. 90% of the proceeds went to a charity for children and woman of domestic violence. And Finn's parents sent us all the ones him and I made together as kids. I didn't let a single one go to waste.

The ornaments are heavy on the dying tree, but it couldn't be any more perfect. My mom sits on the couch, holding a warm mug between her hands, sipping on hot chocolate. She's almost six months sober, and I couldn't be any prouder.

"All right, now for the fun part," Charlie, says, digging into the now empty box of ornaments to pull out a star.

I immediately start shaking my head. "Any more weight on this thing and it'll collapse!" I try to protest, but Charlie wears determination on his face.

Over the past few months, I've noticed our similarities. We share the same nose, his just slightly larger than mine and Chloe's. Both of our legs hyper extend. Chloe pointed it out one day as we were at the lake, skipping stones like we do almost every morning now.

"Charlie!" My mom stands up, setting her mug down and rushing over to him. She balances the star that he set on the top of our sunset-colored-about-to-collapse tree. Her hand rests on his fingertips. Together they hold the base of the star, staring at each other intently.

I want to grab my phone and capture this moment, because I feel deep down this is significant.

I haven't missed the glances they give each other. Or how my mom's cheekbones pinken when he says her name at the end of a sentence.

Charlie's eyes light up and he grins, releasing his hold on the star, causing the entire tree to crumble.

My mom gasps, watching over the puddle of broken branches, ornaments, and the tangled string of lights. "Oh, Charlie!" she says, her tone teasing.

Finn and Chloe silently laugh beside me. I smile so wide it hurts because this is perfect. Finn must feel it too, because he wraps his hand around mine. The stone on my finger reflects the colors from the Christmas lights.

"I have something for you," Finn whispers as my mom chases Charlie around our small home like they're kids. It's everything I've ever wanted, the smile plastered to her face and the strength in her muscles to run. She's even working on opening her own boutique here in Authensville. When I told her about the ornaments and where the money would go, she decided that every profit her store made would be donated to a similar charity.

I glance down as Finn pulls a folded-up piece of paper from his pocket. I take it from him, unfolding the image to find Pete and his new family smiling at me, all wearing matching Christmas pajamas. Even the ducks are dressed for the Christmas card.

"It's perfect." I smile, tears rimming my eyes. Life is good, everyone's happily ever after plays out, along with my own. I've always doubted this moment, but it's here. It's my present, and my future.

"It is," Finn agrees, pulling me toward him and crashing his lips into mine. I laugh into his mouth and see a flash come from where Chloe stands. She's captured the moment Finn kissed me by surprise, in our new home, by our imperfectly perfect Christmas tree.

"It's snowing," Finn whispers against my mouth.

I pull back, eyes wide. I run out the door with everyone I love in tow.

I touch the cold powder with my bare hands, leaving them wet with a huge smile on my face. My first-time seeing snow. I pick some up and throw it at Finn, starting a full-blown snowball fight amongst my family.

Everything is as it should be right here in my happily ever after.

This is the moment promised I've been waiting my whole life for.

The End.

RESOURCES

If you or someone you know is a victim of domestic violence or need assistance in leaving a dangerous situation, please call the National Domestic Violence Hotline: 800-799-7233
Or visit:
www.thehotline.org

If you or a family member are facing mental and/or substance use disorders and need assistance in treatment referral and information services please call: 1-800-662-HELP (4357)

ACKNOWLEDGMENTS

Before I go off on a sobby tangent about the wonderful people who helped support and bring this book to fruition, I want to thank you, the reader, for giving The Moment Promised a chance. I spent equal parts writing this story as I did doubting myself and wondering if anyone would even read it. If you've gotten to the acknowledgements, I've done something right. So, thank you, from the bottom of my heart, for taking a chance on Adeline's story.

My mom. Thank you for the countless hours you've spent listening to me talk your ear off about these characters and telling me to follow my dreams since I can remember. My sister. Thank you for being the proudest sister out there and telling everyone you meet about the book your little sister wrote. This story is for us.

My boyfriend, Michael, from the moment I told you my dreams of writing a book, you've been the biggest cheerleader. Thank you for believing in me even when I don't.

My dog, Gus Gus, you had no idea I was writing a novel every time you barked at the squirrel through the window. I love you. Thank you for forcing me to take breaks. Pixie, you wanted to be next to me every time I pulled my laptop out to write. It always warms my heart. Rosie, my puppy who never seems to run out of energy, I have a feeling you would chew up my book thinking it was a toy.

My beta readers who saw the horrifying first draft of my book. Your feedback and support are invaluable. Thank you.

My editor, Amy, thank you for polishing this book with your attention to detail and great feedback.

If it weren't for my aunt, a New York Times bestselling author, I would never have had the confidence to write my first novel. While you aren't here, I know you were with me every step of the way, guiding me as I wrote my first novel. When I wanted to quit, and it seemed impossible, I had an angel there beside me, cheering me on. There's a piece of you in this book. I know I've made you proud. I love you. I miss you.

Printed in Great Britain
by Amazon

36987419R00189